ONE

It wasn't a rainstorm. It was a deluge.

The rain bounced off the walls. It bounced off the rocks at the foot of the walls. It hissed off the waters of the river flowing round the foot of the walls; and it thumped into the sodden cloaks of the men-at-arms on watch. The wind hurled the rain against the solid defenses as if in league with the army that was besieging the castle on both sides of the river.

The night was everywhere: black, windy, wild.

For the men on the parapets, it was misery. Rain streaming from their clothes, their faces, their hands and their weapons, they sought what little shelter they could from the unyielding stone, while peering through the pelting rain in case the enemy advanced. And they thought of tomorrow!

On one of the walkways, high upon the walls, a little group of men huddled and searched the night, shading their eyes against the rain and trying to pierce the darkness. Occasionally, a winking light could be seen from the odd fire which had somehow managed to survive the torrential storm. There had been many fires to be seen the night before, for Dehrmacht Castle was besieged. The besieging army was still there, but only the hardiest and most sheltered fire had survived this downpour.

On both banks of the river, the armies of Boris, Archduke of Thalesia, a notorious and aggressively greedy ruler, besieged the ancient Castle of Dehrmacht. The castle was situated on an island in the middle of the river, which made it difficult to subdue, but the Archduke's armies were large. They were swollen by many mercenaries hoping for a share in the legendary treasure of Dehrmacht which, rumor said, was hidden deep in the castle keep. The Archduke's attack had been timed for the occasion when King Maximilian's own army was weakened as he had sent many men to assist his brother, Henry, in a war he was fighting against rebels in his own land. Now, after weeks of siege, the Archduke's forces, under cover of siege engines had nearly rebuilt the causeway which linked the castle to the land. In fear for the safety of his only son, Maximilian was sending him away into the night, disguised as a merchant's apprentice and attended only by two of his most trusted servants.

"Perfect weather!" one of the little group murmured, more to himself than to anyone else.

"Yes," shouted another, his voice just audible above the wind and rain. "They must go quickly. They need all the cover they can get. We will go in and start them on their way, although I am sorry enough to see them go."

A little time later, in this foul night, a tiny door opened at the foot of the walls. The door was small but very strongly built, iron-faced and thick. Furthermore, it was deeply hidden in the buttresses of the towers, so that it was impossible to see from anywhere not on the island. It had not been opened apparently, for some time, for it creaked alarmingly and groaned, though it could not be heard much on this night.

Three figures emerged. Two men carried a small boat between them. The third figure was smaller, slighter, just a boy.

Their senses reeled from the impact of the weather. The wind tore at their clothes and wrestled with strong arms to try to overturn the boat before it entered the water. The rain lashed them so that they were wet through in minutes. It hissed in the river, which ran fast and dark and ugly nearby.

Scarcely had they left the door, when it shut fast and, if anything could have been heard that night, strong bolts would have been heard crashing home.

Swiftly the boat was carried to the water, despite the wind. No word was spoken but the boat was lowered and held steady while the boy got in. The men followed quickly and the craft sped away on the current, steadied by the oars wielded by strong arms.

The man in the front of the craft was lean and sinewy, of medium height and weight, with hooded blue eyes, His face was creased and lined; an alert and watchful face, yet thoughtful and careful. Here was a man you could never ignore, the sort of man to whom others turn for advice and wisdom. This was Manfred the Wise, friend of the King, guardian of the King's son, and keeper of many secrets.

The boy was thirteen, slim, but well-proportioned and tall. His back was straight, his features strong and regular, his head high and the habit of command in his eyes. Just now he was keeping his head down, well within the dark cowl he wore, partly to avoid the driving rain, and partly because Manfred said so. His

3

Royal Highness, Prince Rudolph Christian Albert of Dehrmacht, was under strict instructions from his father, the King, to obey Manfred's orders to the letter until they returned to Dehrmacht Castle.

The third in the party was a giant of a man. His massive frame seemed too large for the tiny boat. His huge and powerful muscles bulged and rippled beneath his clothes now as he kept the boat straight in the racing stream. Bushy black eyebrows under a large straight forehead, grew vigorously above slate gray eyes, when at ease, he was inclined to be boisterous, exulting in his great strength. A thick black beard half hid a straight mouth, atop a great square jaw. A broad, flat nose completed a picture of rugged strength, and yet, there was gentleness too in those quiet eyes and, often, humor.

His name was Hans: Hans the Strong, Hans the Brave, Hans the Magnificent in Battle, Hans of a thousand tales of daring and might. This was the Hans of whom minstrels sang in barons' halls, in market places and in taverns throughout the land. To the Prince, he was just Hans, his beloved and trusted friend, whom he loved almost as much as he did his revered and respected father. Hans had taught him to use sword and lance, to handle shield and buckler, to fight with only a dagger and, unusually, to shoot straight and true with the English longbow. And Hans loved the boy, would lay down his life to save his prince, and would fight any foe for the sake of his master.

Such were the men to whom King Maximilian Augustus II of Dehrmacht had entrusted his only son and heir, to take him out of his doomed castle, now besieged for so long, to smuggle him through his own invaded land. They were to take him to his friend and cousin, the Baron Christov de Berenal, in the still unoccupied far north of the country, to await and join the forces of the King's brother, Henry of Felden, still gathering troops in his own principality.

Manfred, at the tiller, grunted as he strove to keep the boat straight against the wind and current. The river was so wild and fast that sometimes it seemed certain the boat would overturn and pitch its occupants out. Suddenly, Hans stopped rowing and thrust his oars stiffly into the water to slow the boat down. In the darkness ahead could be seen a line of dark shapes stretching across the river.

All three knew what to do, for their trip had been carefully planned. They steered their craft up to the boom of lashed logs, set up to prevent any sally or exit from the castle by boat.

Rudolph crouched low. Manfred picked up a crossbow from somewhere beneath him and Hans took a long knife from his belt. With this, he began slicing through the ropes that held the logs.

The thick, wet ropes parted only slowly. It was hard work even for Hans. When the last binding was almost through, there was a sudden jerk and the little craft started to slip through.

Feeling the sudden movement of the boat, the little prince looked up and there, not ten feet away, two stalwart sentries could be seen staring at them. They shouted in alarm and sudden fear as the logs moved treacherously beneath them. One lost his balance and, with a despairing shriek disappeared into the black waters below him.

The other, astonishingly, maintained his balance, raised his crossbow and loosed a wild and hopeless bolt. Almost at the same instant, there was a corresponding twang from Manfred's bow and the hapless sentry fell among the heaving logs.

There were no further problems on the river. Its furious pace slowed and any further guards were obscured by the darkness of the storm.

They traveled along the river until Manfred signaled to Hans that he was looking for something along the north bank. By then, mercifully, the storm had eased and the wind and rain had stopped, so that there was now that lovely calm that often comes after a heavy storm. Just as well, too, for here the country was heavily wooded, with trees coming to the water's edge and, in places, overhanging the waters.

In just such a place, they stopped and scrambled ashore. Pausing only to get their weapons and food, Hans stove in the bottom of the boat and it sank out of sight.

Searching along the line of trees and bushes, Manfred gave a grunt of satisfaction.

"Here it is," he said. "This was the old road to the ferry. Hasn't been used for years, but the track is still here."

They followed him along a track he seemed to know well. It was still more or less intact, though overgrown by brambles and low bushes. These tore at their arms and legs as they stumbled into them in the dark. The Prince hated the coarse, apprentice clothes he was having to wear, but he had to admit they gave more protection here than his soft court finery would have done. His beautiful, new chased silver armor would have helped, but it would not have been easy to walk in.

6

For two or three hours they walked in silence. The rain actually stopped and, in time, they emerged from the wood into gently rolling countryside. It was still very dark, as clouds obscured the moon, but now that they were out of the wood, the ancient path was clearer. Even so, it was muddy, uneven, overgrown and, every so often, they would pass a thicket of trees in which numerous enemies might lurk, thought the Prince.

Manfred walked steadily, even quickly along, while Hans plodded solidly behind the boy. His softly thumping footsteps and the Prince's own increasing tiredness made him think he was walking in an endlessly monotonous dream.

"We are far enough from the castle and any camped Thalesians," said Manfred, "I think we can relax a bit."

"Ho ho," said Hans, "that's better. Couldn't be myself, having to keep quiet all the time."

He turned to the lad: "How are you doing my young lord?"

"Bit tired."

"Tired!" boomed Hans, "at your age? Look at me. I'm not tired. Here, I'll carry you for a bit."

"No, Hans." But Hans was already reaching out for him.

"What did you say? You would love to be carried? I thought you would."

He picked the boy up and tossed him into the air, catching him easily as he came down, and depositing him, upside down across his huge shoulders.

"Hans!" shouted Prince Rudolph, at least he meant to shout, but upside down his throat didn't seem to work in the same way, and it came out in a normal voice. "Stop fooling around and put

7

me down. I'm not a baby, you know."

"Not a baby!" laughed Hans. "I should think not. Weigh a ton, you do, look." He plucked the boy from his back and hoisted him one handed above his head. "You are far too heavy for me to do anything like this. In fact, I don't think I could lift you off the ground. I must be dreaming all this."

"Put me down! Hans, behave yourself."

"Stop fooling around, Hans," said Manfred. "He'll need all his strength for this journey."

"Oh, all right," said the mighty man, "no fun these days. No-one has any sense of humor any more." And he put the boy down.

"You're too big for your own strength!" said the Prince, but at the same time, he knew how gently he had been lowered to the ground, and he grinned at his mighty friend. "You know, Hans," he said, "I'm glad you are on our side."

"For ever, my Prince," and he grinned back. "I'm glad I'm on our side too, for this Thalesian usurper will be defeated in the end, and he is a bad man, when all's said and done."

As they walked on and on, it seemed to the boy that they had been walking for ever. Hans's heavy footsteps seemed to plod rhythmically. He found himself repeating a refrain in his mind:

"Follow Manfred. Keep walking. Mind the bushes (and puddles). Keep walking. Follow Manfred. Keep walking. Keep walking. Oh, when can we stop?"

In his walking dream, he felt himself falling, and came to his senses abruptly, as the shock of cold water up to his thighs woke him completely.

"Not much further, Your Highness," said Manfred, as Hans

lifted him out of the pothole he had stumbled into. "You have to be careful of these holes. Some of them are very deep."

"We seem to have been walking for miles, Manfred. Can we not rest here, or under that tree for a while, and then carry on?" asked the boy.

"No, my Prince. We dare not stop yet. I will show you a resting place soon. We need to be well away from the castle before we can rest with any peace of mind. Even then, there may be roving patrols of the enemy. I have heard that the Archduke has sent recruiting parties everywhere. *They* are our real danger. His Highness's recruiting officers might not be interested in me, or you, but Hans would be a great find for them."

"Hah!" Hans grinned fiercely, "and I would like to be found by them. We should have some fun between us."

The boy straightened wearily and continued to walk. "All right, Manfred. Let's keep going then."

Dawn had slipped in unnoticed and walking was easier . They were back in a wood, bushes thick on both sides of the path, but at least they could see where they placed their footsteps. It was a narrow path so they walked in single file, Manfred at the front, the boy at the rear.

Manfred turned and spoke to his young charge.

"Your Highness," he said, "remember you are a merchant's apprentice, as we may well start meeting people from today. For the time being, I shall not be calling you 'Your Highness', but 'Fritz', as we agreed."

"My lord Manfred, I remember," replied the Prince, with a smirk.

"And *you* will call *me* 'Master'."

"Yes, Master," said the boy, in a funny voice.

"And, one other thing, young feller-me-lad..." But Prince Rudolph never discovered what that other thing was, as Manfred suddenly held up his fingers, saying "Hush! Listen."

There were voices ahead and, suddenly, round a bend in the path, burst a group of Thalesian soldiers.

Hans brightened visibly, but for a moment, Manfred's heart misgave him. Had they been betrayed and all lost! It was quickly apparent, though, that it was just a band of marauding soldiers who were picking up anything they fancied for themselves. It may even be that they were out of the camp without permission, in which case it would go hard with them, if caught.

At first the Thalesians did not see them. Drinking stolen wine they were noisy and raucous. One pushed another into a thick bush and there were hoots of laughter from the others.

It was hard to tell how many there were at first, because of the narrowness of the path. The usual soup bowl of a helmet sat on their untidy heads, leather armor on their chests, partly covered by the red and black surcoats of Thalesia.

The one in front stopped. He had seen them at last.

"Halt!" he said to his troop. "We have some natives here," and he laughed. "I wonder if these will hang as well as the others we met, or will they join our noble Archduke?"

Manfred understood. They were a recruiting party, trying to drum up some support before the big battle started, and to eliminate any resistance if they could not find support.

"That one would make a good soldier, sergeant," said the

fellow behind, pointing at Hans.

"There you are," said the sergeant, "couldn't speak fairer than that, could we. Join us now and have adventure and fun serving our lord the Archduke Boris, or hang miserably from one of these 'ere trees around us. No choice in it, is there?

"I'll even allow the little man to join. He can be a drummer boy or fetch spent arrows, summat like that."

"Hans!" said Manfred quietly, and the big fellow stepped to the front.

Now Hans was a *doppelsolden*, a double handed swordsman. Before he became Captain of the Guard, he and his fellows had fought in the very front of the army, clearing a deadly path through pikemen and knights by means of their long two-handed swords. They were even paid twice the wages for being 'double' soldiers.

As he stepped in front of Manfred, he reached behind his neck and unclipped the sword he carried there. About a hundred and twenty centimetres long, with a handle and an extra part below the quillons (the sticky-out bit) for the other hand to grip. He also had flukes and rings to catch an opponent's sword in closer combat, but its deadly merit lay in its sweeping scythe like action when wielded by an expert.

There could be no doubt about his intention and the sergeant hurriedly re-arranged his men with a great ox-like fellow at the front. "Right, men," he hissed, "rush 'em!"

Hans shouted with sheer delight.

"That's right!" he shouted, "rush 'em. Just what I like. Aha, you're a big fellow to be out by yourself. Mind you don't lose your head over this."

Hans met the rush with a great sweep of his sword that took the unfortunate man's head off in one blow. His heavy body crashed to the ground, spewing a fountain of blood into the bushes. The next man stumbled over him and the return sweep of that flashing sword sliced deep into his face as he fell towards it.

There was no pause between strokes and Hans brought his weapon back in another forward slash which bit through the arm of the next soldier and then deep into his ribs. He fell with a shriek.

The man behind thought he saw his chance, thinking Hans was off balance. He raised his sword, preparatory to bringing it crashing down upon Hans's head. But Hans was quicker and swept his sword upwards, taking his enemy under his arm and across his throat.

Two were left and turned to flee, but the one in front was too late and that terrible blade laid his fleeing back open from top to bottom. The other fled but Manfred's crossbow whirred again, the quarrel hitting the man full in the back and penetrating his heart.

The boy watched amazed. He had heard so much of this big man's prowess, but had never before seen him in actual battle.

"Well done, Hans," said Manfred, while Prince Rudolph was open-mouthed at the swiftness of the destruction that had come upon the hapless troop.

"Poor fellows," rumbled Hans. "They could not have had much experience of war to have rushed at me like that. However," he grinned, "it's my job to teach them how not to do it. Six down and about twenty thousand left. Shouldn't take long!"

Manfred spoke: "We'd better get the bodies out of the way. Hans, pitch them into the bushes while I scrape the path a bit with branches to try to hide what happened here. Hopefully, the Archduke's soldiers will have enough on their hands to bother to go and look for one patrol not returned."

"This one is still alive, Master," said the boy, pointing at the man who had had his face slashed but was still breathing, although he was bleeding copiously.

Manfred moved over to the wounded man and, with one deft movement of his knife, cut his throat from ear to ear.

"We cannot leave any witnesses, and well done, Fritz, for remembering to address me as Master."

The boy was shaken and said, in a small voice "So quickly over and six men dead who a few minutes ago were alive. I wonder if they had families, or children left behind."

Manfred looked at him sternly.

"This is the last time I shall address you as Your Highness, until it is safe to do so again, among friends. Now listen Your Highness, these men have, by their own admission killed innocent countrymen of ours, *your* subjects. *They deserved to die.* They chose that way of life and *their* consciences were untroubled by the murder and misery they had inflicted. We met enemies. It was them or us. This time, thanks to Hans, it was them. Don't waste time or pity feeling sorry for them."

"No, I know you are right, my lord Chancellor," (the boy reverting for a moment to the courtly form of address) " but it was so... brutal and sudden."

Manfred spoke again: "Now, listen my young master... You

have grown up in a castle. All your life, you have been protected. You have fed well, slept in peace, been cossetted, pampered, and few people have dared to deny, or contradict you. Now, although our journey is fraught with danger and, probably, hardship, it will do you good. You will learn that life is not always kind and cosy. Suffering and trouble are bound up in life. You will see that some of your people live hard and unhappy lives. I think you are man enough to learn from these things and my earnest desire is that it will make a better man of you. I may say I talked like this to His Majesty and he fully agreed with me. He did not like submitting you to this danger but, even if there had been another way, he said he wanted you to learn some of the realities of life. He did not want you to be ignorant of how the people in your Kingdom live."

"You talk as if you have sympathy with the ordinary people, the peasants."

"What makes you think they are any different? They do not have riches or power, but they are people like us. They have hopes and fears. They love and hate. They do have feelings, you know. They are not educated, of course, and don't think the way we do, but they are not animals, although sometimes they behave like them. Some want to do good and some don't. They have little or no power and so they, perhaps, don't do as much harm, or good, as noble and powerful folk."

This was new to the boy. He had had no contact with peasants at all. To him, they *were* like animals. They were just creatures he saw from his horse or carriage. He didn't think he had ever spoken with a peasant in his life. He didn't really know if

14

they spoke the same language as they did at Court.

"Captain," he said.

Hans turned to face him, wondering why the boy had addressed him so formally.

"Yes, Your Highness?"

"You have been my friend always. You have heard what my lord Manfred..."

"Master Sandor, Fritz!"

The boy's anger flashed for a moment.

"Patience, my lord. All in good time."

"You heard what our noble lord and chancellor says."

"Yes."

"Do you agree with him?"

"Yes, Your Highness."

Manfred sighed, but said nothing.

"Then how can you laugh and make a joke, when you have just killed four people, ordinary people, who had their hopes and fears, and so on, as my lord says?"

"Your Highness, I have a job to do. I don't *like* killing, but we are at war and these men are our enemies. They are your enemies, Your Highness and your royal father's. I may sympathize with their plight, but that must never sway me from my duty. Don't judge me by my joking words. It is just my way of coping with a grim and dreadful reality. If soldiers think too much about their enemies' suffering, it would un-man us and we would hesitate in battle. *That* would be fatal the other way!"

The boy nodded.

Manfred spoke again: "You, Your Highness, must learn to

15

sympathize with the lowliest of your people, but it must never turn you from your duty. When you are grown up, you will have difficult decisions to make, when one consideration may well conflict with another, but you must learn early to choose to do right, not an easy thing for one from a royal house to do. Make the most of this opportunity. You *will* be going amongst ordinary folk, such as you have never met before in your life. Keep quiet among them, for your speech will betray you, and learn from them."

"How can *I* learn from these ignorant peasants?" the boy asked.

"Not courtly learning perhaps, but there are other things worth knowing. You *must* learn from them, so that you will be a good and wise king when your time comes."

The boy thought for a while and then nodded.

"I understand and I thank you both for the true friends that you are. I know that I can trust you both, even with my life. It seems I have a lot to learn," and he grinned, "but just at the moment, I need to learn to forget who I am and remember our temporary identities, I think."

Manfred smiled and quietly sighed with relief. He knew that his little charge could be stubborn, but stubbornness here might cost all their lives, and the Crown.

"Right, now that these important things are out of the way for the moment, we try to forget our real names and persons. I am your master. You, *Fritz,* are my apprentice and boy, I am Sandor, a merchant from Iflis, with my trusty servant and bodyguard, Vigor."

They finished disposing of the bodies and continued along the path, reaching the end of the wood quite soon. As they emerged, Manfred pointed to a small hill a short distance in front and to their left.

"On the other side of that hill is our inn for the night," he said. "We will leave the path now and go that way. Then we can rest."

So they ascended the slope, skirted the summit and descended into yet another wood, covering the valley floor. Manfred led the way between broadly spaced trees until, in the weak daylight, they saw the dark shape of a large stone house looming in front of them.

"Hans," said Manfred quietly, "go and see if anyone's at home."

TWO

Hans slipped through the bushes round the edge of the building, sword in hand.

Rudolph was cold, tired and hungry. The rough peasant clothes had chafed in so many places that he held himself stiff to avoid further irritation. It seemed a lifetime ago that he had been woken by his servant, Carl. He was feeling sorry for himself but was determined not to show it. His upbringing had lacked a woman's love, as his mother had died when he was a baby, and the ladies of the court had shown little interest in the boy, unless they thought he could win them favor from his father. Consequently he had found his companions among the pages and men of the castle, and his fun in the arts and skills of warfare.

Now Hans was returning.

"No-one," he said laconically. "It seems we have this inn to ourselves. No friends, new or old, no servants or slaves to do our bidding, just us, a rich merchant, his young apprentice and, Vigor, his humble, but mighty, servant."

The Prince looked at Hans quizzically. No flicker of humor showed on those massive features, but the boy smiled. He loved this fearsome man with his, usually, gentle humor.

"Good!" smiled Manfred. "Freedom from company will serve, for now, until we are further along the road. Come, Fritz!

No servants, I am afraid, but a soldier's rest, sleeping where you can, until the night comes and we go on."

"Never mind the servants," said the boy wearily, "I could sleep on the kitchen table, I'm so tired!"

Manfred laughed. "Not on Triffon's table," he said, "I'll warrant that."

The boy laughed too, "No, you're right, Master," and he smiled, pleased with himself for remembering, "as far away from him as possible."

Triffon, Dehrmacht's chief cook, was notoriously bad-tempered and quite contemptuous of any authority, serving the King, he said, because King Maximilian was the only *other* honest man in the Kingdom.

"What is this place, my lord?" asked the Prince.

"Master!" corrected Manfred. "You really do have to remember, Fritz. It's not a game. It could mean all our lives. Better to get into the habit while no-one is near, and then it should come naturally when people are around.

"Now, with regard to this place... It is an old, old hall. Long ago, a robber duke lived here with his thanes and servants. He ruled all this area with great authority, as far as the river, where the previous king's domains began in those days."

"What happened to him and what was his name?"

"His name was Bereca. He was one of a line of ancient and, at one time, distinguished dukes of Tata, which is the name of this district. Somewhere the line went bad and a succession of cruel and wicked men ruled here. Bereca followed in their footsteps. He was feared far and wide. No traveler was safe in this district, unless he paid large bribes to the Duke. In the neighboring areas too, the evil hand of Bereca stretched out to rob, hurt and destroy.

"Great feasts were held in this hall," continued Manfred. "Many great lords were entertained here, not perhaps as bad as Bereca, but willing to eat at his table and share his bounty. That is how he got away with so much, by keeping neighboring lords happy, while he robbed travelers in their lands. He could not bribe the King though, and one day the plague struck here and many died. The King and his son, the present King, did what they had been wanting to do for many years and invaded while Bereca's forces were decimated by the disease. They destroyed everything except for this ancient hall. Hardly a man survived from the Duke's marauding bands... and a good thing too," he finished with a strange, sad smile.

The boy was troubled though as he looked at the long low building, the scene of so much activity, suffering and death. Then a terrifying thought struck him.

"Will the plague still be here? It hangs in the air, doesn't it, Master?"

Manfred grinned. "Well remembered, young Fritz. Men say it does, but I am not so sure. In any case, Fritz, it is very long ago. The air will have been dissipated long since. We are safe."

The building stood on stone pillars, high enough for a man to walk under, and the three companions mounted stone steps to enter the doorless building.

Inside, it was almost pitch black. A little light came from small apertures at the top of the walls and through the ancient smoke hole in the decaying roof. A musty smell was everywhere, but no damp. When his eyes were used to the dark, Prince Rudolph could make out a raised wooden platform at the far end of the room, with a huge and sombre, dust-covered table still stood upon it. In the dim, dim light, the boy could just make out various mounds, bundles and oddments, which no-one had thought worth taking away, though Manfred said the peasants were afraid of the ancient hall's past and kept clear of it.

Prince Rudolph lay down in a corner of the platform with Manfred, while Hans took the first watch on guard. It had been decided that they would all take turns on guard, for the King had insisted that the boy should not be treated differently from any other soldier. So, it was, that after what seemed like only five minutes sleep, he was woken and told to take his watch in the door of the old hall. He did it, and never knew that they cut his time short, for he nodded and dozed all the way through, and Manfred said a whole army could have got past him he was so tired. Then they let him sleep.

Deeply he slept, but not sweetly. He was troubled by an annoying dream. In happier days there had been a cow in the fields near the castle, which had fascinated him. It was enormous with a huge stomach which swayed from side to side as it walked. He and the other noble boys had laughed at it and called it Droopy. In his sleep now, he dreamed Droopy was lying on top of him, her enormous stomach stopping him moving in any direction. He tried to turn but it was no good, and then he woke up. And he still could not move. A strong hand was on his shoulder, holding him down. He tried to sit up but he couldn't.

A rasping voice sneered above him in the darkness of the

hall.

"Ah!" said the unfamiliar voice, "the young puppy is awake, and wriggles. We'll soon put an end to that," and the Prince felt a ringing blow across his face.

"Keep still you young rascal, and answer a few questions," said the voice.

"Quietly, you fool," hissed another man, apparently at the other end of the room, nearer the door, "he may have friends near."

"Yes, indeed," thought the Prince, "but where are they?"

Blind rage overwhelmed him for a moment. He had never been struck wantonly before in his life. In his arms training, of course, but never by an unwashed peasant. Such an act would have been punished by death. His cheek stung but that did not bother him much. He had had to endure much more than that from the blows of staff and the blunt, round-ended practice swords.

He could see that it was light outside but the windows in the hall were high and the interior of the hall was black. His eyes were becoming used to the dark and Rudolph was able to make out something of his enemy. He saw a heavy-jowled, thick-set man, unshaven, unwashed, with bleary eyes. There was a strong odor about him and the Prince realized, even through his anger, that this was what had made him think of Droopy. The man seemed to have slept in a cowshed. His clothes were ragged and the boy knew he was one of the roving vagabonds that were to be seen nowadays.

The man had started to wave an evil-looking knife in front

of his face. "Now, my beauty," he said softly, menacingly, "tell me where you're from, what you're doing here, and whether you've got any friends around here."

The Prince made no answer but started to slide his hand down under his blanket to see if his dagger was at his side, as it always was. Even in the court of so enlightened a monarch as King Maximilian, the danger of the assassin was always there, and the Prince had been taught to sleep with a dagger within easy reach. This wise precaution paid off now amply. His hand closed round the dagger's handle and he slowly withdrew it from its sheath.

"Come on," snarled the ruffian, "I'm not waiting all day.

"'Ere!" he exclaimed suddenly, whisking the blanket off. "What's going on 'ere?"

At that moment, the little prince lunged, straight upwards, at his side. The years of patient teaching were rewarded as the man stiffened and uttered a deep groan.

The boy wriggled out of the man's way and jumped to his feet, but the man was mortally wounded and toppled over on to the floor. There was still the other fellow to beware of, and a sudden rush of footsteps from the door reminded the prince of that unpleasant fact. A lumbering shadow lurched at him out of the gloom. He ducked and twisted and made for the lighter patch which was the door.

Not a moment too soon either, for the second man was almost upon him. He ran through the door, down the stone steps and into the clearing outside. He heard his shout and was aware of heavy footsteps behind him.

The Prince dived towards the wood but the bushes were thick and brambles tore at his legs and clothes. Fear gave him strength and energy, and he hurled himself at the bushes. He knew he could not escape though. He was running from a grown man and he was bound to be caught in time. Anger welled up within him again. The son of the King was not used to running away. So he turned and faced his enemy, dagger in hand, and clear blue eyes flashing.

The man came at him, a slight smile touching the edges of his mouth as he realized the boy had stopped running.

"Now I'll get you, you little rat, and you won't stick me like you did poor Niko. I'll feed your miserable bones to ..."

An angry roar interrupted him and out of the bushes stepped Hans.

"What about *this* rat?" snarled Hans. "What will you feed my bones to, you miserable carrion?"

The fellow's face paled and he turned to run, but he was too late. He was almost cut in half as Hans's huge sword flashed in the morning sun and sliced across below his ribs. He fell to the ground, a massive cavity in his body spewing blood and gore on to the ground.

Hans did not even wait to see his opponent fall but turned to check that the Prince was unhurt. He came swiftly over to his noble charge and smiled a slow smile at him.

The boy looked sternly at Hans and at Manfred who was standing slightly to one side watching them.

"Where did you go, both of you? I needed you."

Manfred shrugged: "We heard voices, and movement

24

outside. We saw the beggars approach, but didn't think they could do you much harm, and there were others, men-at-arms, on the road, and we had to know where they were heading. We were afraid to stop these ruffians too soon, in case the other men heard, and turned to the old hall to investigate."

"You left it long enough, *Master.* If I hadn't had my dagger, I might have been in trouble."

"Yes, but you *did* have your dagger and, quite frankly, *Fritz,* I would have thought you could take care of yourself, at least a little, after all the training you have had."

The prince was miffed. He thought he had behaved exceptionally well and bravely, and that he deserved some praise for his achievement. He would have been praised at the castle. He did not know yet that much of the castle praise was worthless flattery.

"Take care, Master Sandor, that you do not mistake the present fiction for the reality," he said. "I am sure my father did not entrust his son to you so that you could take unnecessary risks with him."

"He apprenticed you to me and gave me absolute freedom in my treatment of you. You would do well, young Fritz, to remember *that!"*

Rudolph scowled, but said nothing.

"You see, Fritz, *he* trusts me, and you must do the same, just as I trust Vigor... totally."

If Manfred was distressed at the incident, and its consequent danger, he hid it well.

Hans was pleased.

"Our little *apprentice* shows promise. He might make a soldier yet, eh, Master?"

But Manfred was of a serious mind. "He'd better, considering the present state of the world," he grumbled.

Both the men were pleased that the Prince had managed the situation so well, but Manfred was not one to praise very much, and he thought the boy needed a little humbling.

Somewhat shaken, but comforted a little by the solicitude of Hans, the young prince looked around him. There was a curious stillness in the clearing, which had such a short time ago been full of violence and sudden death. The sun was warm and pleasant, the insects buzzed peacefully in the air, and all would seem to be well with the world. Only the outstretched body, still, sticky and already attracting flies, spoke of man's unpleasantness to man.

Manfred looked at the body carefully to see if anything could be learned from it. He appeared to be just what they had thought, one of the many wandering villains roaming the countryside and taking advantage of the law's current distractions. The man was well built but dirty, with heavy features, a thick overhung brow and a cruel and sneering mouth. He was dressed in the usual baggy leggings and tunic of the country peasant.

"Who was he, Manfred?" said the boy softly, a little awed by what he had done.

Manfred shrugged. "A wandering beggar, young *Fritz,*" emphasizing the boy's alias, a trifle angrily.

"The other one, is he dead, too?" whispered the Prince.

"I don't know. We'll go and see." And with scarcely a

glance at the dead man, Manfred started towards the hall.

The other beggar *was* dead.

"Bury the bodies of these beggars, Vigor, or hide them. I shouldn't think anyone will bother about two dead rogues in these troubled days, but the less interest there is in this old hall, the better for us."

Hans lifted the body effortlessly to his shoulders and crossed to the door.

"They deserved to die, Master. They tried to kill me. Maybe they were hired assassins, sent by the Archduke to get me."

"No, Fritz. They were just beggars, wandering to see what they could pick up or steal. Unfortunately, they ran into something they did not know about and they had to die." Manfred did not sound sorry, but he did not gloat over the deaths either. He had seen many men die, some deservedly, and others more unworthily. If these had been brought before him at the castle, for judgment, he would have had them hanged, without a thought. They were unlikely to be missed.

Manfred spoke again. "As soon as the sun goes down we will go on our way. We won't need to travel at night for the whole of our journey, just these first few days, until we're clear of the castle's domain."

They sat peacefully at the door of the old hall, watching the birds and the insects, enjoying the early morning warmth of the sun. The hall was truly in a lovely spot and the boy felt his spirits lifting as he relaxed. He thought of his father, and missed him already. Had the Archduke attacked the castle yet? he wondered.

27

How long could his father's men hold out in the face of sustained assault? They had watched the enemy soldiers dragging up massive tree trunks and timbers. The men said they were to build a makeshift bridge across the river. His father had said they would take the castle the day after he had left, which was today, he realized with a start.

The boy sighed. He knew that his father's men would fight tooth and nail for the King. They were intensely loyal to Maximilian, but he only a token force with him in the castle. Most of his men were away, fighting with the King's brother, Henry of Selden. Of course, they would hasten back when they heard what was happening, but by then the castle would have fallen. Archduke Boris had chosen his time well. Kings were not always as good as Maximilian, and his men were not anxious to exchange his rule for the foreign Archduke's, especially as tales of his cruelties were common knowledge amongst the countries around. No, thought the boy, they would not give in easily.

And *he* had killed a man, himself unaided. He felt a little awed by the thought but, with the insensitivity of a boy, was suddenly immensely proud of himself. And then, for he was not a cruel boy, felt ashamed of himself and just a little bit sorry for the unknown peasant who had tried to rob him. Well, he thought, I guess he deserved it. After all, he would have killed me.

Manfred interrupted his wandering thoughts.

"Hist! Hans is speaking to someone. Come, my Prince, this time we will stay together. We will go into the hall, until we see who it is." And so, they melted into the shadows.

THREE

At about the same time as Hans, Manfred and the young prince were fleeing the castle, what appeared to be a bundle of old clothes stirred slowly in the damp grass on the edge of a village a few miles distant. The bundle groaned and gingerly moved each limb in turn. *Well*, thought the bundle, *there seem to be no sudden stabs of agony, so no bones broken.* On the other hand, he thought ruefully, every bone ached badly, so they could all be broken and he might not know the difference.

The man, for such the bundle was, moved cautiously on to his knees and began to give thanks, quietly but audibly. "I thank you, heavenly Father, for letting me suffer just a little bit, compared with your holy son, Jesus. But, Father, there is still much work to do. Please will you strengthen this poor body, take away its hurts and give me strength and courage to carry on.. Have mercy on the people in this village. Forgive them and let some at least believe truly in your beloved son. Then it will be worthwhile." He began to feel better already, he thought, and although he still ached, his courage rose and a deep feeling of joy and peace flooded his being.

He was still on the edge of the village, where he had been flung, unconscious, after the beating. It was dark now and the villagers seemed to have gone to bed. He had no idea how long he had lain there but was wise enough to know that he should not stay. He was surprised they had left him. They may have thought he was dead, or would be by morning. In any event, he was sure they would be back.

Very slowly and painfully, he pulled himself upright by a friendly sapling. Thinking of the savagery of the attack on him by the not so friendly rustics of the village, he thought it must be a miracle that he was still alive, let alone no bones broken. It had been at the instigation of the local priest, of course.

It was strange that nearly all the opposition came from the priests. You would think they would welcome a fellow priest coming into the village to teach the people Christian truths, but they did not. He supposed they saw him more as a challenge to their position and authority, much as the Jewish leaders had seen Jesus as a challenge to theirs. The villagers had been friendly at first and he had noticed that some had listened intently, drinking in his words and nodding their agreement with some of the things he had said at least. Then the crowd had fallen silent at the approach of a portly and sleek priest of the church. They had bowed before him, parted and let him through. He had listened without comment for a while but then had peremptorily ordered the people to their homes and then roundly upbraided him as a heretic and for poisoning (as he put it) the people's minds with pernicious and false doctrines. When he attempted to argue with the local priest, he had waved his arms and a number of the men of the village had appeared and gave him a severe and systematic beating. It was so thorough that he wondered if they were called on to do this regularly. They certainly seemed to be practiced at it.

So now here he was, frankly surprised to be still alive, and grateful that his injuries had not been more permanent.

Time to go, he thought again and began to move away towards the woods that closed tightly upon the village. A sound suddenly startled him and he stiffened. A figure slipped from between the huts and resolved itself into the form of a young woman.

"Father," she said in a low voice. "Thank God you are not dead. I thought they had killed you."

"I thought so for a little while, myself," he said with a painful smile.

"I loved what you said, before Father Altruus came and stopped you." She hesitated and then went on "I *did* what you said, too. I turned away from all my sins and trusted the Savior with all my heart. Now I *know* the Lord Jesus died to save me."

Despite the pain, Bertram beamed upon her in the moonlight.

"Then, my child," he said, "it was all worthwhile. God bless you, my dear. Continue to pray and ask him to guide and help you. Er... are there any others you know who have believed, like you?"

"Well there are some who were very interested."

"What is your name?"

"Eothra," she said.

"Well, Eothra, try to meet together and talk to these others about Jesus and what he has done for you. Pray for them and the Lord will draw others to himself. It will also encourage you and help you to grow as a believer. I wish I could stay and teach you but maybe the Lord will allow me to come back to you one day and do that."

"You must not stay tonight," she said, frightened at the thought. "They will surely kill you if you do."

"Yes, I know, my child. I am reluctant now to leave you, but I know that I must."

"What is your name, Father? For I want to pray for you and have a remembrance of you by name."

"My name is Bertram, Eothra, Bertram of York, which is a city in England."

"Thank you, Father Bertram. Here, I have brought you a little food to help you on your way, for it is high time you were gone. I will not forget you," and she thrust a bundle of food into his hands and hurried off into the night.

"Goodbye, my child," he murmured and he, too, disappeared along a path into the woods.

He wondered too about the advice he had given her, to meet with others. In the face of the violent attack he had received, he did not think Father Altruus would take very kindly to a group of his villagers meeting without his supervision, even if it were just to pray. He shook his head. Would this wonderful gospel ever be accepted by the church which was supposed to preach it? Well, *he was* a duly ordained priest, and there were others, even some knights and noblemen, who believed and followed this pure gospel. Maybe one day, those high in the church would embrace these truths, but it was a long way off yet.

His aches and pains re-asserted themselves and he winced a bit as he hobbled along the woodland path. *Must find a place to rest for a bit, but a little bit further still from here,* he thought.

FOUR

Morning found the priest curled up on a bed of bracken just off the path he had followed for miles in the dark. He was cold, stiff, and sore from a dozen cuts and bruises. He was also hungry, and he ate the last of the food Eothra had given him the night before. Shifting painfully to his knees, the unusual priest spent some time in prayer before continuing his journey. He committed his day to the Lord, prayed again for peace in the country and, thinking of his non-existent stores, asked for provision on his way.

A short time later, he came upon a clearing in the forest and saw the stone walls of what looked like a fortified hall, evidently no longer lived in. Pushing his way past a large bramble threatening to overwhelm the path completely, he stopped abruptly. Immediately in front of him lay a man. Roughly dressed, a gaping wound in his stomach showed clearly how he had died. No need to check if he was dead, thought Bertram, the fellow had been almost cut in half.

Looking around, he could see no-one, but he realized he was in a dangerous situation. Whoever had killed this man must be still close and it was reasonable to assume it was they he heard in the hall. He gritted his teeth and prayed again for safety. Then he continued his way across the clearing.

He stopped again as round the corner advanced a giant of a man. Fully a foot taller than Bertram, broad as a barn door, dressed in the work-a-day clothes of a serving man, he carried what appeared to be another dead body across his shoulders. A massive sword was suspended from a cloth sling across the giant's chest.

Hans, for of course it was he, did not see Bertram at first because of the body across his shoulders, but he saw a slight movement out of the corner of his eye and swung immediately round. He cast the body to one side and drew his sword, all in one sweeping movement. For a moment, they stood, each weighing up the other: the fair-haired, bright eyed, man of God, in his worn and much patched priest's robe, and the man of war, glorious in his strength, ready for any foe, towering over the other.

Hans slowly lowered his sword. "A priest!" he breathed, "a little late for these carrion, I'm afraid, Father. What doeth a priest out here so far from his church? These are dangerous times to wander alone."

"Or even in pairs," said Bertram, indicating the bodies. "Who were they?"

"Who knows? Rogues, vagabonds, outlaws, they tried to kill my master, thinking he is richer than he is, no doubt."

"Ah, they must have been desperate indeed to tackle such a one as you."

"Had they seen me first, they might not have bothered. We don't always live and learn by our mistakes, do we Father."

"You are careless of other men's deaths?"

"They had murder in their hearts. If I had not killed them,

they would surely have killed others. Save your sympathy, master priest, for those who deserve it."

"I have sympathy for all men, good and bad. We all need the Savior's forgiveness. Indeed, he said he came to save not the righteous, but sinners."

The priest continued: "Who is this master you spoke of?"

"I am," said a quiet voice, and Manfred stepped into view, "and who is it that wishes to know?"

"My name is Bertram, a wandering English priest."

"Ah, that explains your accent," said Manfred. "My name is Sandor and I am a merchant. My servant, Vigor, and my apprentice, Fritz, make up our little party."

"And what makes you travel these lonely roads, Master Sandor, in these troubled times."

"Oh, I had to visit my sister and do some business in her town, but really I am come from Iflis in the north."

"Ah, yes. I am hoping to visit Iflis at some time. It is a prosperous city I believe."

"Very," said Manfred cheerfully, "it gives me a good living, being the northern-most city in the kingdom. It is a good place for trade."

Hans was studying the man's bruises. He had seen enough pain and wounds to recognize someone who was nursing a tender body.

"You have been wandering into other battles, I think, English priest."

"I am afraid so," smiled Bertram painfully, "rather more involved than usually. I wonder if I might rest in yonder hall, I could do with a little ease for a while."

"Surely," returned Manfred, thinking that as he was not yet sure of this man, it would be an opportunity to find out more and decide how far he was to be trusted. "Have you broken your fast, Father? We have enough and you are welcome to share our meal."

"Aye, gladly I will. I have eaten, but meagerly, and have not drunk since last night," and he accompanied them into the ancient hall.

Manfred introduced him to his apprentice, 'Fritz', and explained that he was a wool merchant traveling on business. As they talked, Manfred observed the man closely, deciding whether he was genuine or a threat to them. He seemed sincere, but Manfred was a suspicious man and thought before he acted on trust.

"Forgive me saying so, Father, but you are a strange one for a priest, not like any I have met I think. And, isn't it unusual for a lone priest to be wandering in a foreign country?"

"Yes, it is unusual, but not unheard of. I studied at Oxford under Master John Wycliffe, a brilliant scholar. Through him, I learned to respect the truths of the Bible and to understand that I should go from place to place teaching as many ordinary people the ways of Jesus as I can."

"But the church does that anyway," put in the Prince. "Our country has a church in every village, or almost."

Bertram was surprised at the boy speaking out in front of his master.

But Manfred was quick to respond: "Quiet, boy! How dare

you speak before your elders. You have many lessons to learn before you finish your apprenticeship."

Prince Rudolph flushed red, his eyes flashed and he swung on Manfred. Just in time, he remembered and dropped his eyes: "I am sorry, Master. I forgot myself."

"Aye, that's better. I took him as a favour to his father," he explained to the priest, "but he has been over-indulged at home and I am afraid it will be a hard job teaching him."

"I don't mind the boy talking. He has a point worth mentioning too. You would think the boy would be right, and yet it is nearly always at the instigation of the priest that I am beaten, whipped and, twice now, stoned."

It was unusual for a youngster to speak intelligently and give an opinion so freely in front of his elders, but he was wise, this priest, and kept his counsel. "Aye," he continued, " many of the village priests are uneducated and barely worthy of their calling. They need as much teaching as the people and are full of superstition, falsehood and downright heresy. Also, mother church has to be honored and paid for and many of the villages are poor and can hardly afford the tithes and dues demanded of them, so they develop little understanding of the God who loved them and gave himself for them."

Manfred knew that what he said was true. "So, Father, the bishop has sent you to add to the teaching of the church in various places. Do you have a license to wander where you will, or are you confined to certain parishes the bishop knows are particularly wanting?"

"Ah, my friend, I wish it were so. I have no license from any bishop, only the command of God. No. I am afraid, not many bishops look kindly on the work I do, and these bruises you see come from one parish priest in particular who objected to my teaching the people in his parish."

"And still you teach?" asked Hans. "It needs a rare courage to defy the might of our *holy* church. *I* would not like to try it."

"I must. It is my calling," replied Bertram simply, and then, because he was embarrassed, "this meat is good. Is it venison?"

"Yes, it is. I know what you are thinking, how did a merchant get to eat of the King's venison? Well ..." said Manfred, "several of our nobles are allowed to hunt the King's deer and one of them is the noble baron, Maresh. I have business dealings with Lord Maresh and as a favor, out of his profits, he pities me and gives me of his meat."

The Prince was enough of a boy to choke on his laughter as he heard this, for Manfred *did* have business dealings with Baron Maresh at court. The pair played cards regularly and the poor baron would have been hard pushed to give away a rabbit out of the profit he made out of Manfred, who invariably won handsomely. He did as invariably return it after, but it was always a keen source of jesting between the pair.

Hans roared out loud. "Aye," he said, remembering his assumed role, "the lord Maresh was ever a generous man. He even shows kindness to us servants. And, of course, he is gentle born. Not many gentle folks would even talk to us servants much, except to order us about. And that makes me think, Father, if you don't mind, Master, will servants be servants in Heaven? Will they have to do extra years in purgatory?"

"There is no such place," said the priest in rags.

"No such place!" exclaimed all three together. This was an outrageous thought.

"No, if you really belong to Jesus, you go straight to Heaven. If you don't, you won't. It is as simple as that!"

"O-o-oh yes!" sneered Manfred. "And you come against all the teaching of the church and tell us there is no purgatory. Why every priest I have ever met preached purgatory."

"Yes, and how did he say get out of it?"

"Well, by living a good life and by having masses said for your soul."

"Were these masses performed free of charge?"

"No, of course not. They had to be paid for, like everything else."

"Exactly. It is just an invention of the church in order to make money. There is no mention of purgatory in the holy Scriptures. The Lord Jesus never mentioned it. He even said to the dying thief 'This day you will be with me in Paradise.' No mention of purgatory, you see."

"Do you say this sort of thing everywhere you go, Father?" asked Hans.

Bertram laughed. "Well, yes, if I am asked."

"No wonder, you have many bruises. I am surprised you are still alive, Father."

"Frankly, my muscular friend... often, so am I."

They laughed politely with the priest, but each was wondering about him in his own way. Manfred was suspicious, and yet if a man wanted to be thought a priest who wasn't, he wouldn't make up such foolish notions. The Prince was thoughtful. This ragged man made sense to him, and he liked the way he looked at you, as if he was really interested in you, and meant what he said. Hans was frankly impressed.

"You know, Father, with your courage, I would almost offer you a place in my..."

Manfred coughed meaningfully.

"... noble company of bodyguards," he finished, and laughed loudly.

"noble company of chatterers! And I don't mean the priest," sneered Manfred, but he was intrigued by this strange man. He had a low opinion of priests and bishops, and had many a time wished to administer justice among them, but powerful though he was, he could not stir against the might of the church.

He spoke again to Bertram: "These are dangerous times, Father, and I prefer to travel at night. If you wish to have company along the road, you are welcome to travel with us, unless you are in a hurry to continue."

"Indeed, Master Merchant, I think it would be beyond my small strength to go on my way before nightfall. I will accompany you then right gladly."

So they sat in the sun in the clearing, chatting and dozing as the day wore on. Manfred and Hans were not as dozy as might appear as they were ever alert for travelers approaching and were ready to disappear into the darkness of the hall if need be.

But no-one else came near and their day was restful and pleasant.

As the evening came on, they gathered up their things and,

41

the priest being rested and more or less free from pain, the four set out from the old hall. Manfred realized that the priest's presence might be useful to them, as a priest might well travel the road with a rich merchant.

FIVE

Three days later, they had reverted to traveling in the daylight, after two difficult nights spent negotiating woods and fields in the dark, and difficult days finding somewhere to sleep which would not arouse too much suspicion. Now the four walked along a pleasant woodland path. The sun was shining and filtered pleasantly through the overhanging trees. It was a beautiful day and, if recent events had not been so horrifying the young prince would have been cheerful. As it was, although his heart was heavy about his father, he found himself beginning to hum quietly.

Manfred looked at Hans, who glanced at the boy. A ghost of a smile flitted across the rugged countenance, but he said nothing.

The morning passed and they found a little glade in which to rest and eat their lunch. After, they stretched themselves out on the grass, cropped short by generations of rabbits. Out of respect to the priest, Manfred asked if he would give a blessing on the food they were going to eat.

"I'm not sure that I can bless the food, as it is inanimate," said he, with a smile, "but I can bless the One who gave it," and he did.

All four seemed inclined to relax and enjoy the day and the meal. Hans and Manfred were now as sure as they could be that there was no treachery in the priest and, truth to tell, were enjoying his company.

The Prince spoke up. "Master," with a little smile to himself, which Bertram did not understand. "It must be pleasant to be a peasant." Then he realized what he had done and smiled again. "Hey! That rhymes." And he said it again, rolling it round his tongue, and varying the words slightly.

"It could be pleasant to be a peasant. It should be pleasant to be a peasant ... but I bet it isn't really," thinking how peasants were at the mercy of their lord, dependent upon his nature, his whims and fancy. Still, that was how it should be and the lords of his acquaintance were mostly reasonable men. But Manfred had returned to his original theme.

"Only when doing ...nothing but chewing!" replied Manfred, smiling,

"Or thinking and lazing

When the bright sun is blazing."

Their strange priest then joined in:

"Pleasant to be a peasant?

When famine and wars

Take all that is yours!

Even friends and relations

Perish, in wars between nations.

"Sorry, my masters," he continued, "I have seen too much hardship these last few weeks to envy them."

"Yes," said the boy, "but it's not so bad when the country is at peace. The common people have nothing to worry about except to do their work and earn their honest living."

44

Bertram looked at him seriously. "You seem to have had a privileged childhood and, I would judge, have never really had to go without."

The Prince was stung by this. "Why, I have often had to..."

But Manfred butted in here "I think the good priest meant go without food and shelter, not other sacrifices that even merchants' sons have to make from time to time," he said emphasizing *merchants'* sons. "Also, young Fritz, you *have* had a privileged upbringing in that you have been allowed to air your views before elders far too freely, in my opinion. While you are with me I think you must try to keep your tongue more under control. I don't think it is good manners, myself, for one so young to speak so freely."

"Oh, I'm sorry, Master" and he blushed "I will try to do better in future."

"That's better, young man. See that you do," and Manfred made a pretense of glowering at his erstwhile apprentice.

"Father Bertram," rumbled Hans, "how were you thinking of traveling across the country. You do not seem to be rich and even priests must eat."

"Well, I suppose the answer is that I trust the Lord to provide for me as I go. That is the plain promise of Scripture. In more practical terms, the Lord does seem to have His people in different places, and all sorts of strangers and individuals have given me just enough to keep on with my work. You, yourselves, are an example of such kindness, and the night before I met you, a young maiden from a village came to me and gave me enough to sustain me for the next phase of my journey. So it has been through all my travels so far.

"Not all priests are rich or high-born, as I am sure you must know. You are a merchant, Master Sandor, and come from a prosperous city, where I imagine you have a fairly wealthy priest, but that is not universal. Many earn a poor living unless they have rich patrons or relations. However, it does not matter. As I mentioned earlier, I follow the teachings of one, Master Wycliffe of England, who has taught us that those who would serve the Savior amongst the common people should go without money or riches and share the life of the poor and the needy. There are now several of us in Europe and many more in England. We preach a pure and simple gospel. We help the poor wherever we can, and we teach the Scriptures, which are able to make even the poorest, wise unto salvation."

Manfred listened to this speech and searched the man in front of him with steady eyes. The fellow sounded sincere, although Manfred held a low opinion of priests, being used to self-serving flatterers at court, who loved rich and gorgeous robes, and were always asking him for favors that other men would have disdained. That was one good thing about the evil Archduke's approach, he thought grimly, most of the priests and bishops had left the castle when the size of the enemy army was known.

This, he thought to himself, is the strangest priest I have ever met.

"Sir priest," he said, "almost you persuade me to become a more faithful son of the church."

"Not that, Master Sandor, I do not wish you to become a faithful son of the church, but a follower of our Lord Jesus, in spirit and in truth."

"Yes, well, that as well," said Manfred, embarrassed, and turned away.

Still, the Prince, he noticed, was becoming more and more friendly towards him and seemed to have relaxed completely, treating him almost as a father figure. Well, that would do no great harm. The boy could do with some disinterested friends.

The priest jerked him back to the present. "Your apprentice has unusual learning, and capacity for words, in an unlearned boy."

"Yes," said Manfred nastily, "he does have a tendency to talk when he should keep his mouth shut. I have noticed that. Still," he said, remembering the fable, "it has to be said, in fairness, he is not an ordinary apprentice. His father is very rich and has seen to it that he has had a good education, unusual for people in our class I know."

"And yet," said Bertram gently, "I wager you have had a good education too. You are not like other merchants I have met. You are much more interested in the ... oh, I don't know ... the things around you: people, things happening..."

Manfred laughed "Oh, I am definitely unusual. My friends say so all the time, some not kindly, but business is business and must be attended to, even if I would like to be a gentleman of leisure. Where would my fortune be if I idled away my time chatting and gossiping as some do? When I am on journeys like this, there is time to take an interest in people and to chat, but if you could see me in my counting house, you would change your tune."

For an hour they followed the stream, but then branched off deeper into the forest, as the stream meandered towards the west and, therefore, did not suit their purpose, their path lying east. It was a wide path and must have been much used in the past, perhaps before the archduke came and men stayed home when they could. Even the wandering tinkers and gypsies, seemed to have left these areas for safer routes until the times should change. The boy found he was really enjoying the walk and he hummed to himself as he walked beneath the lofty trees. He listened to the birds, he enjoyed the delicious scent of wild flowers, seemingly all around, and Father Bertram pointed out to him various ones he knew.

Hans and Manfred trod silently on, with the easy, effortless gait of the seasoned soldier. Manfred, at least, would have been happier on a horse, but Hans was happy to walk. Indeed the others had to remind him that they did not have his long and powerful legs and beg him to slow down for them.

All four were occupied with their own thoughts, when a piercing scream startled them and brought them to a halt. It came again and again, then was silent.

Manfred and Hans looked at each other.

"In front of us along the path, I think," said the priest. "Come quickly, we may be able to help," and he ran towards the dreadful sounds they had heard.

"Stay close to us, my Prince," said Manfred in an aside, "and hazard not your life, I beg you."

They ran to follow the priest and soon came upon a clearing and a pitiful sight.

A man was writhing in his death throes as he hung from the leafy branch of an oak tree. A girl of fourteen or fifteen was crouching behind another tree and crying bitterly, while she tried to evade capture by a burly soldier in a rough tabard of red and black. Near the foot of the tree lay what appeared to be a bundle of old clothes, very still and quiet. Three or four others, also in red and black, stood grinning and watching, and another sat upon a horse, a slow smile upon his square and weather beaten face.

Onto this scene burst, first the ragged priest.

He raced to the dying man and, before the startled men at arms could stop him, his knife flashed and the rope was cut. The man fell heavily to the ground below.

Bertram then turned his attentions to the man chasing the girl.

"You scoundrel!" he shouted. "Have you not done enough mischief here. In the name of Mother Church and of our blessed Savior Jesus, I command you to leave her at once."

For a moment it looked as if the priest's audacity was going to work. The man turned open-mouthed and stared at him, while the other troopers were similarly startled.

But it didn't last long. The one on the horse recovered his wits first.

"And who are you to question and even *command* the loyal servants of His Royal Highness, the Archduke of Thalesia?"

"My name is Bertram, a priest duly ordained of Mother Church, and I tell you that if one of you touches that child, I will call down the curses of Heaven upon his head."

One at least of the soldiers turned pale at the threat, for these

49

were superstitious days and the curse of the church was no small thing to reckon with. However, he on the horse was not so impressed. He sneered at the gaunt scarecrow in front of them.

"We care nothing for the curses or blessings of 'Mother Church'."

He grinned viciously. "Now we will see if you really believe what you say. You should be glad, Master Priest, for we are about to send you to your heavenly home, which you all profess to like so much, yet are ever anxious not to go there too soon. Too kind for my own good, I am."

He smiled again and shouted to his men, "Kill the priest, and stop fooling with the girl. Take her and be done, but first ... the priest," and he urged his horse towards him.

Then the others arrived in the clearing. Distracted by Bertram, the first the soldiers knew of their presence was a quarrel from Manfred's crossbow hitting the horseman in the throat. He fell with a hoarse cry and his men turned to face their enemies. Hans took the nearest one with a mighty blow of his sword, which left the man lifeless on the grass. He then parried the sword thrust of the second man who attacked Manfred as he struggled to reload his crossbow. The man recovered and swept his sword sideways in a vicious undercut to try to take Hans's arm off. Again, Hans parried and thrusting his great bulk against his opponent, brought the massive pommel of his sword down upon the man's head, crushing his helmet and felling him to the ground, where he lay still.

Manfred had by this time reloaded and looked up quickly to see the first man at arms chasing the priest who was running across the clearing towards them. Manfred's arrow struck the soldier's chest with a resounding thwack, the impact knocking him off his feet, so that he lay moaning on the floor.

Behind Manfred came a startled cry and his blood ran cold as he turned to see Prince Rudolph on the ground, a soldier standing over him with his sword raised above his head. Manfred's bow was unloaded and he knew that Hans was too far away to reach the Prince in time. Just as the man started to bring the sword down in its horrid sweep, a brown bundle struck him squarely and swept him off his feet. Bertram the priest had intervened again.

The two men rolled over and over, but the soldier was more than a match for the gaunt priest and he soon began to get the upper hand. By that time, though, Hans had reached them both and plucked the soldier effortlessly off their friend. He flung him to one side and waited for him. But the man saw that his party was devastated and that Hans was a fearsome opponent. He lay there groaning and offered no more resistance.

Hans inspected one or two of the bodies. "Thalesians!" he spat out, "underpaid, underfed, under-trained; not much good as soldiers. I don't know how they would get on if they met some of the soldiers I have fought against in my time. Remember when those brigands attacked us in Palentia. Now *they* were really fierce. These poor fellows would have been in trouble against them!"

Rudolph could not quite see how they could have been in much greater trouble than they were now, but Manfred was ruminating on their enemies.

"I suspect the Archduke keeps his best for the army near the castle. However, I did not think the recruiting parties would have got this far east. Strange really, and the one in charge is not a second class soldier. I wonder if he has another mission and is recruiting along the way." He looked at Hans, "Well done, my faithful friend, again! But it would have been disaster without the priest. If *he* had not been here..."

"Ah yes," said Hans with a sombre look. "All would have been lost without him today."

"Yes, indeed."

Manfred took a quick look round at the clearing. The man who had been thrown by Hans was groaning, but the others were unmoving and appeared to be dead.

Bertram was kneeling by the man whom he had cut down from the tree and was bathing his face with water. The girl was crouching by the tree where they had first seen her and was rocking to and fro, moaning quietly to herself. The Prince, although a little pale, and apparently none the worse for his ordeal, was on his way across to Bertram. Manfred himself walked over to the boy who was his special care and charge.

"Are you all right?" he asked quietly.

"Yes, I am. Master, the English priest saved my life, didn't he. And to think I was suspicious of him for a while."

"He did. We owe him more than we can tell him, at least, at present."

"I'm going to say something to him, if only to thank him."

"Be careful, *Fritz*," was Manfred's only comment.

The boy went over to the priest, who looked up at him.

"I think he will be all right. He will have a mark round his neck for the rest of his life but, otherwise, he will be none the worse. Now for the girl." And he started to get to his feet.

"Father," began the Prince hesitantly.

"Yes?"

"You saved my life and I thank you most sincerely. I'm afraid I was a little suspicious of you when we first met."

Gentle blue eyes regarded the Prince steadily. "You were right not to trust me at first sight. This is a dangerous time and, as your master said, the roads are full of vagabonds.

"And *you*, young man, if you are an apprentice, I am a Welsh rabbit! However, your secret, whatever it is, is safe with me. I will not betray you and, if you will have me, I will be your friend."

The boy looked into the gaunt face before him and smiled. They said no more but shook hands and were friends.

"One day, Father, I will thank you properly for your bravery," the boy muttered. But Bertram was on his way to the girl, who was sitting weeping quietly, still by the tree.

The Prince was impressed by this man. Thin and spare he was, but he seemed to have plenty of energy when it was needed. And although he seemed old in the boy's eyes, he had recovered quickly from his tumble and from adventures that would have tried many young men. To a lad that had been taught all his life to respect courage, the priest's actions had been praiseworthy all through.

Now Bertram was kneeling by the girl, talking gently to her, calming and consoling her. At one point she pointed hysterically to the pathetic heap which was obviously her mother, and Bertram shook his head gently. He led her gently to the peasant lying on the ground, and she kissed him and helped him to sit up, leaning against the tree that had nearly been his death. He seemed to be recovering. He kept coughing and rubbing his neck, where there was a livid weal. He gazed at his daughter and then looked around in bewilderment, uttering a short, agonized cry as he saw his dead wife, lying not far from them both.

Hans walked round to inspect, with the point of his sword, the red and black clad figures, lying on the grass of the clearing. He stopped at the man, who was still alive and bound him swiftly but securely with rope he had found on one of the soldiers.

Manfred came to question the fellow. His voice was quiet, but there was that about him that brooked no argument. His eyes searched the man's face and his questions seemed to probe his heart. He found that the man came from Unterkrau, a village far to the west, and had been captured by one of the Archduke's raiding parties. He had been 'persuaded' to join the army. The man they had saved from hanging showed the nature of the persuasion. He had chosen the other path.

Manfred wondered what was the best thing to do with him. They dared not trust him, yet Manfred was loth to kill yet more people, and in cold blood. That was the difference between the noble Archduke and his own royal master. The King was of a different stamp and had striven to rule his lands with justice and mercy, according to the rule of law and not with arbitrary cruelty. No, they would take him with them and leave him at a village Manfred had in mind.

"Apart from him, they are all dead," Hans said gruffly. "I will hide the bodies. It would not do to leave them here where they can be found so easily. The Archduke's men might come looking."

"Yes, Hans, old friend, that might be a good idea. Before you do that, I will pick up a sword. I will keep my bow, but I felt its inadequacies just now, when our priestly friend joined in. If it had not been for him, our mission would have been in vain, and would have ended in dishonor in this clearing."

"Yes, my..." but Manfred put a warning finger to his lips as Bertram began to walk over to them.

"The man and the girl want to be left. He says he is Peter, from Trilsound, a village not far from here, and he will go there. He says to leave his wife and he will bury her."

"No," said Manfred. "That would take too long by himself. There may be other patrols this way and their ways would not be pleasant with him or his daughter if they find this mess here. We will help and we will be quick."

"He wishes to mourn her properly."

"He can mourn her properly later. If he delays now, there may be more to mourn for than he wishes."

And so it was. The bodies of the soldiers were well hidden in the forest and the poor woman duly buried.

Manfred chose his blade carefully from the dead soldiers' weapons, and slung it from his belt. Reluctantly, he decided he would leave his crossbow behind. He would miss it but it was too slow for these abrupt skirmishes. Truth to tell, he was a better swordsman than bowman, but he fancied himself with the crossbow. He thought he had a good 'eye' for it. But no, a sword would fit in better, and after all, in these lawless days, it was not unusual for a merchant to be carrying a sword when he was away from his home.

Bertram thought about going with the man and his daughter, but said he had heard of a large village, called Peslok, where they had no priest and, therefore, perhaps be more open to the gospel. *What a tragedy,* he thought, *that those who should be foremost in preaching the gospel, were foremost in persecuting those who did..* He shook his head sadly and decided he would speak to Sandor, the merchant.

"Master Sandor. Do you know a village called Peslok? I heard that it is quite a large village, at present without a priest. I am thinking I might go there next. What do you think?"

"We are passing through Peslok, and I am sure you would be welcome there. I have known the Reeve there for many years and he is a good man. However, I think you might be better accompanying Peter and his daughter first. I think they need some support and their village would welcome you too, I am sure. It is not far from Peslok. You could go there first and then go to Peslok. I will tell the Reeve at Peslok to look out for you and ask him to make you welcome. And, Father, I thank you for saving my young apprentice's life. I am fond of him and would not like to tell his father I had lost his son."

Bertram brushed aside the thanks, saying it was nothing. He responded to the suggestion of following on to Peslok. "It would be a pleasant change to be welcome for once," said Bertram, "and it would enable me to take the gospel to two places instead of one."

"Why do they need the gospel?" asked the Prince. "The church has been in our land for centuries and I was hoping you could come with us. I wanted to ask you about England."

Bertram gave him a serious look. "They need to know about Jesus' love and, I am sorry to say, Mother Church has often taught them that their money is more important than His love for them. But you and I are friends, aren't we, and we will meet again one day. And one day, I will tell you about a friend who will never leave you."

"Sir Priest," interrupted Manfred, "we owe you more than I can say, for saving the boy's life. If we are ever in a position where I can help you, be sure I will."

So they said their farewells, and Manfred slipped a few coins into the priest's hand.

"After all," he had said, with a slight smile, "I would not want you to die of starvation before I can pay my debt."

Hans placed a ponderous hand upon the priest's shoulder. "Father, I am beginning to understand why you are somewhat bruised and battered. If I begin to be bored with serving my master," he nodded at Manfred, "I'll come with you. I have a feeling it would be quite exciting."

Bertram grinned his thanks and bowed, then turned back to the man and girl, still sitting disconsolately on the grass.

The Prince, Manfred and Hans set off again, returning to the path they had been on before the incident in the clearing, but this time they had their prisoner with them. By now it was late in the day, and they were miles away from Manfred's planned resting place. He decided they would camp in the forest.

The prisoner was called Alfric. No, he had not been a soldier before the Archduke's men had come. Yes, there had been others conscripted with him. Where were they now? He guessed they would be back in their camp. His had been part of a larger force, sent out to scour the villages for food for the army and for recruits. This had been just one of the bands. The leader of all the recruiting force was a knight called Count Murden, a formidable and cruel leader. Even his own men were afraid of him. Could Alfric be trusted not to escape if they untied him? Oh yes, he had never really wanted to work for the Archduke, but loved his country and was loyal to the King. Had he a wife? Yes, she had run away with the rest of the village women when the Archduke's soldiers had come. No, he did not know where she was now.

It all sounded reasonable to Manfred. After all, faced with the choice between serving the foreign, apparently all powerful ruler, and being hanged, which would most peasants choose? Manfred guessed that in most men's minds there was not much difference between serving one autocratic master and another. He decided to release him. He seemed anxious to go home and the last they saw of him, he was wandering off, rather sadly, towards the south, where he had said his village was.

Manfred turned for a last look at Bertram sitting with the two peasants. He shook his head wonderingly. The priest was by far the most ragged of the three.

SIX

The resonant knock of an axe echoed through the quiet woodland. Rhythmic and regular, knock upon knock; a man worked alone in the stillness of deep forest. Birds saw him, and the sun warmed him. Insects buzzed and busied themselves. Wild flowers spread their sweet fragrance through the woodland. Timid beasts hid from man's activity, but he worked on, unheeding of the creatures around him.

At last he finished.

Breclan, Keeper of the King's Forest of Klein, stopped work. He put on a rough coat, shouldered his axe and a quiver of arrows, picked up a long stout bow and walked cheerfully away from his work.

Breclan was away from home this night, deep in the forest, away from any dwelling. He had made a rough shelter and tomorrow he would return to his beloved Elena and their growing brood of children. He thought about them now as he strode along: Elena, with her long blond hair and gentle ways; Garth, his first born, strong, like his father, but going to be taller, he thought; Ilya the next, gentle like his mother. He worried about Ilya in this modern brutal world. *He would be better at court*, he thought. He thought then of Irena, full of mischief. His mind strayed to the youngest: Palki, Lotte, Gertrude and baby Ivan. Oh well, plenty to keep Elena busy while he was away. Still thinking about them, he arrived at his shelter in the wood, prepared a simple meal and soon slept the sound sleep of the outdoor worker.

Next day saw him early awake and soon back at work. Normally he would not do these routine tasks but he knew the threat facing the Kingdom and he found it easier to think his plans through when he was swinging his axe alone in the great forest.

He stopped suddenly, gently deposited the axe and noiselessly fitted an arrow to his bow. A throaty clucking and a rustle ahead sounded like supper to the experienced huntsman. A loud whirring noise came from the ahead and a fine cock pheasant broke from the bushes and took flight. It happened quickly, but Breclan was ready and loosed his arrow while the bird was not more than a dozen yards above him. He grunted his satisfaction as the arrow struck and killed the bird. He stuffed it into a cloth sack he had with him, and continued. He worked until noon, looked at the trees he had thinned, nodded to himself and shouldered his axe.

This part of the forest was deserted, deliberately so today, for he had tasks to perform away from the eyes of others. Although at least five hundred foresters worked for him, for the most part they worked away from this area. Indeed, most of the men hardly knew of its existence. The forest was vast, and only his lieutenant, Huw, knew roughly the area in which Breclan worked alone from time to time. He was on his way home, all tasks completed, and was glad to be out of the lonely part he had been in. The trees still grew thickly together though, and the undergrowth was dense. He picked his way along an unseen path until, at last, the trees thinned a little and there were more open spaces.

Short and stocky, Breclan was almost as broad as he was tall. Stories of his great strength abounded along the edge of the forest, where the villages were. It was even said that he had fought a bear unarmed, and that the bear had been glad to escape, but stories are easy to tell, and grow with the telling.

Now he could hear water ahead: the same stream, grown a bit, from which he had drunk that morning. His eyes gleamed and he scratched his hooked nose. Not far to go now. He lived in a long house on the edge of the village of Kleinar, still deep in the forest. Near to his house, was Huw's hut, and then the rest of the foresters' rough dwellings clustered together in the village. Other villages there were, with other foresters, scattered along perhaps forty miles of the edge of the forest.

The smell of honeysuckle came to him and he wrinkled his nose with pleasure. Funny how after all this time in the woods, the simple pleasures still moved him.

He tensed as he heard voices and movement not far away. It must be strangers, he thought, although he could not see them yet. Not even his own foresters should be in this part of the woods today and he had given orders that they should be thinning young saplings the other side of the village. He decided he would try to place himself between the strangers and his home before he showed himself. He also decided that he would see them before they saw him.

He moved swiftly in a flanking operation between the strangers and the river. Happily, they were not used to the forest and were moving slowly compared with him.

"Three of them, I think," he muttered to himself.

When he reached the position he wanted, he climbed into the fork of a tree and, fitting an arrow to his bow, waited.

In a short while, a figure appeared from behind a tree, closely followed by a smaller and then a much larger one. Breclan loosed his first arrow and Manfred stopped dead as a white goose feathered shaft thudded into the trunk of a birch tree next to his head.

"As you value your lives, stop there," shouted Breclan. "State your business in the King's forest."

Manfred tried in vain to see the speaker and looked at Hans, who shook his head. He could not see him either. He gave up and shouted back.

"Breclan! Is this the welcome you always give your friends and old comrades in arms?"

"Come forward slowly. Make no attempt to draw your sword, and I will see who you are that claims friendship with Breclan of the King's Forest," was the unpromising reply.

"Oh, don't be so grizzly, you old bear!" laughed Manfred, but he kept his arms well clear of his weapons as he moved carefully forward with the other two. "It is Manfred of Tata, with Hans of the King's Guard and... a friend. Have you forgotten our voices so soon?"

They had come clear of the trees now and Breclan could see them plainly. His hands flew to his bow and five arrows sped so quickly it was hard to distinguish between them as he fitted and fired them to stick quivering in the ground in a semi-circle at their feet. He then jumped down, flung aside his weapons and ran towards them, enveloping Manfred in a hug that left him gasping.

"That will teach you to call me a bear, my lord Manfred of Tata," he grinned, and then hurled himself at Hans. But Hans was ready for him and moved with him so that they rolled together onto the forest floor. The Prince watched open-mouthed as they fought and grunted, each trying to gain the mastery of the other. Suddenly, with a twist of his massive frame, Hans threw Breclan to one side and then landed on top of him to pin him to the ground by his shoulders.

"Mercy, you great oaf!" cried Breclan, laughing. "Can't you take a little playful wrestling, a loving hug from an old friend!"

Hans slowly got to his feet, brushing the twigs and grass from his jerkin. He then stooped to haul Breclan bodily to his feet. "Arr," he growled, "I just thought I'd humor you for a little to get rid of some of that excess energy you have. Comes of not having enough to do, stuck out here in the back of nowhere. Got to do something with your time, haven't you."

Quite unabashed, the sturdy woodsman turned to the Prince and seized him, lifting him high in the air and grinning at him broadly.

"And who is this, Manfred? A fine, sturdy lad, fine eyes, straight limbs, good features, too good looking for *your* son," and he laughed uproariously at his own joke.

"Tell you what," he said, "for a small sum, I will enlist him as a King's Forester in training, and teach him all I know. Course, it will cost you a bit, but I know you must have a bit stashed away, with all those years you have been at court, rich friends and all that, you know."

"This," said Manfred coldly, but with a twinkle in his eye, "is Rudolph Christian Albert of Dehrmacht, son of Maximilian the Good, Prince of Gerden, Archduke of Branza, Lord of the Southern Islands and Count of Tiros."

Breclan became instantly serious and put the boy down with a bump. Then he knelt before him.

"Your Highness, I am your obedient and loyal servant," said Breclan. "I beg your pardon for my liberty with your Person. I have loved and served your royal father for these many years and the loyalty I owe to him I also owe to you. I pray you will forgive my presumption and accept the loyalty of myself and my people."

"Manfred," said the boy sternly, "is this wise? Was not my identity to be kept secret?"

"Your Highness," said Manfred, "this man is one of his Majesty's most trusted servants. In this man's house, as in few others, you may be yourself, but we will still be Sandor, Vigor and Fritz, in front of the villagers. You can relax and be at ease, although there may not be all the comforts of royalty, I fear."

Breclan was still on one knee before him.

"In that case," said Prince Rudolph, laughing, at least partly from relief, "good woodsman, if you can feed our royal person with something warm and tasty, you will have our most gracious pardon.

"You may rise, but remember that our forgiveness is dependent upon a meal."

"And you shall have it, Your Highness, a hearty meal, although I know we cannot provide the sort of feast Your

Highness is used to. Our life is quite simple here, you see, sir. We do not have the sumptuous banquets of the court but fairly simple food. Plenty of it, though," he grinned.

Manfred spoke "Just one thing, Your Highness. Breclan is no common woodsman. He is nobly born and is entitled Count Breclan of Klein."

The Prince hastened to make it right and apologised, addressing him as "my lord Breclan".

SEVEN

Breclan led them through woodland glades, along hardly marked paths, beside chattering streams. He seemed on familiar terms with the King's Counsellor, Manfred, and with Hans, and the Prince wondered at it. Breclan was pleased to see them, chatting to them about old friends and experiences shared, even teasing them over incidents in the past. The thing that puzzled the Prince was that he had never heard of this man who made so free with these men of the King's household. Manfred, for his part, acquainted his old friend with their situation, and the need for secrecy.

Although boisterous at first, Hans seemed subdued. He was obviously pleased to see his old friend and comrade at arms, but he was quiet. Rudolph noticed but dismissed the thought and enjoyed the beauty around them.

At last, with the day well on, they came by various paths, to an island, on which stood a long, wooden manor house, with no windows, but horizontal slits near to the roof and a single hole on top. Through this, a steady stream of blue smoke issued. Trees surrounded the house, but none were close, for all around there was a cleared space of level grass. Just inside the ring of trees was deep ditch, with water channelled from the river, which lay to one side. Rough wooden bridges lay across the moat, one on each side. Over the nearer one, they passed.

Men and women were working in the clearing. As always, animals seemed to be everywhere. As they passed, the people stopped, the men bared their heads and the women curtsied. Breclan was very much the lord of this village. He would ask Manfred about it later. He smiled to himself as he realized how much he had to learn and how much he might have missed if he had stayed in the beleaguered castle, and then he sighed as he thought of his father and wondered how he was.

Small children were playing in the clearing and a group of these ran from near the house. They made straight for Breclan, with shrieks of delight. Breclan swept two or three of them off their feet and greeted them with a hug and a kiss. Then, depositing one on each broad shoulder and a third on his back, continued a triumphal journey to his home.

Prince Rudolph watched with interest and a slight undefined sadness. His father loved him dearly, but he had never been able to behave with such abandon with his son, although he might well have longed to do so. Hans did, occasionally, but it had to be out of sight of prying eyes. The court would not understand.

This man, Breclan, was a strange mixture. His face was that of a battle-hardened warrior: fierce, stern, unyielding. His body was strong beyond most men and the Prince was sure that he would have shot them out of hand if he had thought them enemies when he first met them in the wood. And yet, underlying that grim exterior there was a certain sense of bubbling fun, never far below the surface, ever waiting, it seemed, to burst out. And, he noticed, the strain that had been upon Manfred and Hans since they started out, had dropped away from them both since they had encountered their old comrade. Hans was almost, but not quite, chatty.

Rudolph watched the woodsman now and almost regretted he was a prince. Breclan was a veritable softy with the children and, it seemed, not just his own. And they loved *him* too. He was surrounded by a large band of these small brown urchins. They squealed with delight as he danced his way amongst them. He fell! No, he was pretending, for their pleasure, and then, as gently as any mother, he placed those he was carrying upon the ground. Then, again to the Prince's astonishment, he rolled upon the ground himself. Instantly, all the children hurled themselves upon him and he disappeared under a mass of small wriggling bodies. There were confused rumbles from the floor, amongst the shrieks and squeals. Then, slowly, the whole mass began to rise. Breclan arose, with children clinging to him from every particle of his clothing and his body. His face was red, he panted a little, but he grinned from ear to ear, as he looked at his two friends.

"Ah!" he said. "This is the stuff to keep you young. I never feel a day over sixty with all these little ones around." And he roared with laughter again.

"Down then you young vagabonds," he cried, "let me attend to my business," and children poured off him like water from a leaky bucket. He shook himself and then stopped. Coming towards him was a boy of about Rudolph's age. He bowed his head slightly and then stood before Breclan, who stood and looked steadily in turn at the boy.

"Well?" he growled. "Young man, give your report."

"Sir," the boy replied, "all is well. The village has been quiet and undisturbed. The men have worked in the south-western quarter as you commanded. They thinned the trees, cut much wood for the winter, and Mark, the farrier's son, hurt his arm when he fell out of a tree. But he's all right now," he added belatedly.

"Oh, and Mother says, if you don't come and introduce your visitors soon, there will be no venison for you tonight," and the boy grinned.

Breclan pretended to be cross.

"How many times do I have to tell you not to mix your business with family matters. And now come and say hello to your father."

And the boy whooped and flung himself onto Breclan, who hugged him and lifted him high in the air, as he had the Prince when he met him in the wood.

"And, Father," said the breathless lad, "I can now hit the gold on the target at eighty yards!"

"That *is* good, my son, I must see you do that tomorrow. And broadsword?"

"Yes, Father. Ilya and I have practised daily, also with pike and quarterstaff."

"Hmm! It seems you have done well. And now I want you to meet someone.

"Your Highness, this is my first-born son, Garth. I would dare to hope, Sir, that one day you might allow him to serve you, as I have served your father in times past, and in the present.

"Garth," he continued, "this is a great day for us, for this is the King's son: Prince Rudolph, son of Maximilian, heir to the throne of Dehrmacht."

Garth knelt before Rudolph, who felt he should say something, although he was full of confused thoughts, but Garth was still kneeling and the others were waiting, expectantly.

"I am glad to honour the son of any man whom my father honours, and feel it a privilege already to have the loyalty of such an one before me."

On a sudden impulse, he added rather shyly to the boy,

"I hope you will not just be a subject to me, but perhaps, my friend," and he reached out his hand to the lad to rise. Garth took his hand and kissed it as a sign of loyalty, and the Prince knew his offer of friendship had been accepted.

Breclan and the two servants of his father smiled. Somehow they were pleased with their little prince. He had managed to say the right thing, and yet he had meant it too. He had never had a real friend of his own age and he liked the look of this sturdy son of the woods who, like him, was learning the arts of weaponry at an early age. Then he had another thought.

"Tomorrow, when you show us your archery, perhaps we could practise broadswords together, as you and your friend have been doing."

Some of the common people had stopped working while this had been going on and Breclan now spoke to those who were within the compound.

"My people, we don't often have visitors here. These men are very old friends of mine. You will honour and respect them as you would me. This is the merchant, Sandor," for Manfred had already told him their pseudonyms, "Vigor, his bodyguard, and his apprentice, Fritz."

Breclan's son, Garth, was delighted to be in on the secret, and grinned broadly at Rudolph.

"Tonight, we will have a feast in the hall," Breclan continued, "so root out Platik, and the other musicians, and we will make it an occasion."

There was an excited buzz amongst the villagers and they hurried off to spread the word and to make themselves ready.

Together they went into the hall, blinking as their eyes became used to the darkness. The smoke, too, seemed to be everywhere, despite the hole in the roof. In fact, the smoke, as in all these places, seemed to go everywhere *except* through the hole meant for it.

Manfred's plan, as he explained it to Breclan, was to get his young master to safety with a powerful baron in the far north of the country. His name, Christov of Berenal, cousin to the King, was well known to Breclan, who agreed that it was a good choice, as his loyalty to the King was unquestioned. There, they were to await the arrival of Henry, the King's brother, and Prince of Selden. He was at present raising an army to join the men of Selden, who were already assembled with a large force of Maximilian's men. They had been sent to quell a rumoured invasion of that country, which was now known, of course, to be a ruse to weaken the kingdom for the Archduke's invasion.

Boris, Archduke of Thalesia, had, of course, foreseen the return of the Dehrmacht army, and the probable intervention of

Prince Henry, but he had gambled that, with possession of the fortress of Dehrmacht, and its reputedly vast treasure within, he would be able to hold what he had taken. Unfortunately, so far, he had found very little treasure in Dehrmacht. He was convinced there was some somewhere, for the kingdom was rich and prosperous, but he had not found it yet. Perhaps it was only a rumour after all.

EIGHT

The young prince enjoyed the time at Breclan's hall more than he could have told. Manfred repeated that Breclan was, in fact, of noble birth himself and a baron in his own right, ruling over all the land of the forest in the King's name. More than once he had been offered high office at court but had always asked to be excused as he loved the rough open air life of the woodsman. He had also served in the King's armies in the past with great distinction and Prince Rudolph remembered hearing tales of the formidable valour of the Woodsmen of Klein and their fearsome leader, whom men called the Wild Boar of Klein. Now he had met him, was sharing his home, and, he found, he loved the man, and he loved being in the Great Hall of Klein.

Until now, Rudolph had not had much to do with other children, being an only child, the Heir Apparent, and growing up in the king's court. He had been taught alone by tutors, diplomacy and politics by Manfred, and military skills by Hans and other members of the King's Guard.

Now he was surrounded by the children of the hall and the children of the village, for Breclan drew little distinction between them. He began to forget a little his dignity and his future role, which had never been far from him. For a short time, he began to relax. He seemed to benefit so much that Manfred quietly altered his plans and allowed them to stay at Klein several days longer than he had intended.

Also, Rudolph had never known a mother, and Breclan's wife, Elena, was beautiful, gentle and kind. He sat near her at the High Table. On this occasion, the older boys of the family, Breclan and Elena, and the three guests only sat there, so they could enjoy some freedom of speech. By rights he should have had a privileged position at the High Table, should have been given the choicest food and been able to distribute morsels from his plate to favoured ones around him, but this could not be. The servants and even the villagers would have noticed if he had been given privileges of rank, and he only a boy. Elena asked about his life at court, particularly wanting to know what the great ladies there were wearing. He said that there had not been many ladies there lately, as they had fled at the rumours of war. She sensed his need for some of the softnesses of feminine company. Every boy needs a mother, and he took the motherless boy to her heart and showed him many kindnesses. His heart in turn was touched and his iron hard self-discipline softened a little. Manfred saw it and approved.

Hans was still quiet though. Breclan tried to draw him out, reminding him of encounters in the past, and he did seem to shake off his gloom for a while.

"Remember," said Breclan, "that day on the edge of Gringlemoor, when we were set upon by Tata's men? And that great ape with an enormous beard was about to cut my arm off?"

"Hah! Now that *was* a battle," said Hans. He would have roared it, but he had to keep his voice down because of the

75

villagers nearby, although the whole place was full of shouting and noise. There were even some dogs having a fight over a piece of meat somewhere. "The Thalesians we have met so far would have perished miserably fighting Tata's men. Did I fight that bearded oaf? I can't remember now."

"Can't remember!" said Manfred scornfully. "Nearly cut him in two, that's all." Then, relenting a little... "I suppose there have been rather a lot of battles, haven't there, old friend."

"Well, it's strange really. Yes, there have been a lot of battles, and yet, I am almost ashamed to say it, I have enjoyed them. Oh, I have not enjoyed seeing friends cut down, men I have known and worked with, but the physical challenge and the thrill of battle..."

Prince Rudolph leaned over: "Aren't you ever afraid, Hans?"

"Ho, yes!" roared Hans, then he quietened a bit, "Yes, I am afraid sometimes, if I start to think what might happen, especially just before a battle, if we have time to think and worry, but once it starts, I seem to forget all that. It's like a sort of challenge of strength and skill. It's me against the opponents that come against me. Can I be quicker, stronger, more skilful than they? I suppose the day will come when I won't be as strong or quick..."

"Not you!" put in Manfred, "not yet. It will be a long time before you lose your strength, my mighty friend."

Hans smiled at this: "Well, just so long as I can still beat my lord Breclan in a friendly wrestle."

"Friendly!" cried Breclan. "Last time we wrestled, not counting the little tumble in the woods just now, I ached from my bruises for two weeks. You nearly pulled my leg off. I think I have been limping ever since."

"Nonsense!" put in the Lady Elena. "He walked around boasting about what he would do to you next time." Breclan was making faces at her, to keep quiet, but she grinned and carried on: "Said he could fight two like Hans any day and that he had only been beaten because he had slipped on a wet patch of grass."

"Oho!" roared Hans.

"I thought you loved me, my lady," groaned Breclan.

"I do, my love, I do, but I love the truth too."

"A return match then," said Hans.

But Manfred was having none of it. "No, not this time, I have too many things to talk about and we cannot afford to have either of you injured just because of silly vanity."

The Prince spoke to Ilya, Breclan's second son. He was not sturdy like Garth but slimmer, taller, like his mother.

"So, you have training in warfare too, Ilya?"

"Oh yes, Your Royal Highness," replied the boy, a little nervously. He was younger than Prince Rudolph, by about two years. "I am not very good, though, not like Garth. *He* is really good, especially at archery."

"What *are* you good at then, Ilya?"

"I can read," said the boy, "although we are a little short of books here. I seem to spend a lot of my time reading through old manuscripts about the ancient laws of the forest and who has right of tenure, and all that sort of thing. Why, my father now lets me settle disputes among the foresters. He says I know the laws better than he does... I do too!" This last he said with a twinkle in his eye and a mischievous glance at his father.

"Perhaps you could become a law-maker when this war is over."

"Oh yes, I would like that, sir, but I would need more education than I have at present."

The Prince agreed and then turned to Garth: "Ilya says you are really good at archery. We will have to have a competition and you can show me your skill, and then we will have a fight with broadswords, 'cause I am better at that than archery."

"Yes, that would be fine," said Garth, "I would enjoy that."

They had the archery shoot the day after the next day. The Prince had been half afraid that Manfred would step in to forbid the competition, as he had with the men. Manfred stayed quiet though. Rudolph wondered if that was because it didn't matter as much if *he* were injured, although in his heart he knew that was not so. As Breclan had said, Rudolph found that Garth could shoot with an English longbow or Italian crossbow, straight and true, far better than he. In fact, the lad was a better archer than many men. But he, the Prince, could beat Garth every time in swordplay. After all, he had held a sword almost since he could walk and had been taught by the best in the land. He could also hold his own with pike and quarterstaff, although Garth had inherited his father's strength and gave the Prince knocks that made him gasp. Garth forgot his awe of him, almost, and they became firm friends, going off into the woods together, chattering about this and that, their different lives and the things they saw around them. The little prince kept Garth vastly amused with his descriptions of some of the great people of the court, while the woodland boy showed Rudolph secrets of the forest, the habits of animals and birds, the nesting places of birds and the dens of some of the animals. There were bears in the forest and Garth warned the Prince about disturbing them and the wisdom of leaving them to their own devices. Neither of them ever knew that one of the men always followed them into the forest, flitting silently from tree to tree behind them, ready to come instantly to their aid if danger should follow. In fact, a small band of men followed the follower in case the danger should ever be more than one man could handle. The ever careful hand of Manfred was behind this.

The village children all swam like fish in the river round their home and Rudolph watched fascinated. True, his home too was surrounded by a river, but it was deep and swift flowing and no-one ever swam in it. He bravely tried to swim with the other children, but came up coughing and spluttering. Still, he went in every day and began to learn a little of the ways of water.

Manfred allowed them seven days, for he knew the boy needed to rest and relax. At the end of the seven days he told the Prince that on the morrow they would journey into the heart of the forest, but that they would return to the hall to say their farewells.

"Can Garth come with us, Manfred?"

"Not into the forest, my Prince, not yet. One day, he may be one who shares this particular secret, but for the present, no."

Then, of course, the boy was full of questions about what it was he was to learn, but Manfred was not to be drawn. Indeed, he said, it should not even be talked about or mentioned, and that he, the King's son, must speak of it to no-one without permission.

"But who *is* 'chosen', Manfred, "and how will I know

them?"

"The King's Council know *of* it, but not its details and ... there is the Keeper of the King's Secret. No-one else knows of it."

"It sounds very mysterious, Manfred. Who is the - what did you call him? The Keeper of the King's Secret? *I've* never heard of him."

"Remember no-one talks about the secret, so it is not surprising you have never heard of the Keeper."

"Then who is it? Actually, I think I might know."

"Breclan is the present Keeper."

"I thought it might be," said the boy thoughtfully, "so that is why he lives out here in the wilderness, when he could have a place at court with my father."

Manfred laughed. "That is only part of the reason he lives here. He loves this life and *he* would certainly not call it a 'wilderness'. I don't think your friendship with Garth would last long either if he heard you call his beloved woods a wilderness. I thought you had begun to learn in the last few days here that life can be pleasant and enjoyable without all the luxuries of the King's palace."

"Yes, I have really, Manfred. I spoke without thinking, and you are right. My father must have a high regard for Breclan for him to hold such a secret."

"He does, Your Highness. Only a man who could be trusted on his life could be Keeper ... Breclan is such a man."

"So, where are we going tomorrow, and are we coming back to the hall? You see, Manfred, in some ways, I think I have been happier here than at almost any time in my life, except for my father not being here."

"Yes," said Manfred slowly, "I understand that, my Prince, and that is why we have stayed so long. I had originally planned to be here just three days. However, it has not been time wasted and ... tomorrow, Breclan will show you the King's Secret. Until then my Prince, you must be content, and wait."

NINE

They set off early the next morning, just the four of them. Garth and Huw, Breclan's lieutenant, listened carefully to Breclan's instructions for the care of the hall and work for the men.

He led them in the direction he had come the day they had arrived. After walking for about an hour, however, Breclan broke away from his route that day. They found it hard going after a while, as the way was densely tangled and thickly overgrown in places. He explained he had several different routes but that he varied them so in order to confuse anyone who might try to follow him, although, he added, he trusted his foresters absolutely.

He stopped often, motioning them to silence, and listening intently for long periods before continuing.

All day they travelled, until at last they reached a similar shelter to the one in which Breclan had slept a week earlier. It had taken them somewhat longer than it usually took Breclan and they crawled inside and fell asleep instantly, apart from Breclan, who lay and listened to the noises of the woodland night and then, he too, slept.

With the dawn, they awoke and breakfasted. They had eaten cold meats and bread so there was no fire to put out. Breclan made sure there were no signs of their presence, and the party resumed their journey.

About midday, they arrived at a clearing in the forest. They had come from the south east, and any slight path there was, lay across the clearing and away to the west. Two great oaks stood in the centre of the clearing.

"Hans, old friend, we must ask you to remain here until we return."

"I understand," said Hans.

"The reason for this, Your Highness," continued Breclan to the prince, "is that although Hans is a member of the King's Council, there are only two people in the Kingdom who know the exact location of the secret. It is the King's wish that you should know, and that there should be one other, separate from us, in case my lord Manfred and I should both die at the same time. The secret must not be lost, you see. The King himself knows, of course, but his own life is in danger and the times are perilous, so he wished you to be shown."

The boy was more excited than he could say, but he listened carefully and agreed to keep to himself all that he was told.

Breclan moved between the two oaks, Manfred and Prince Rudolph following. Breclan spoke again,

"Your Highness, you are about to be shown the Secret of Klein. Its presence here in the forest is the reason why I, Breclan, true descendant of the Barons of Klein, am able to call to arms more than three thousand men. I live in the solitude of this forest, when my sons and I should, by rights, be living the life of gentle folk. Not that I resent this life," he said with a grin, "truth to tell, I love it. With regard to this secret, Boris of Thalesia would give half his kingdom to know it, for it is… the great treasure of Dehrmacht."

"But how am I to find it again in this great forest?" asked the prince.

"These oaks are known as The King's Trees to all my chief foresters, though they do not know their significance. If you ever needed to come here, you need only send for one of my chief foresters and leave him here while you go on."

"Go on where?" asked the Prince, gazing in bewilderment at the forest all around them.

"There is a simple formula to remember, provided you begin in the right place. Now, stand here in the exact middle of the two trees and look straight ahead. What do you see?"

"Trees!" said the prince.

"Yes, what kind of trees?"

"Oh, I don"t know, they all look the same. No, wait a minute, there are two in front of us which are a silvery colour."

"That is right. They are birch trees and we must walk between them. Once through them the formula is always 'Three on the Right'"

"Three on the Right," repeated the Prince.

They advanced to the birch trees. The Prince cast a quick glance behind at Hans, faithfully standing with his back to them, almost hidden as he was by the two birch trees they had passed through.

Breclan continued to speak:

"The treasure is hidden in a large cave and the path to it is hidden by trees. So, we pass between the birch trees and what do you see?"

"Oh, Breclan, more trees!"

"Look more closely, Your Highness."

"Still trees, but somebody has been doing some cutting here, haven't they?"

"Yes, *I* have, Your Highness. Now look for a tree with three branches cut on its right-hand side."

"The boy looked at the trees in front of him. He saw that several had had branches lopped off.

"Here's one," he said.

"No," said Breclan, "that has only two missing on the right, and one on the left."

"Ah, yes, I see," said the prince, looking more carefully at the trees. "I see it now. It is this one, isn't it."

"Yes," said Breclan. "Now go to its right and there is a tree leaning across. Lift it."

Manfred did so and, to the Prince's surprise, it moved easily out of their way, to reveal a path. They followed it, moving the branch carefully back into position.

"Remember, "Three on the right" is the key," said Breclan, as they walked along a narrow path, bordered thickly by trees and bushes on both sides.

The path opened into a rocky gully, strewn with boulders. In the centre of the gully was a boulder about the size of a small table. Just beyond it was another larger one, and then beyond that a third larger still. The floor of the hollow was strewn with boulders, but this line of three standing slightly to the right of the entrance to the gully, stood out because of their peculiar square shape and their size.

"Three on the Right," murmured Prince Rudolph.

The boulders led them to the rocky wall of the hollow, where a heap of rocks lay, to which Breclan walked. He moved to the left of three particularly large rocks and disappeared.

"And we follow," said Manfred."

Rudolph went with him to the left of the rocks and saw that there was a narrow passage behind them. It was just wide enough to walk in one at a time and there was Breclan waiting for them.

The passage led into gloomy darkness and, at the entrance anyway, there were not torches. The Prince supposed that was in case anyone managed to find the passage and would not suspect there was anything more.

"It is dark at first, but it gets better."

Breclan's teeth gleamed in the dim light and he beckoned them to follow him. From the receding light of the entrance, which was not very bright anyway, being partly obscured by rocks, the passage seemed to come to an abrupt end. They followed Breclan to the end, however, and there he stepped sideways into darkness. They were close behind him and they saw that there was a narrow opening right at the end of their passage, hidden from any casual observer. Indeed the passage narrowed and seemed to peter out. They squeezed through after him and then it really was dark. Prince Rudolph realized that this was probably the blackest place he had ever been in. No light from anywhere relieved the inky darkness, not so much as a pinprick. Breclan's cheerful voice came from close in front of him.

"It's not as bad as it seems," he said. "Your Highness, so that you could do this yourself if no-one was with you, feel your way past me and keep your hands on the right-hand wall."

The Prince did as he was told and, of course, bumped right into Breclan, who grunted but said nothing. Rudolph continued to grope along the wall and discovered that the passage seemed to have become much wider. Then his hands met some sort of obstruction, which felt like wooden sticks.

"I've found something sticking out of the wall," he said. "They feel like thick sticks and ... ugh, they're sticky!"

Breclan chuckled close behind him. "That's right, Your Highness, they are torches. Pull one out and I will light it. I have brought some tinder on purpose for it." The Prince did so and then jumped as Breclan struck sparks and, after a few attempts, lit a small bundle of dry grasses he had brought. He held these to the torch and soon it was blazing merrily and illumining the whole cave. "Better take a couple more, Manfred, in case we need them."

The cave was dry, littered with rocks and rubble, with many projections and protrusions from the walls, but it was dry.

"Nothing here," said the Prince, "what's next? Or have we come to the wrong cave?"

Breclan and Manfred looked pleased.

"That's what we want people to think, but go further in and explore, Your Highness. Here, take the torch."

And so he did. When he reached the far wall of the cave, still nothing was obvious, but searching carefully, he discovered that there were further passages beyond this cave. He found three, and, by the light of the torch, the one in the middle seemed particularly lengthy. Furthermore, he discovered that there was a further supply of torches some way along it. This must be it, he thought, and called out to the two men.

"No, not that one, Your Highness. It does indeed lead somewhere, but not where we want today. Remember the rule at the beginning?"

"Yes, of course, three on the right."

"Yes. Well, is there a third passage on the right?"

"Yes, there is, but it looks poky."

"That's the one," said Manfred and Breclan together, and they came across.

The young prince entered the third passage, which did seem poky as he had said. However, he again found that just as it seemed too narrow to go on, there was a sudden opening on the right into yet another cave. At the far side of this smaller cave, there were three openings each one barred with a massive door, studded with ironwork. Each had a large keyhole, and at each side of each doorway, there was a bracket holding an unlit torch, doubtless ready to be lit.

"Oh," said the Prince, "we need a key, but this time I can guess that it is the door on the right which we open."

"You have learned well," smiled Breclan, "but this is the one occasion on which it does not apply. The men who contrived all this long ago, figured that if someone got this far they might have worked out the three on the right rule, so this last time, it is the door on the left we must try, and ... I have the key! Here you are, would you like to open it?"

"Thank you. Yes, I would."

"It's the largest one, here," and Breclan handed him a bunch of keys, one large one protruding in his hand.

The boy took the key, fitted it into the keyhole and tried to turn it. He grunted and struggled but could not move it.

"It is too stiff for me, I'm afraid," he said, rather disappointed.

"It's too stiff for anyone at the moment. There is yet another trick to get past," and Breclan lifted his hand and pulled on the right-hand bracket beside the door. The Prince watched as the entire bracket swung out in Breclan's hand. Breclan continued to pull until the bracket was at right angles to the wall.

"Now you do not need the key, for keys might be lost. Turn the handle of the door three times to the right, and it will open."

Prince Rudolph did so and the door opened easily. He walked in and the others followed. They were in a chamber of moderate size, whose walls were lined with chests: large, heavy, iron bound chests, some of wood, some of iron. There were sacks too: on the floor, on the chests, and piled on top of each other. There were also three or four large figures, covered in heavy cloths, standing against the wall.

"Here it is, Your Highness, the Secret of Dehrmacht. Go and look. None of the chests is locked, although the keys to them are here on this ring."

There, in the gloom, lit only partially by the flaring torches, Prince Rudolph gingerly lifted the lid of the nearest chest without anything on the top.

It was full, to the brim, with jewellery of various kinds: necklaces with gems winking in the flame of the torches, diamond clasps, bracelets with rubies glowing in the semi-dark, gold rings, here and there a tiara pushing up through the smaller items. The sight was breathtaking in its wealth and glittering beauty.

"Are they all like this?" gasped the boy.

"No, Your Highness. Some contain rich cloths, velvets and silks, beautiful gowns, robes fit for a..." here he smiled in the dim light, "a prince, or a king! Others are full to the very brim with gold coins and, there, if you look closely at that wall, you will see something a little different about it."

"Oh yes, I see, it is not like the other walls of the cave, it is made of bricks, isn't it."

"Ordinary bricks?"

"Yes, but yellowy, not red clay bricks, but a sort of yellowy colour. They're not..." the prince blinked in the half-light and gasped again. "They're gold, aren't they, Breclan."

"Yes, they're solid gold, Your Highness, and there is more than one layer of them building that wall."

"But where did all this come from?"

"It has been here a long time, collected by your great, great grandfather during his wars against the great robber barons of Grisombda. He decided that as they had collected their riches from others, he would not spend it himself but store it in case there was a great need in the future, either of the kingdom or of the people. Now, at this time, it would seem there might be a need for some of this to hire mercenaries to repulse the ignoble Archduke."

"What about Tata?" asked the Prince, with a sideways glance at Manfred.

"Yes, some came from Tata," said Manfred, "but it is now *all* the ancient treasure of Dehrmacht. The Duke of Tata renounced all rights to the treasure, and gladly. It belongs to the King, to him only and his heirs, theirs absolutely to do with as they will." This was said with some vigour, Manfred's eyes blazing in the flickering light, so that the Prince looked at him in wonder.

The Prince's eyes continued to wander round the room, taking in all its riches. "What about those small chests there?" he asked.

"Those contain spices from the East. Some of the larger ones have weapons in: swords and daggers, inlaid with gems and precious stones. The smaller figurines around the cave are statuettes and ornaments of different kinds, of gold, silver, ivory and alabaster."

"What are those, Breclan?" pointing to the large figures covered in protective cloths.

Breclan withdrew the covering from one of the figures.

It was a suit of armour in steel, slightly dulled, but as they looked closely, they saw that it was exquisitely wrought, with small moving parts at the joints, beautifully patterned and chased with gold on the breastplate, shoulders and greaves. Such a suit would have cost a small fortune, only to be afforded by the very richest noblemen, even kings.

The Prince gazed in awe and then wandered from chest to chest, looking at the rich bounty that was in each one, unveiling priceless jewellery and ornaments, some of which appeared to be very old.

Then he turned again to Manfred. "It seems, my lord, that you have given up too much. Do you really not want your rightful share of this magnificent treasure? Few men would refuse such an heritage."

The boy was troubled, and in his lonely childhood there had been few people so important to him as Manfred and Hans. There amid the torch-lit wonders of that ancient cave, the boy took Manfred's hands in his and looked quizzically into the older man's troubled brown eyes, as he asked his questions.

"My Prince, mine is not an honourable heritage," sighed Manfred. "Also, I have my life. Ordinarily, it should have been forfeit. To return your words, there are not many men who would have spared a worthless brat, brought up in that wicked hall of Tata, but your grandfather did, and I will ever be grateful for it. Indeed, many urged him to make an end of the whole murderous brood, but he spared me and, in fact, one other, a kinswoman. No, I have no claim to this treasure. It was ill-gotten and it is right that it should one day do good. It cost its former owners dear, I am afraid. I give it up gladly.

"I grew up, learning every art of trickery and treachery, all the usual arts of war, the sword, the bow, mace and lance, and others. Where others were taught the old laws of chivalry, I was taught to lie, to steal, to play weak or dead, and then to strike: to win, by fair means and foul. Others, of course, of noble birth, do such things too, but for me, as for my fathers, it was our way of life, from the cradle to the grave."

"Your father," whispered the boy, "was he executed?"

"Not exactly. Not by your grandfather anyway. Seeing the

forces arrayed against him were too great to defeat, my father, true to his nature surrendered, intending to use some trick or cheat, to regain his power and wealth. He knew your grandfather was an honourable man, and as the King had promised safe passage if he surrendered, my father knew he was safe.

"However, justice was waiting for him, all unknown. A young man from Selden, now Prince Henry's land, had lost all his family and wealth in a recent raid from Tata. As my father walked from the hall, through the ranks of soldiers, the young man stepped forward and cut him to pieces then and there.

"The King was terribly angry, for he felt his word had been broken. The young soldier was sent for and sentenced to death, but when the King heard his sad story, he pardoned him on certain conditions."

"What were the conditions, Manfred?"

"You will be surprised, my Prince. You see, the King, who had a kind and generous heart, like your father, felt that I was too young to be blamed for the wickedness of my family, although there were those who said I should perish with the rest of my house. The King over-ruled them and gave instructions that I was to be brought up at court, and educated in all that was good and decent and right. Truth to tell, I had early been sickened by the evils of my house and had prayed that if there be a god, he would give me a chance to break from the unspeakable things I had seen and heard. Well, I still don't really know if there is a god but my prayer was certainly answered, although I am sure a priest would find much wrong with it."

"But what about the conditions for the young soldier?"

"Ah yes," with a smile, "the young man who had killed my father, was given the task of caring for me and being my teacher, though not my master, I was too high-born for that. In his wisdom, he thought it would do the young man good to try to turn me into something better, and me good to see at first hand a little of the suffering my family had caused. Because the young man was an honest and upright young fellow, he showed me more kindness than I ever deserved and great patience with me. In time I grew to love him, and your family who never failed to show me courtesy and kindness. The young man and I became firm friends, and ..."

"And his name is Hans!" the Prince burst out with a cry of delight.

"And his name is Hans," smiled Manfred. "I felt the disgrace and evil of my family so much that I renounced my dukedom and all my lands, but the King would not let me renounce everything and insisted that I keep my baronry and some of my estates. He said it was not right that I should be destitute and that some of our ancient lands should remain in my possession. So there you have my whole sad and sorry tale."

"It's not so sad or sorry," mused the Prince, "for it has given us two of the best friends king or prince could ever have."

"I thank you for that, my Prince, from the bottom of my heart and I rejoice that when the sad day comes that your noble and gracious father leaves us, he will have a worthy successor in his son. "

Breclan came and interrupted them.

"Your Highness, Manfred has passed to me your father's

command that twelve sacks of gold be removed from here and given to Prince Henry for any payment of mercenaries that may be necessary. With your permission Hans, Manfred and I will take the sacks and hide them close to where we slept."

Agreement given, some time was spent in carrying the sacks to their resting place, well hidden, to be picked up later when the foresters marched to fight for their King. That night, they sat in Breclan's private quarters behind the high table in the great hall. Plans were made for the future. Breclan was to call in his woodsmen and, leaving a small force to guard the homesteads and the forest, would march to meet Prince Henry and the King's loyal forces as soon as possible. There was still a need for secrecy as it would not do for Breclan's men to be attacked before they were ready.

For a short while the boy forgot his anxieties and played with Breclan's children. Just now, he was chasing Irene, who had been teasing him with grossly exaggerated respect for his position.

Manfred took time off from the discussion to observe his young master. He was glad the boy was able to relax. He knew the strain everything had been for him recently and he was glad that here, at least for a little while, he could be a child. There had been little opportunity for the boy to enjoy childhood as he grew in the artificial atmosphere of the court.

Time drew on, the light faded and Manfred ordered everyone to bed as they would start early next morning.

Daylight saw them awake and dressed ready for their journey. They breakfasted and picked up sacks full of good things for their journey. They were armed as before: Hans with his huge sword at his back, Manfred with his sword, and Prince Rudolph with his sword strapped to his side. Goodbyes were especially difficult for the boy. Never before had he known friendships free of the stifling atmosphere of intrigue and favours at the court. Here he had felt liked for his own sake and not because of his position. Being with the children had been a treat he had never known before and he felt his heart would burst as he said goodbye to Garth, Irena, and Breclan's gentle wife, the Lady Elena. She flung her arms around him, kissed him on both cheeks and fled precipitously into the house. Irena giggled but she, too, kissed him shyly and he noticed her eyes seemed moist. Garth clapped him on the back and whispered "Father and Manfred have said that I will be going to serve as a page in the castle as soon as the war is over."

Rudolph beamed his approval and hugged his new friend.

"That will be wonderful. I will really look forward to that. Let's hope the war is over soon."

The little party set off, guided and escorted by Breclan and a half dozen of his foresters, they were led to the edge of the huge forest and then watched out of sight along the high road to Blecklinghaus.

TEN

Blecklinghaus was a city on a hill.

Around it, the plain was flat and fertile, after the hills from which the Prince and his friends descended. The Prince had never seen the city before, though he had heard of it. It had been known as 'The City of Thieves' in times past and was still turbulent. It no longer relied on highway robbery for its living but instead had prospered on the spice trade passing its doors, as it lay on the main highway through the kingdom, linking the mysterious East with the prosperous West. He was astonished now as he looked at it, drawing closer as they walked across the plain along the highroad, not alone despite the early hour, as many peasants and farmers were taking their wares to market there.

It was a rabbit warren.

As they drew nearer, the Prince could see that houses were built one on top of another up the hillside. Some were literally built on the crumbling walls of older houses. The wall of the city was itself built of houses, but this was not unusual, most were. The windows, very narrow, looked out across the plain, the entrances of the houses within the labyrinth of streets inside. Towers stood leaning at crazy angles from the wall, many painted bright colors, so that they looked like giant sticks of colored sugar, the whole effect amazingly haphazard and higgledy-piggledy, crushed together, as if some giant hand had leaned upon it.

In the middle, at the top of the hill and surmounting the whole town, was a rugged round tower, surprisingly and rather garishly painted in gold, so that it glinted and shone in the early morning sun.

Manfred, watching the boy's reaction, broke in upon his thoughts. "It is said, Your Highness, that no stranger can find his way round its jumbled streets and alleys and, indeed, at the one gate into the city, men make their living simply by being guides to the strangers who arrive. Men also say," he continued with a smile, "that beneath the city lies a maze of tunnels, so that although there is only one visible gate in and out of the city, there are said to be other exits known only to a few."

As the sun rose and the morning advanced, they could hear the city alive with movement. A dull murmur, even a roar, could be heard, of voices. The sounds of activities, much and varied, pursued within the town, reached their ears. More and more they could distinguish the shrill cries of street sellers, shouts and voices of women and men within the houses of the wall, and the shriller cries of children playing.

They were now very near and the city loomed over them as they began to climb the narrow ramp leading to the massive iron-studded gates, now standing wide open for the day's business. A window opened in a house high up in the wall, a woman's voice shouted something quite unintelligible and a bucket ejected its filthy contents into the air, to splash and trickle disgustingly down the inward sloping face of the house below.

Manfred thought wryly that it was a good thing this part of the country was noted for its heavy rainfall. Indeed the smell of the city hit them like a soft wall as they came to the gate. They wrinkled their noses, while other travelers, more prepared than they, produced scented cloths which they held to their noses as they entered.

A group of guards sat lazily playing dice just outside the gate, passing insulting comments about the well-to-do, and sneering at the poor, who passed them by.

Another group of men, some in rags and tatters, exchanged jests with the guards , and rushed upon wealthy strangers to offer their services as guides to the teeming city. Noticing the rich clothes of Manfred the merchant, one of them, smaller than the rest, with a wizened, lined and seamed face, looked keenly at the two men and the boy, and approached them.

"Do you need a guide, your honors? It's a hard city to find your way around in. Better to have a friend with you, who knows his way and how to look after you."

"Aye," said Manfred, "we could do with someone. It is many years since I was here."

In fact, it suited Manfred's purposes very well to have a guide, as one purpose in coming to Blecklinghaus was to discover the feelings of the people and whether this strategic town would remain loyal to the King. So Shiffon, as he was called, was hired, and immediately led them to a long, low building: an inn, apparently in great danger of collapsing under the weight of a merchant's house built partly in the wall and partly on the inn. No-one seemed remotely concerned about this, however, so

99

without further thought, they followed their guide through a gaily painted doorway into a room of immense darkness within.

The room was low-ceilinged, long but narrow. An oak trestle table ran most of its length and a large fire burned in a hearth on the wall away from the entrance. This gave some light and candles were lit along the table.

The room was packed, so that they had to elbow their way through to find space at the table. Their guide seemed to know exactly what to do and disappeared, to emerge soon after with steaming platters of hot food and tankards of a warm, sweet ale.

Conversation surged around them and they were questioned about where they had come from, what their business was, and a hundred other things the curious thought to ask. They knew their story well of course by now, but Manfred had been insistent that the little prince was to keep silent, come what may, in case his manner of speech should betray them. Manfred and Hans listened carefully to all that was said around them concerning the war. The general opinion seemed to be in favor of the King, but one or two were loud for the invading Archduke. Manfred felt that feelings were running high and that there was tension in the town.

One man was telling a group of men, in a loud voice, how he had heard that the Archduke was very generous to cities that yielded to him.

"Aye," said another, "I heard what he did to Grillo in the western borders, when they yielded to him. He was so generous he gave half the men four inches of cold steel."

"Yes," a tall thin fellow added "and took away their wives, so they wouldn't have to feed them anymore. That's true kindness, that is," he finished, to general laughter.

"Ah, he couldn't do that here," put in one, evidently a stranger.

"Why not?"

"Because he'd never find them in these streets and alleys," he replied, to more laughter, and Manfred thought the tension had eased some.

A large, well-fed man, whose eyes seemed to slide slowly over everyone, stared at the young prince.

"Let's hear what the younger generation thinks," he said, with a sneer. "Who are you for, pretty boy? Should our gracious King, or the noble Archduke, tremble to think your sword arm is lifted against him?"

Prince Rudolph stiffened and his face burned, but he kept silent and Manfred's quiet hand rested lightly on his arm.

"Leave the boy alone. He has been taught not to speak before his elders."

"Don't be a spoilsport, Master Merchant, even boys have an opinion. Come on, speak up," the man continued roughly. "Who will you pit your puny might against?" and he laughed a long, sneering laugh, which some of the men joined in.

"Ah, leave him alone, Sylrac," said Shiffon uneasily, for Sylrac was a notorious bully. "He's only a lad. He doesn't know anything."

"When I want you to answer, Shiffon, I"ll ask you. Until then, keep your nose out of it," snarled Sylrac.

Shiffon's hand went to his waist and a long knife started to slide out of his waistband. A man nearby grabbed his arm and twisted it up his back, holding him in a tight grip.

"Ah now, you wouldn't want to spoil Sylrac's little bit of fun, would you, Shiffon? Just sit quietly for a minute and don't interfere with what is not your concern."

Manfred answered. "These are questions too hard for us for us to be bothering ourselves about. I'm too busy earning a living to bother about the high doings of kings and princes. I just do my job and leave the quality folk to do the worrying about wars and that."

"Hear that, lads? It's not often we are called the 'quality folk' although it's long overdue, I'd say."

By now, he had an audience, and he seemed to be well-known to the regulars there. He had a habit of not looking directly at you at first, but sliding his eyes towards your feet and letting them creep up until they came to rest insolently upon your face, showing his contempt for all creatures except himself and his cronies. His eyes had reached Manfred's face, and he was about to make another disdainful comment but he hesitated and turned back to the lad.

"Has no-one taught you, you ignorant peasant brat, that when your elders and betters ask you a question, you answer it!" he shouted. Swiftly, the fat man leaned across, grabbed the front of the prince's rough jerkin and pulled him out of his seat towards him. "Now, an answer, Archduke or King? Who should reign?"

Manfred started out of his seat, but he was seized by two fellows and a knife held at his throat. "Stay still, wealth has its place, but here Sylrac rules," hissed a voice.

Then the earthquake occurred.

The man holding the knife at Manfred's throat was flung across the room, the other man let go of Manfred quickly and backed away from him, as if he had the plague. Two others blocking the way to the Prince were each felled by a blow on the head, and a massive hand fastened on the fat man's throat.

Hans had joined the discussion.

The mood in the room was mixed. Most of the men could not care less about Sylrac. Some would be positively glad if he were bested, but he had a few nasty friends who would help him if they could. Just now, though, they were showing a marked reluctance to interfere on his behalf. Sylrac was a big man but Hans handled him as if he were a baby. He was helpless in the giant's hands and was starting to turn a rather unhealthy colour. Peculiar gurgling noises were coming from him.

"Come, Vigor," said Manfred, quietly, "we must leave this charming group. Better let our new acquaintance live, as it might cause trouble."

Sylrac was indeed close to death and, collapsed retching and gasping on the floor, when Hans released his iron grip.

The four slipped out of the inn and found Shiffon grinning cheerfully at their side.

"Sylrac has been asking for that for a long time," he said. "Every stranger that comes in he picks on, provoking them to a fight. He's particularly fond of baiting boys."

"I noticed," growled Manfred.

"The trouble is he's got some nasty friends and one or two rich strangers have disappeared without trace. The burghers don't like it, but Sylrac seems to get away with it."

"How does that happen?" asked Manfred, though hardly interested.

"Friends in high places, I guess!" said Shiffon. "I'd better get you away from this area for a while."

He led them through a warren of streets, all narrow, some with just enough space for a cart to get through others only wide enough for a man.

"Are you all right?" Manfred murmured to his youthful lord. "That was an ugly moment."

The boy nodded. Then he grinned. "I wasn't worried for a moment. I could see Hans' face!"

"What an enormous number of people, Manfred," he suddenly remarked, "I have never seen so many packed into so small a space."

Shiffon kept close by them guiding them deeper into the city. The streets teemed with people: buying, selling, talking shouting, squabbling, just generally living. This must be one of the strangest cities in Europe, he thought, and important to whichever side could claim its loyalty. It was, apparently, ruled by the mayor and burghers, but Manfred knew there was another, unofficial, but much more powerful ruler. And that is why we're here, he thought.

"I know what you are thinking," he smiled, "and yes, you are right, I *have* been here before. My family has connections in this city" and he smiled, a little sadly, the boy thought. "Just a minute," he said, pausing. "Listen!"

They could hear singing. It seemed to be coming from one of the nearby houses and it was singing like they had not heard before. It was not drunken singing, nor yet the beautiful plainsong of the church. There seemed to be a fervency about it which was hard to explain. Manfred decided to ask their guide.

"What is that, friend Shiffon?"

"It is a strange group, master. Everyone is talking about it. A priest, like no priest you ever saw before, came to the town and preached in the market place. Some listened to him, some made fun and some just pretended he wasn't there. Anyway, a group gathered round him and that is their meeting. They say strange things happen there and, indeed, a friend of mine goes there and has become quite a different person. I couldn't believe it really. He is so different."

"In what way?" asked Manfred.

"Well, different in his character really. He doesn't swear any more, doesn't drink much, doesn't beat his wife, doesn't steal, works hard ... in fact, no fun at all now but, he seems really happy. Says this is what he has been looking for all his life. It's astonishing really. I'll take you in if you like. They welcome strangers."

Manfred agreed as he had more than half a suspicion that this was their friend, Bertram the Englishman. Shiffon led them into a large house. The man at the door was a big man, strong and sturdy, who looked at them steadily, gave them a slow, but friendly, smile and told them they were welcome. Hans put his hand at his back to make sure his sword was handy, ducked his head and entered the low room, following Manfred and the Prince. It was packed. About fifty people: men, women and children were there. They were singing. It was obviously some sort of hymn or psalm but it was strange to the ears of the three friends. There was a life to it and, really, jollity, compared with the singing they knew in the cathedrals of the realm. Anyway, all the hymn singing they knew took place in chapels and cathedrals, and there the choirs sang, not the people. These were common people. Furthermore, judging by their faces they were ecstatic about it. Some of them had their eyes shut, some had smiles on their faces and there was an atmosphere of peace and joy in the place. None of them had ever seen anything like it before. And, as Manfred had suspected, there was their friend, Bertram, the priest, standing at the front, seemingly oblivious to everything but the hymn he was singing.

It came to an end and another astonishing thing happened. One person after another started to pray. And they prayed just as if they were speaking to a person in the room with them. The prayers were personal, concerned with everyday things and yet they were certainly addressed to God, for they talked to their 'Heavenly Father', 'Dear Lord Jesus', and so on. Manfred and the Prince were frankly astounded. These people were not priests, yet there was a priest present and he didn't seem to mind the ordinary people praying. It was unheard of.

Suddenly the Prince's ears pricked up and he nudged Manfred "Listen!" he said. The big man who had welcomed them at the door was praying:

"And Lord God, we ask you to remember our King in this difficult time. Give him deliverance from all his enemies and grant to our land again the blessings of peace."

There was a loud Amen from the people in the room. Prince

Rudolph was encouraged and beamed on the man who had prayed.

But it was time to go. Manfred was whispering in his ear that he still had things to do and that they should be on their way. He turned to their guide. "Shiffon, take us out of the square to the house of Velda, if you know it."

Shiffon sharpened at once and he looked at Manfred. "I know it, master, but how do *you* know it? More importantly," he added softly, "does Velda know you?"

"Do as I say," commanded Manfred.

"Aye, master, on your head be it if she doesn't."

ELEVEN

Considering for a minute, the little man nodded to himself and, beckoning them to follow, he dived back into the maze of alleyways leading away from the house where the meeting was taking place.

They were now on the eastern side of the town and their way had been downhill.

Their guide had stopped, evidently in trepidation.

"Now masters," he said. "Yonder lies Velda's dwelling. Pay me now and let me go, for Velda does not welcome visitors and I would not want her to know that I led you to her. Pray do not reveal to her that I did so."

Manfred agreed and was about to pay him when Hans intervened.

"Stay!" he rumbled. "You say you have led us to the right house, but this one you pointed to is naught but a ruin."

The man grinned for indeed Hans spoke the simple truth. They had arrived at the houses making up the east wall of the city, and the one their guide had pointed to seemed crushed beneath the weight of another building on top.

The upper buildings in the wall were curious, for if the street did not run by the door of the dwelling, as it often didn't, paths to the upper buildings were built on to the fronts of the lower buildings in order to reach the higher entrances. This was the case of the house the guide had pointed to, for a path ran round and up the lower structure and another up the side of their destination, which seemed to be flattened by the houses on top.

"Nevertheless," insisted Shiffon, "that is the house. Look, see the opening a short way up that path there, go no further up but in there. That is not the actual house but t'will lead you to the place you seek." The man was near panic, the Prince realized, and was almost trembling. "Masters," he continued, "are you sure this is your pleasure? You are stepping into great danger. I dare not go with you and I dare not tell you more. Have a care and give up this plan."

But Manfred firmly kept to his purpose and said they would go on. He looked with distaste at the route before them. This particular path was perilous in the extreme, as it was unfenced yet sloped and twisted quite as much as the paths to other houses, which did have stout railings.

"I wonder who lives up there," said Hans, glancing at the house above their target. "He will have few visitors anyway," he finished.

"Perhaps," replied Manfred. "That does appear to be the house we seek so let the man go. I have been here before, long ago. He has guided us truly."

"Thank you, good sir," said Shiffon, "may you be welcome to Velda," and he vanished.

Manfred led them up the path to the crushed building above the first house. The upper story of the house they climbed seemed to have largely disappeared. Lower window frames were bent and pushed out of shape by the weight above. Thick parchment filled the windows instead of glass, but it had bellied and twisted, sticking out here and folding inwards there. The door frame seemed half the usual height, the posts leaned at crazy angles and the lintel seemed about to fall on the unwary.

"Your friend does not spend much money on the house, it seems," said the Prince.

Manfred replied to the Prince's comment, with a smiling "And yet men say the person who lives here is rich."

"Aye, and somewhat feared, to judge by our friend, Shiffon," mused the Prince. "What do you think Hans?"

"We shall see soon enough," he muttered, but he touched the sword at his back, as if to reassure himself that it was still there and ready.

The door was off its hinges and, truly, the whole building looked derelict and unoccupied. With difficulty, Manfred pushed past the leaning door. Hans followed, pushing himself through with an effort which seemed likely to bring the house down on top of them and the Prince brought up the rear. Through the doorway, they found themselves in a dusty wooden chamber and a stout door facing them, upon which Manfred knocked four times, pausing after the third.

Nothing happened.

"We"re wasting our time, Manfred. For once you have misled us, my friend. There is no-one here." The Prince spoke in his clear, cultured voice.

Manfred whirled on him and shouted "Quiet, boy! How dare you question your master thus? Truly I am your friend, for no other master would suffer your insolence as I do. Say no more or you will be severely beaten."

Prince Rudolph shrank from his friend and bit his lip. He blushed and looked down.

Manfred repeated the peculiar knock and waited. "Once more, I think," he said, and knocked - three knocks and then another knock after a short pause.

This time, after a few seconds, a voice spoke, seeming to come out of the very wall.

"You are observed," said the voice.

The boy jumped at the unexpected voice and Hans glowered round threateningly, but there was no-one to see.

They waited and, after a while, the voice spoke again.

"Who visits this house uninvited? State your business quickly and begone!"

"Tell your mistress - 'Tata calls!'" said Manfred, apparently unimpressed.

"Wait!" was the single word vouchsafed to them.

They waited.

Not long and the unseen voice said "Enter, Tata, if such you be. If not, despair!"

The door before them swung open and they passed through.

A swarthy, short, but well-built man stood before them. His hair, eyebrows and beard were jet-black, his nose hooked, and his eyes slate blue, and hard. He did not smile but pointed before them to a narrow staircase, at the top of which stood another fellow holding a lamp.

Hans was restless. His warrior's eyes had immediately seem that both these fellows were well armed and he sensed that others

111

were nearby. Manfred saw his friend's unease and gently laid a restraining hand on his arm.

"Bring up the rear behind His Highness," he whispered. "It will be all right, for us, but it is truly a dangerous house."

The servant stood aside to let them pass and, as they did so, two more came from an alcove, to follow them up the stairs. The fellow at the top opened another door and led them into a long room, dimly lit with dark alcoves and recesses along its length. At the end of the room, a woman sat alone.

Most of the light came from a large, mullioned window, occupying much of the end wall and looking out over the plain below the city, so the house was one of those built into the city wall. All the light was behind her, so that they could see little of her, but she could observe them closely as they advanced towards her.

The door shut quietly behind them and Hans noticed grimly that it shut after the servants had passed through with them, so that they now stood behind them. His hand was ready to flash to the sword at his back, as he saw curtains moving slightly in one of the dark alcoves that stood along the room.

The young prince too had spotted a man's hand moving behind a curtain as they walked up to the table. He shuddered involuntarily. It was altogether a frightening and unnerving experience. The tension was almost unbearable and then they reached the table.

The woman's appearance and dress were scarcely less frightening. She was shrouded in black so that nothing of her form and little of her face could be seen. A shadowy outline

112

looked out at them from the cowl of her hood and the young prince seemed to be aware of a pair of sharp dark eyes assessing him, almost seeing through him.

"Who claims admittance in the dread name of Tata, when Tata died long since?" The woman's voice was soft but dry and menacing. Nothing moved in the chamber though the boy still had that feeling that many unseen eyes watched them. Hans looked as if he was ready to tear the place apart. Manfred alone was looked untroubled. He threw back his cowl and let the light shine on his face.

"Ah, my lady aunt, Velda, uncrowned ruler of Blecklinghaus, feared princess of unnumbered subjects, has it been so long that you do not know me?"

The woman leaned forward to peer more closely.

"Manfred? Can it really be..." she went on wonderingly, "Duke of Tata, Count of Bellair and Tringum, Baron of Disteina, Lord of all Tresty and Dannheim and, lately I hear, unheard of honor for one of your house, King's Friend and trusted counselor?

"Is it you, Manfred? I loved you once, though you were too young to return my love."

"It is I, noble lady, but all the titles you have listed I have long renounced, save only the last."

The woman threw back her head and laughed loudly and scornfully.

"That sounds like youthful folly, lord duke. But, if it be really you, tell me where your father's knife wounded you when you refused to lie to the King's messenger?"

"On the left forearm, mighty Velda."

113

"That is right. Now show me the scar and if it be not there you will have scars enough before you die."

Manfred pulled up the sleeve of his rough tunic and there was the old evidence of a wound, which must have virtually opened his arm from elbow to wrist.

"And who saved me from worse, my lady, when my father would have had me hanged on the spot?"

"Yes, " she sighed, "and you repaid me by entering the King's service, sending me neither sign nor token these last fifteen years."

Manfred spluttered a little and replied indignantly, "Noble Aunt, you well know my latest messages went unanswered and I gained the impression that I was ... perhaps, um, too respectable for your tastes."

She laughed again, this time a genuine sound of amusement.

"Ah, Nephew, only member of my family now alive, see how I still love thee. I knew that my friendship would not help you in the King's service and, though it hurt my poor old heart, I thought it better that you should be free of my encumbrance."

"Never that, Aunt beloved," and the little prince was surprised to see that Manfred was genuinely moved and fond of the grim-looking woman before them.

Then she turned and clapped her hands. Servants appeared immediately.

"Open the shutters," she commanded, "and bring food and drink for my friends. Honor them as you would my self for this is all the family I have. See too that you honor this man for his own sake for he is truly a great lord and the son of Tata, of whom you have heard much."

Manfred was alarmed.

"My lady, I am travelling incognito, I dare not become known."

Velda laughed again.

"These, my servants, can be trusted to the death. Each one would die willingly before he betrayed my trust. Your secret is as safe with them as with myself and, now that I have spoken to them, they will serve you in any way that lies within their power."

The servants withdrew, soon to re-appear with plates of sumptuous food, accompanied by goblets of delicious wine, which were laid before the travelers with every mark of respect and honor.

Velda, now revealed by the light, was a striking woman, who must have been truly beautiful in her youth. Even now she retained the fine bone structure that had given her beauty. Her forehead was high and her eyes clear and shrewd. She had great grace of movement and, the Prince noticed, her every command was instantly obeyed by her men. She questioned them closely about their presence in Blecklinghaus and Manfred told her all. She was much amused by the presence of the prince and looked at him closely and not unkindly, merely remarking that his father might be somewhat concerned had he known his present company. She greatly admired Hans and tried to persuade him to join her retinue, promising him he could name his own wages and position, but she did not appear to be surprised when he refused and, indeed, later said she had expected naught else.

They stayed there two days and talked much. Prince

Rudolph was amazed to discover that her power spread far and wide, mostly among a strange class of wild and lawless fellows who appeared to thrive in the cities rather than the countryside. Her net extended even beyond the borders of the country with her agents and loyal followers in Unterhals itself. Manfred knew it, of course, and knew that her active support would be a huge asset in the current struggle for the kingdom.

"And if I agree to help your king, lord duke," for she refused to accept Manfred's renunciation of his titles, "how will you reward me, or my followers?"

"I will write more often," Manfred smiled.

"Ha, you have at least inherited some of your father's roguery. Not enough though, my friend, not by a long chalk. Now Manfred, I am a business-woman. Speaking frankly and perhaps crudely, what is in it for me? My spies tell me that an embassage from Thalesia is at this very moment in the town, visiting that fat fool, the mayor, to enlist support and men for their cause. His Highness of Thalesia does not know, as you do, who wields the real power in Blecklinghaus."

Manfred was stunned to learn that the Archduke's men were already in the city, although he knew it had always been likely and, his rewards and service would probably be more to the taste of these lawless citizens than those of good King Maximilian. However, he hoped his old friendship with the lady Velda would still bear fruit for his King.

"His Majesty is well able to pay you and your men, Velda, if I cannot appeal to your loyalty."

"Now Manfred, you cannot do that, as you well know."

116

"His Majesty will pay you well, for I know that your power and influence are great. Three thousand marks, or four, or five, depending on the support you can offer."

"That is certainly a persuasive argument. I have lived my own life here, virtually a queen in my own right. I have shown little loyalty to any king and do not need to. However, the old king was kind to me once. I have not forgotten that. My followers are loyal to me and if I call them to fight for the King, or for the Archduke, they will do so. But gold interests me somewhat and it interests my people even more. I must think on this. I am not attracted to the Thalesian. Methinks he would prove an untrustworthy ally. I have heard what he did to the Count of Instrom, who was his vassal. I will think more on it."

Lady Velda looked at Rudolph.

"He is indeed a bonny lad. If I were not such a wicked woman, I would agree to help his father just because he has a worthy son, but," she sighed a little "I am what I am and will do what I wish."

Prince Rudolph smiled at her and thanked her but was unsure whether she had said anything of real note to him.

"Enough!" she said, as if ashamed of herself. "I must return to myself or my followers might not know me.

"See, Your Grace," this to Manfred, "should I repay with kindness your betrayal of many years ago?"

"My lady," protested Manfred, "when have I betrayed my friends? But I trust you are jesting."

"You did betray some of them, Manfred, when you swore fealty to Maximilian whom you have served faithfully these last

... twenty years, is it? What about Marco the Assassin, Lord of Crawmor? Or Jimnon the Red of Tura? Or, even, Piroc of Blecklinghaus, my liege lord, and ... father?" she said softly, all the while gazing intently into Manfred"s face.

"My Lady, you know all about all of these, and I know you do not need to ask. There was no betrayal here of these you speak of. I hated them all, apart from Piroc, and made my views known frequently, even to you, when you were younger. Indeed Marco and Jimnon both swore they would cut my throat from ear to ear if it were not for my father. Jimnon in truth said it every year from the time I was fourteen, if I remember rightly. Come now, Aunt, your father was one of the few I respected for he never slew a helpless man and was never strong with the weak. He died in open battle, as you well know, and I bathed his wounds as he lay on the field of Kragga."

"Was it you did that? I had forgotten."

She smiled suddenly. "I will decide soon. Who knows, a new friendship with the throne of Maximilian might lead to unheard of blessings for the poor of the land!"

She turned to another subject as they sat at dinner that evening. She usually ate alone for she was a lady and had none of her class for company but with the three friends there, she took all her meals with them. The Prince was astonished at the opulence and luxury of her table. It compared favorably with his royal father's provision at home. A variety of meats, both fowl and flesh, were in abundance, with many exotic fruits and sweetmeats, which he particularly enjoyed, as he did at home.

"You visited the mad priest when you first came into the

city. What did you think of this strange servant of the church? I am finding it hard to make up my mind about him though I am not normally a lover of the clergy," she continued. "It seems to me that their faith is a fine weather thing for the most part and an affair of convenience. Their principles too often vanish when the prospect of gold is dangled before them, but this one is different. He also seems to have a strange effect on people. One of my own servants, a most trustworthy villain, called Cryllan, came to me and told me that he would no longer serve me as he was determined to follow Jesus.

"Have you ever heard anything like that before! I told him he could still serve me and follow Jesus. Did I not already have one or two priests who willingly did my bidding whenever I spoke to them, but he was insistent. Even when I said that no-one left my service except through death, he still persisted."

"So, my lady, what did you do?" asked Manfred, with a slight smile, for he knew that, despite her fierce ways, she respected courage.

"What could I do with such obstinacy? He could not be changed so I thought I had better let him go," she sighed, then with wry indignation, "and do you know what he said?"

"No, madam."

"He said he would pray for me! I nearly *did* have him executed then but while I was gathering my wits, he left me. Now, what do you think of that?"

Manfred thought a minute. What a powerful thing this was, to make a man risk his neck to pursue the thing he believed to be right, and this not a high minded nobleman but a man who had probably lived outside normal laws most of his life.

"I am impressed," he finally said quietly. "As for the priest, he did not appear to be mad to me and we owe him a debt which can hardly be repaid."

"Do you?" her woman's interest aroused. "How could a poor priest serve the King's Friend?"

"He saved my life," put in Prince Rudolph.

"I am more than ever impressed by him then. And was the mighty Hans there too? Did he allow your life to be put in danger?"

So the whole story had to be told to her and she listened with interest.

"I think I will visit this man myself ... or rather, I may have him visit me." She smiled a sardonic smile.

The Prince realized that she was not as bad as she pretended to be but had been so soured by men's wickedness that she continually adopted a sardonic attitude to hide her disappointment. Furthermore, he dimly suspected that if she did meet someone truly good she would honor and respect him, hence her treatment of the servant who had joined Bertram. He wondered if the devotion of her servants *was* solely due to fear of her as she might have them believe, or was there something deeper there.

"My Lady Velda," put in Manfred, "with your permission we must leave tomorrow. It is Sunday and the beginning of a new week. I would fain be on my way in the morning. But, before we go, I would like to visit Bertram the priest again. I am impressed by him. Such a man would be an asset to my lord the King and I think would be a help along the way. Also, with the news that Thalesia's men are in the city, it is time we left."

"You are safe while you are in this city. No one would dare harm you while under my protection," she said coldly, "but if you would visit Bertram, you must go now as the day is already far gone."

Manfred bowed his acceptance.

Lady Velda called one of her servants to her: a tall, silent man, dark in countenance, grim of mouth, strong of arm.

"Aspin, you know the meeting place of the priest, Bertram? Where Cryllan goes habitually now?"

"I know it, my lady."

"You will take my friends there, stay till they have finished their business and then bring them back to me here. Then," she said, turning to Manfred, "you can sleep and be on your way when you will in the morning."

Manfred agreed and they followed the grim Aspin into the darkening streets of Blecklinghaus. Bertram's lodging was well away from Velda's palace in the wall and they threaded their way through the maze of houses. There were still people about: neighbors talking between doorsteps, across the streets from the low casement windows and, from time to time, standing in the time honored way at street corners in groups discussing all the city's multitudinous affairs. Occasionally, a dark figure or two started out from a doorway, but seeing the grim figure of Aspin, always faded back into the shadows. Inside the houses, there were voices and laughter, shrill cries and stern warnings. The day was still light, but not for long.

As they drew near Bertram's home, they began to hear again the sound of singing. Here the building was well lit already, the windows were open and many of the local people were gathering to watch out of curiosity. In such a close knit city, nothing much could be done in corners and Bertram saw no need to keep his message secret.

In such a city of wickedness, he had found a ready welcome for his gospel and his seed had fallen on very good ground. Nowhere in the kingdom had he found such a willingness to listen, and many had believed.

The house was packed. Aspin's grim presence ensured that a way opened into the room where Bertram was leading the worship. Without him, Manfred knew, they would have had no hope of getting near their friend the priest. They squeezed into the room. Several people smiled at them though, of course, they knew none of them. Prince Rudolph recognized the man who had prayed for the King last time and was now singing with the rest of them.

The hymn stopped and Bertram stepped forward to speak. A few people had brought rough chairs with them and sat. Some sat on the floor and some remained standing.

"My friends," said Bertram, his eyes roving gently over the multitude, "I am so glad to be able to tell you tonight, this first day of the week, that a small group of us have started translating the Scriptures into your own language. I will not be able to stay long but I will see the work started and hope to return again to check its progress. Alexander here, indicating a black haired, pleasant featured man, will oversee the group in my absence, as he has a good grasp of English and is used to writing. When finished, of course, it will mean untold blessings for your country. We will have it printed on one of the new printing presses and you will be able to read the Scriptures for yourselves."

The Prince thought about this for a moment, much surprised. It had never occurred to him that it would be a blessing for ordinary people to have the Bible in their own language. It had just been a book priests had used and had read in Latin. Scholars too could read it but the ordinary people, never. He thought it was a very interesting development and resolved he would talk to his father about it as soon as he could.

Bertram started to read from the Scriptures. He had a copy of Master Wycliffe's English Bible with him and translated as he read. He had not got far when voices spoke loudly near the door. There was a disturbance there and the young prince saw armed men burst into the room. They pushed people to one side and through their midst, strode a black-haired ruffian similar to the one they had seen in charge of the soldiers hanging the peasant.

TWELVE

Black Griffo he was called. He strode to the centre of the room and seized Bertram by the front of his robe.

"You are under arrest, holy priest. Your bishop says you are a heretic and must be taught to see the error of your ways and these poor people here must be shown that you have led them astray."

The Thalesian was a grim warrior. Manfred looked at the Captain and thought quickly. He had seen this type before; a hardened soldier, probably raised from boyhood in some castle yard, veteran of many battles: hard, cruel eyes, tight, unyielding mouth. Under his basin-like helmet, a thatch of thick, black hair stuck out at all angles. It jutted from his eyebrows and matched the thick, full beard that almost hid the cruel mouth. The beard was unusual as it was split on the left side by a livid scar, running from ear to chin. The scar would have been largely covered by the beard but it had been trimmed so that the scar showed clearly. It had not been allowed to cover it, presumably because its owner thought his scar was more effective uncovered. Certainly it gave him a cruel and terrifying look, which few men would think of defying. Chain mail could be seen on his arms and shoulders, while a massive breastplate of dull iron sat upon his chest. A sword hung at his left side, a long thin dagger at his right.

A murmur of dismay rumbled around the room. Manfred lifted his eyes to the windows and saw they were lined with crossbowmen where, before there had only been sightseers. He groaned. Hans, too, was alert for any chance but he also looked at the windows. Resistance now would be futile. Griffo had planned well. He was speaking again.

"So sad to see so many good people led astray by false doctrines. How nice it is for me to be able to turn you all back to right thinking and doing. You have been sadly misled. However, confident that you have seen the error of your ways, I will allow you to come with me and join the glorious army of His Royal Highness the Archduke of Thalesia."

There was another mutter from the congregation and a little talk among themselves. The thickset man who had prayed for the King stood up.

"This priest, whom you call heretic, has taught me the true way of Christ. I see no error in his ways."

"Well said, Cryllan," one or two shouted.

Griffo turned and looked at his sturdy figure and broad chest, his unyielding mouth and smiled.

"A peasant turned theologian. What a dangerous heresy this is!" he sneered. "Don't worry though. You will join my little band, and I will make sure you have time to change your foolish ways."

Then his eyes fell on Hans: "Wait, who is this? A fine budding soldier, if ever I saw one. You will make a great addition to our glorious, all-conquering army." Hans scowled angrily and looked as if he would tear Griffo apart. "Ah, now, now! No rebellious thoughts, please. It is useless to resist," he said, motioning towards the windows.

His gaze continued over the room, resting on Manfred.

"Ah! A merchant. Now what is a rich merchant doing amongst all these ordinary people. Don't tell me you too have been led astray, Master Merchant."

"I am not rich, sir," said Manfred in a wheedling tone, "just a poor man, trying to earn an honest living. I heard the singing here, was curious, and came in to see what was happening. I see now that I was mistaken and will go on my way, with my apprentice and servant."

He went to go towards the door. Griffo gestured and two soldiers blocked their way immediately.

"Not so fast. By the look of you, there could be a place in our army for you, too."

"I am a respectable merchant and, furthermore, I have powerful friends. It would be a mistake to trifle with me."

"Oh, it would, would it? I care nothing for your powerful friends. I have an even more powerful one. He is His Royal Highness, the Archduke. Match that! And... hand over your purse. I'll wager it is worth having. And it is better with me than with you."

Aspin now stepped forward. He stood insolently in front of Griffo.

"Stay," he said, "these three are not to be harmed. They are my charges and you will let them go free."

"And who might you be?" Griffo sneered at him.

"Ask the people about you. Ask *them* if I am to be trifled with. Ask *them* if I am worth listening to."

The Thalesian captain glared fiercely at the cowled, black robed figure of Aspin. "All right," he said, "I will."

He faced the people gathered unwillingly before him: "All right, you frightened sheep. Who is this peasant before me?"

They shuffled and groaned.

"Come on, answer me. Is he so frightening? Look, he is but a man, he can bleed," and he thrust Aspin's arm with his sword, so that the blood flowed. "See, he is not so frightening."

Somebody in the crowd said, trembling: "He is Aspin, Velda's executioner. There will be bad things done, if you harm him."

Griffo laughed and contemptuously pushed Aspin out of his way. He reeled backwards for Griffo was a powerful man, but he recovered quickly. A sword appeared in Aspin's hand so quickly that Griffo was caught unprepared and would surely have died then but for the bowmen at the windows. There were whirring sounds and the quarrels from three crossbows struck Aspin full in the chest. He was dead before he hit the floor.

"Enough of this," snarled Griffo, "I will waste no more time. You are all under arrest."

He turned to go. Then he thought better of it and turned again to Manfred.

"Your purse," he said curtly.

Manfred could offer no resistance and handed over a small bag of gold. Griffo hefted it, examined its contents, looked satisfied and put it into a pouch slung at his belt.

Then the whole group were marched through the darkened streets of Blecklinghaus.

Aspin's body lay in the gloom of the priest's lodging.

THIRTEEN

Griffo of Tastag, marched up the short flight of stone steps to the main hall of the Golden Tower of Blecklinghaus. He was well content. He had not known who the priest was that the mayor had suggested he arrest but he had seen an opportunity to press soldiers into his master's service, which was his mission. He had the mayor's permission and the bishop's blessing and, he thought, no one would miss the unfortunates he would recruit. It had turned out much better than he had expected. He did not much like the mayor. He was over friendly to his taste but he had to admit he had been useful to him in this matter.

His Worship and Excellency the Mayor and Governor of Blecklinghaus sat near a huge fire in the warm and comfortable Great Hall. Rich and expensive tapestries draped the stone walls and the floor was covered with the usual sweet smelling straw. Heavily carved oak tables were graced with comfortable chairs where, on occasion, the worthy counselors of the city met, feasted and debated the town's concerns. However, the Council had not met recently and, as this was also the Governor's residence and as he combined in his person the office of Governor as well as that of Mayor, Porteus Balic sat alone with the remains of his and Griffo's evening meal. A lone servant stood near his master to attend any of his needs.

Balic was of average height and build but his physique had suffered through over indulgence at the table. A once handsome face was now puffed up and piggy eyes peered out through his folded lids. He smiled a cordial welcome as Griffo strode in.

"Ah, welcome back, friend Griffo! Did all go well? Our good bishop will be pleased with you. That crazy priest was bothering him with his dangerous and strange ideas." He turned to the waiting servant. "Go, Carl, but wait within calling distance." The servant bowed his acquiescence and disappeared through a nearby door.

Griffo eyed his erstwhile friend with some distaste. He thought it a liberty that this fat merchant should treat him so familiarly. A rough and brutal man, he respected soldierly strength and nothing else. He had no time for this fawning politician though now it was politic for him to pretend otherwise.

"My dear fellow!" continued the cheerful mayor, "come in, get warm, a cold night outside, come here by the fire. I doubt you had any opposition from these religious peculiarities?"

"Not much" was the curt reply. "Some half-witted fellow ordered me to stop and attacked me, but he was easily disposed of."

"Ah, foolish fellow, foolish fellow," sighed Balic, as he might have done over an erring schoolboy. "Who was he, just out of interest, I get to know some of the hotheads in the town occasionally."

He said he was a servant of some woman called Gelda or Velda ... some such name. It is of no importance."

The color drained from the mayor's large round face and he

stared appalled at the grim soldier in front of him. Griffo went on, not noticing the mayor's discomfort.

"Yes, it was nothing to worry about."

He laughed. "He said I should fear for my life if I defied his Gelda. Ha! Did he think such as I would be frightened by mere threats, I who serve His Highness of Thalesia? Why I have torn apart better men than he with my bare hands."

"What have you done?" whispered the mayor.

"Eh? What do you mean? You don't mean you are scared of this fellow and his idle threats. Anyway, he can harm no one now. He is dead."

"You fool!" hissed the mayor in a low voice. "You have acted too hastily in this matter. If this man was a servant of Velda, as it seems from your words, you have offended the most powerful woman in the land. You and I are both in danger of our lives because of your action."

"Pah! Nonsense. How can one woman wield such influence? What can she do? Can any woman pit her puny strength against armed soldiers of Boris of Thalesia!" His fierce, bearded face flushed with rage. "*You,* Mr Mayor, are an old woman and *you* can be as frightened as you like, but I am a man and no woman is going to frighten me."

His Worship the Mayor rose with a snarl. His friendliness dropped like a mask and his mild rheumy eyes became hard little chips of blue. "You are a fool, Griffo. You speak of what you do not know. This Lady Velda rules a small army. She can, and probably will, have every man in the city at your throat within minutes. Most of the townsfolk would follow her to the death. I

131

tell you this. If you do not leave now, immediately, you are not likely to live until the morrow dawns. In addition to this, she has numerous followers throughout the land. Gipsies, vagabonds, cutthroats, outlaws, footpads and many of the poorest folk acknowledge her suzerainty and she can call on aid at the furthest extremities of the country. *I* was appointed by her. My power and authority depend upon her and now you, you stupid, arrogant, puffed up cockerel ... you have put my very life in danger. One last thing I will do for you, no two. I will give you a guide to help you get clear of the city, for if I don't, you will die this night. If I help you, there is just a chance that you might escape and even, though I have little hope of it, I might escape her wrath myself. The other thing I will do is to give you some advice. Let your prisoners go. If they are really under her protection, she will not rest until they are safe and free."

"Never!" snorted Griffo. "I will leave the town but I will not leave the prisoners."

"On your own head be it then," said the mayor soberly. Then he turned to the doorway that his servant, Carl, had used earlier, and he shouted for him. The man appeared and the mayor spoke urgently to him for a few minutes. Then he turned back to the Thalesian soldier. "I have given Carl instructions to show you the way through one of the tunnels out of Blecklinghaus. It emerges well to the north-east of the city and should give you a good start on any pursuit that may be organized. Now, go ... quickly."

"Pursuit!" spat Griffo contemptuously, but he turned and followed the wary Carl as he descended to the courtyard.

FOURTEEN

After their arrest, Bertram and his people had been herded roughly into a kind of guardroom at the foot of the tower. They heard a bar being put across the door and laughter and talk amongst the guards outside. Manfred, of course, was furious with himself for allowing them to be put in this situation. Hans was unusually quiet and anxious. He was willing to fight for his young master to the last drop of his blood but, at present, he knew the odds were impossible, even for him.

He and Manfred cast their eyes over the darkening room. There *were* windows but they were high up in the walls and very narrow. Even the prince could not fit through them. There was no hope that way.

Prince Rudolph himself was a little subdued but was also fascinated by Bertram and his people.

They were singing!

Soon after the door had closed, Bertram had started to sing a hymn, in a loud and confident voice. The others joined in - they evidently all knew it - and it was not a sad and gloomy song either. It was an amazing contrast to the attitude of Hans and Manfred, seasoned and courageous warriors though they were. The young prince looked at the faces of the people, some of them women and children, and they seemed ... happy! How could this be? Some of them definitely had smiles on their faces and pretty well everyone he could see looked at peace with the situation, especially Bertram, who must be facing death at Griffo's hands.

Then this strange and, it must be said, admirable man, prayed.

"We thank you, heavenly Father, as the hymn said, that you are in control of all things and that you bring good out of everything. Thank you for letting this happen to us. Thank you for taking care of us. Help us to be faithful to the Lord Jesus Christ, whatever happens. Please give courage to us all, and wisdom and grace, and we will see your glory in this matter. Amen."

He looked up and smiled at them all. Manfred was amazed at his serenity. Their eyes met.

"Master Sandor! I am sorry you got mixed up in this. It isn't really your quarrel. I am used to the church objecting to me but *you* have not offended them."

"I fear, Father Bertram, that this has little to do with the church, and more to do with settling old scores. I am not so concerned about myself but I fear for the lad. His father entrusted him to my care, you see."

Bertram, with his youthful face and gentle eyes, looked at the young prince and nodded.

"Don't worry, my friend, I believe in my God and I have a feeling this is not the end of things for us just yet. There is more to be revealed."

"That is all very well for you, Father, but I am not sure I have someone watching over me like you."

"Are you sure, Master Sandor? Look back and see if there

135

were not times when you should have come to disaster and did not. Many have found that our heavenly Father was looking after them even when they were not aware of it. I well believe you might find it the same, if you think about it."

As Manfred was thinking about it, and realizing there might be some truth in the priest's words, he heard the bar being lifted off the door and Griffo's men entered the room.

"All the men" they said, "Out!"

Some of the women cried out a little at this but their menfolk comforted them and tried to put on a cheerful countenance for their sakes. They were roughly hurried out of the room and assembled in the courtyard.

Night had now definitely fallen and it was dark outside. They heard the bar being put back on the door and the men wondered when they would see their wives again. Then, from within, they heard the sounds of the hymn they had been singing earlier ringing confidently out again.

"My brothers," said Bertram cheerfully, "we cannot fail. With such a group praying for us, the Lord will be glorified in this and, I am assured, we will come to little harm. The Lord will have mercy upon us and will hear the prayers of his loved ones. Be comforted and uplifted. Take courage and remember 'Greater is He that is with us than all that can be against us.'"

Prince Rudolph looked at Manfred's anxious face and smiled. "Listen," he said, as the men around him joined in the hymn with their wives. "Don't worry, Manfred, I believe in Father Bertram and I am glad we are with these people."

A harsh command from Griffo interrupted their thoughts and

their singing, and the prisoners were marched out of the courtyard and into the narrow streets around the tower. Soon they entered what appeared to be an ordinary building, through a store room, into a basement where a trapdoor in the floor was already open for them.

Manfred and Hans, always looking for a chance to turn the tables, were dismayed to see that there were at least sixty soldiers in Griffo's group. He can't be leaving any behind, thought Manfred, which means he is leaving Blecklinghaus for good.

Cryllan, the man who had spoken up for Bertram, was standing near them. "They are using Bletcher's Tunnel," he whispered. "It is the longest of the tunnels and leads to the north-east."

"How do you know?" asked Prince Rudolph.

"Why, I grew up in Blecklinghaus, young master."

"Ah," said Manfred, "you are the one who said he wanted no more sin and was going to serve the good priest there."

Cryllan smiled a little. "Mm, you know about that, then? My lady wasn't right pleased about it at the time. My heart was in my mouth 'cos she has a short way with those who defy her. My wife knew though. She said 'You stand up to her, Cryllan, and she will be all right.' She were right, too, my dear Annie. I wish I could think she were at home now. It makes my blood boil to think of her shut up in that room, but I'm with Bertram. I believe in Jesus, I do, and I think things will work out all right. But, if not, then so be it. I'll not go back on what I believe, Jesus being my helper."

Manfred was impressed by the man's stalwart courage. Then Cryllan spoke again. "I also think my lady Velda will have

137

something to say when she hears of Aspin's death. She is not one to let that go by unavenged."

"Get on there," a harsh voice rasped, "and stop the talking."

FIFTEEN

Her servants quailed before her anger. Fifty-three years old, hair prematurely gray, thin featured, with good cheekbones, a woman who ruled in a man's world, her eyes flashed fire at the men around her.

"Aspin is dead? Killed, presumably by this Thalesian, and my guests taken. Taken! From *my* town, under *my* protection, under the very noses of *my* people. How could it happen?" She struggled to get her anger under control. She thought rapidly.

"Out of every five men in the city, I want four out looking for them. See to it, and quickly! I am going to the Tower, to see if I can find out more."

Velda turned to a twisted, gaunt man standing near her. Of average height, he appeared smaller because no part of his body appeared to have grown straight. His legs were bowed, his back bent, his chest seemed to face a different direction to his feet but the outstanding feature of this curious man, was that his head was twisted on his neck and, in fact, lay on one side as if perpetually inclined to sleep. His eyes were bright and sharp, though even his face seemed to have joined in the general attempt to make people think he was coming from several different directions at once. He was clad in light body armor; a sword hung at his left side and a long dagger at his right. Everyone knew he had suffered on the rack at one time and that he had been cut down from the hangman's noose by Velda's men. Since then he had risen to become Velda's chief of staff and was both feared and respected, far and wide.

"Wrynak!" she said. "Get a group of men and follow me to the Tower as quickly as you can. Choose skilled archers but men who can handle a sword if need be as well. I know I can rely on you."

"Aspin was my friend, my lady. I will not be long." He bowed and was gone.

Someone brought her a richly ornamented cloak. She swept down the long hall of her house and into the streets. Men outside stared and removed their hats as she passed. Women curtsied. Not often did the lady Velda enter the streets of Blecklinghaus unannounced. Everyone in the city knew of her, of course, but few had ever seen her. They revered and feared her. Most loved her and many had experienced extraordinary kindnesses at her hands. Very few hated her.

The iron bound gates of the Tower were open when she arrived and the guards saluted her as she passed. They felt more allegiance to her than to the mayor and governor. Suddenly she stopped.

"What is that?" she said. The crowd, which had followed her wonderingly, stopped and listened too. They heard clearly, but not too loud, the sound of singing. It was coming from a building to the right of the Great Hall.

"It's women singing, m'lady. Sounds like hymns."

"The doors are barred, m'lady," said another.

She gave orders for the bars to be removed and the doors opened and light streamed in upon the twenty or so wives and children Bertram's little band of followers. They immediately crowded round her and she had difficulty hearing the tale from so many wanting to tell her at the same time.

"You mean they took your men prisoner because you listened to this English priest? And, this Thalesian said it was on the orders of Bishop Theodore?"

"Yes, m'lady," they chorused.

"Sounds strange that such a man as this Thalesian should be concerned to serve the church in this way... unless," she thought, and then she understood, he would gain recruits for his detestable army. Not if I have anything to do with it, she thought grimly.

She turned to another of her servants, a thin, scholarly man, in the robes of a clerk. "Take the names of these women, Pelan, and see that they are compensated for their distress. Now, you women, get you home and see to your children. I am sure their night away will have been excitement enough for them for now."

"Please, m'lady," said a pretty, middle-aged woman with two children clinging to her skirts, "what about our menfolk?"

"Don't you worry, Mistress Agatha, I will be doing something about that, you can be sure."

"I knew you would, my lady. Cryllan is amongst them, too," put in another.

"All the more reason to get them back, Annie, although I was not best pleased with Cryllan last time I saw him, if I remember rightly."

"No m'lady," said Annie demurely, but with a little smile on her face.

Despite her fury, Lady Velda's eyes twinkled briefly. "I wouldn't mind wagering that his wife told him what to say, you know, Annie."

"Well, m'lady..."

"I knew it," said her ladyship grimly. "Men I can control, but with a woman at their backs... Enough, we are wasting time. Is His Excellency the Governor in the Great Hall?"

"Yes m'lady," came response from a servant boy brought out by the noise of the crowd.

She stormed up the steps and into the beautiful Great Hall of Blecklinghaus. Pale and trembling, the governor and mayor came to meet her.

"What have you done, Balic?" she snapped.

"My lady, I can explain. I didn't do anything. Honestly, my lady, it wasn't my fault..."

She silenced him with a gesture.

He was much bigger than she but he wilted as she advanced grimly.

"How did Thalesians come to be in *my* city? You let them in, probably, even *invited* them, yes?" She did not wait for a reply. "Who gave him authority to arrest the townsfolk in that meeting? *You did!*

"At least," she shouted, "you should have informed me, but you didn't, because you knew I would say no. You were probably paid to let him 'recruit' some of the townspeople. I can see by your face, I am right, and you hoped I would not know or care about a few men who disappeared."

She was pale with anger as she faced the unhappy man who stood awkwardly before her. "Is it possible you do not know who rules this town? Have you forgotten who put you into this position?" She paused and thought again. "You must have listened to that fat rogue, the bishop, and decided you could help him *and* provide recruits at the same time. Knowing you, you probably got paid by the bishop as well!"

"No, no, my lady," cried the unfortunate mayor.

"Yes, yes, your Excellency," she continued, with heavy sarcasm. "Worst of all, when you knew he had murdered my servant, Aspin," her voice rose again, "you helped him to escape! Which tunnel did they take?" she asked abruptly.

"I don't know, my lady," he stammered. Why he lied is difficult to understand. It may be that he was trying to say that his guilt was not as great as Lady Velda said. She was not deceived.

"What!" she screamed. "Do you still defy me?"

She turned to a dark visaged man behind her. "Gilflower," she said. He was sturdy, a little over-weight, a square stolid face, not at all resembling any flower. "Gilflower," she said again, motioning him towards the mayor.

He seized the mayor's substantial leg, twisted and lifted and the man was on the ground. He grabbed the mayor's hair, pulled his head back and pushed the point of his dagger into the mayor's throat, drawing blood.

Balic shrieked. "I'll tell you, m'lady. It was Banister's, m'lady."

"Banister's," she murmured, "on the northern edge of the city, but leading to the west. No..." she said, "I don't believe it.

143

They would have had to pass through several streets to get there and they would have been seen."

She glanced at her man. "Banister's?"

Gilflower shook his head. "T'ain't likely, m'lady, one of us would have seen 'em."

"You're a fool, Balic. Why lie to me? Cut his ear off, Gilflower."

The mayor shrieked and struggled but Gilflower held him firmly and, neatly and expertly, cut the man's ear from his head.

Balic screeched in pain and screamed. His screams were heard in the courtyard outside and men and women looked at each other.

Lady Velda was inexorable. "Which tunnel?"

"Belcher's," he sobbed. "It was Belcher's."

She thought again. "Yes, that makes sense, near at hand and heading in the right direction. When did they leave?"

"Two hours before midnight," the mayor replied.

Velda pursed her lips. "If only we had known sooner. They will be far on their way by now."

"What do you think, Gilflower, can we catch them?"

"Not with a large force, m'lady, takes too much time to muster enough men. I'd say a small containing force, to stay with them until we *can* catch them up."

His mistress agreed and then went on. "Tell Wrynack what we have learned. He will take his men and go on ahead while you take care of things here and muster our people everywhere. I have a job for them to do. Tell Wrynak to harass these Thalesians. Give them no peace. Tell him to see that no harm comes to my guests."

144

He bowed his assent, although his mind was racing. Never before had he heard of Velda's people being summoned from all the corners of the kingdom. He didn't even know that it could be done although he suspected that it could.

"One last thing, Balic," and he quailed at the word 'last'. "What is the name of this Thalesian soldier, the captain?"

"Griffo, my lady, Griffo of Tastag," he answered miserably. Then "My lady, have pity on me. I did not know. I did not think you would mind. It wasn't my fault. I didn't know about Aspin."

He pleaded with her, on his knees, but she turned away from him, her face implacable as she addressed Gilflower again. "Hang him!"

"No, my lady!" he wailed and begged again for his life. She was having none of it though and, still very angry, added "and the bishop!"

"The bishop, m'lady?" Even Gilflower, hardened as he was to violence, was shaken. "He is the leader of the church. Some of the people won't like it."

"Pshaw!" she snorted. "*He* is not the church. He is corrupt, greedy and cruel, and I think you will find that most of the people will be glad to see the back of him." Another thought struck her. "And give his money to those women we released today. That seems to me more like the church. See that it is done, Gilflower. I have spoken."

Gilflower bowed, flung the mayor's ear into the fire, gruffly indicated the mayor to his men and marched through the watching crowd to the door.

The mayor and the bishop were hanged before midday. The

people were astonished and turned out to watch, but they were not dismayed and treated the event as if it were a public holiday.

SIXTEEN

Morning found them many miles from Blecklinghaus. Black Griffo had taken the unfortunate mayor's warning seriously enough to keep them moving and they had now been walking for several hours. The boy found it especially wearisome as he trudged along for mile after mile until, at last, Griffo called a halt. They sank wearily to the floor, guards as glad to stop as the prisoners were. Griffo alone seemed full of energy and, indeed, was in high good humor. He had a goodly group of healthy men for the Archduke and, perhaps more importantly in his eyes, he had at least three people in his clutches who would make fine soldiers. Hans, of course, Cryllan, and he recognised the fighting qualities and courage in Manfred. He came over to them soon after they had stopped. The boy had fallen asleep immediately and lay on the grass near Manfred.

Griffo looked back frequently, thinking of the mayor's warning, but there was no sign of any pursuit. *Just the fussing fears of that old woman, the mayor,* he thought contemptuously. But he was wrong and if he had stopped and looked for just fifteen minutes more, he might have seen a small cloud of dust on the horizon. But he didn't.

Griffo stopped by Manfred and kicked him viciously as he sat. "Now, good merchant," he sneered, "although an unfortunate one I think, there will be little time for you to rest. Like all *good merchants* you no doubt like your comforts. There will be precious few of those, I think. I wonder if you have any more gold on you. You gave up your purse rather easily."

He beckoned to two of his men and motioned towards a nearby tree. It was countryside, thick with gorse bushes, but with the occasional tree, standing tall among the yellow bushes. They took Manfred and stripped him of his outer clothes, which he then searched.

"Hah! I knew it," Griffo shouted in triumph. "*Two* more bags, and stuffed with gold pieces. You must be a very rich merchant indeed, and fancy trying to keep them from me. You will pay for that, my man."

Manfred knew what was coming but was helpless to prevent it. Hans squirmed and seethed but, again, could do nothing. There were just too many guards and he dared not endanger the Prince. Griffo whipped him until his back ran red with blood and, eventually, he fainted from the pain and loss of blood. He hung from his tied hands, his back a raw mass of red meat. Rudolph could not look at him and wept openly. Hans was pale under his rugged outdoor tan but said nothing.

A little, jolly, red-faced man from the church, spoke up. His name was Eric, round from too much eating and not enough exercise, got to his feet and approached Griffo. "Your honor," he said, "yon fellow has had enough. May I have your permission to cut him down and bathe his wounds. He will be no use to you dead, you know."

Griffo's face darkened with rage and he whirled on the little man, striking him to the ground and kicking him again and again, until he begged for mercy. Then he cursed him for daring to question him as to what he was doing. His little dark eyes glanced around and lighted on Hans.

"You'll do," he said, "you're big enough. Take that whip and teach this fool a lesson for attempting to teach me my business.

Hans lumbered to his feet and shuffled over to the soldier, taking the whip off him, as the man grinned in anticipation. Hans then returned to Griffo and poor Eric, still groaning on the floor.

"Whip him, you big oaf, and see that you do not spare."

Hans raised the whip and brought it sweeping across Griffo's face and shoulder.

"No," said Hans, "I will not do your dirty work for you."

By then Hans had delivered many blows and Griffo was writhing on the ground.

The soldiers hurled themselves upon him, and Hans threw them off as if they were made of straw. But there were three score of them and even Hans went down under the sheer weight of bodies

"You fool!" said Griffo. "When I have finished you, you will wish I had killed you. Come off him, you men.

"Talmek!" he called to his sergeant.

Talmek was tall and thin, but sinewy. His face was lean, expressionless, with deep, black eyes, like little stones. He bowed before his captain.

"Cover him with two bowmen."

"Yes sir."

Hans was still on the ground, panting.

One soldier struck Hans a vicious blow in the back with his spear butt. Taking hold of his man's spear Griffo struck Hans across his head with the shaft so that his head jerked to the side, then he struck again on the other side, and again, and again, back and forth, back and forth, until the mighty Hans lost consciousness. Even then Griffo seemed unable to stop for a while but continued to thrash the unconscious mop of black hair on the ground.

"Sir," said Bertram, "if you continue like this, there will be no men left for your master."

Griffo turned evil eyes towards him. "Ah yes, the priest," he mused, "a priest who challenges the power of the secular authority. What can I do with you, my holy friend?" He looked at four of his men. "Cut down the merchant and hang this priest from that tree. Never know when a good tree will come in useful," he grinned.

Bertram paled but he looked at him steadily. "I am ready to die, but are you, for your day will surely come? If you, instead of me, were to die today, do you know where you would be going?"

"Yes," sneered Griffo, "into the ground, like a rotting turnip, and so will you Sir Priest, only sooner than I. That's the only difference."

"Not so, Captain Griffo, for that *is* your name isn't it. I know whom I have believed and, if I die today, I have His assurance that I will be with Him in heaven."

Cryllan stepped up. "Sir," he said. "I beg you not to harm this man. He is a man of God."

Griffo looked annoyed at this new interruption and regarded

Cryllan with some disfavour. Then he looked at him with astonishment as Cryllan continued. "If you must hang someone, hang me. I have been a thief and a vagabond from my youth, richly deserving punishment, but this man has done nothing but good. Take me instead."

Griffo stared at him. "Now this *is* a wonder. Never before has a man begged me to hang him. Ah well, I am too soft-hearted, I suppose. I never could resist an earnest request. Hang them both!"

His men stepped forward and, in a trice, ropes were round their necks and they were led unresisting to the tree, where Manfred still slumped unconscious.

"Take courage, Cryllan," said Bertram. "I do not feel our time has come and yet, if it is so, we will meet our glorious Savior this very day.

"String them up," growled Griffo brutally.

"Wait!"came a cry from the road. "Captain Griffo, don't harm them."

Everyone turned to look. Unnoticed in all the turmoil among the prisoners, a large man, red-faced from his exertions, was hurrying towards them along the dusty road. Prince Rudolph recognized him as Sylrac, the bully from the tavern. He could not imagine what Sylrac could be doing here. Griffo regarded him sourly. He had met him briefly in Blecklinghaus and, indeed, Sylrac had tried to do a little recruiting for him amongst the habitues of the tavern where he spent so much time. He spoke to him now.

"What are you doing here? And why should I not harm these

men?"

"My lord, I have heard rumors in the town that some of your prisoners are not all they seem to be ... that there might be rich ransoms to be gained for some of them." Griffo's eyes gleamed with interest. Not a poor man at all, but with a very sharp eye for increasing his wealth, he at once saw that there might be truth in Sylrac's words. What he did not know was the true worth of the prisoners he had in his hands, or that Sylrac had been deliberately fed information by Velda's clerk of affairs, Pelan, on Velda's instructions, for just such an eventuality as this hanging that Sylrac had so wonderfully interrupted. "There are two men, a boy, and a priest, who may be more than ordinary people, one man indeed who is reputed to be fabulously rich."

"Don't hang them ... yet!" he said to his men. "Bring them over here to join the others while I think about this."

He walked over to the prisoners and gazed wonderingly at Hans, still unconscious, Manfred, covered in blood and barely conscious, the priest, unafraid, looking at him now with clear brown eyes, almost with pity in them. Cryllan, prepared to die for this priest, why? Perhaps because his family is very rich and Cryllan's family would be rewarded if they heard of his sacrifice. In Griffo's mind, no-one did anything for nothing. And the little fat man, Eric, who had wanted to bathe Manfred's wounds. Would he do that if Manfred were not rich? Yes, there might well be something in that fool Sylrac's words. He thought some more, especially about Manfred. Those villagers had seemed very respectful to him and he was dressed in merchant's clothes and didn't everyone know that merchants were always rich. Who else

152

would there be? He was not sure, but he would keep them a bit more carefully now.

"All right, Sylrac, you may be right. You may be wrong, of course, but you would not be so foolish as to bring me false information, would you?" Sylrac paled a little but stood his ground.

"I believe it to be true, Captain."

"Mm, all right. You will, of course, come with us, won't you." It was not a question, and Sylrac joined the unhappy procession, herded by the soldiers along the dusty highway.

SEVENTEEN

No-one saw the first soldier die. He was near the back of the column and he just disappeared. They were passing a little wood and he, by name Stoggi, nipped into the wood for a minute. He never came out and they were a fair way along the road before his friend, Alglis, realised Stoggi had not come back. He quickly told his sergeant, who in turn told Griffo, but Griffo was pre-occupied, thinking about his prisoners. He just roughly said to forget it, that he would catch up later and then he would be for it.

Manfred and Hans were in a sorry state. Hans was conscious but dazed and had to be supported by two of Bertram's largest followers: the faithful Cryllan and a strong young fellow called Ticval. Manfred struggled valiantly but his back was so painful that he seemed to pass in and out of consciousness, his hazy vision trimmed with red. Bertram and Prince Rudolph supported one arm each. They dared not touch his back.

Late in the afternoon, they reached the end of the great plain of Blecklinghaus and the road entered pleasant woodland. A smithy stood here and a few rude cottages. The procession halted and, at the point of soldiers' pikes, all the men were herded towards the smithy. Griffo entered the rough stone building, which served as shelter to the fire and brazier, the heat pushing at them though they were still outside. The exchange between the blacksmith and Griffo sounded as though they were hot too.

The smith emerged. He was a youngish man, with fair complexion, hot and flushed from the forge, untidy, light brown hair falling in a shaggy mop on all sides of his head, a loose shirt, open at the front revealed a broad chest and ample muscles. He had a broad forehead, straight eyebrows and blue eyes, which, just now, looked angry.

Griffo indicated his prisoners. "There they are," he said. "Shackle them!"

"It's not my kind of work," said the smith angrily. "I shoe horses. I don't chain men. Anyway, it would take a week to shackle all of them, and a pile of iron."

"Not all of them, you bumpkin, just those I point out to you," indicating Hans and Manfred.

"I don't like it. It's not work I do."

"You're a smith, aren't you? Do as I say, or it will be the worse for you."

"I'm a free man. You can't make me do anything."

"Don't be a fool," said Griffo, waving a brawny arm at his men. "I can make you do whatever I like. Who is to stop me? In fact, you can count yourself fortunate that I have let you talk to me for so long. Now shackle them or I'll burn you and your smithy to the ground."

Reluctantly the blacksmith returned to his shed. A brawny lad came out with him and together they set to work on their reluctant clients, who were sat in the shade of the cottage wall and waited their turn. It took the rest of the day. Hans was chained first.

As Malka, the blacksmith saw his massive frame and rippling muscles, he smiled, "I am not surprised they want you chained. I'm thinking they'll feel a lot safer. I'm also thinking you'd make a fine blacksmith, if you ever fancied the job."

"A little too hot for me," said Hans hoarsely, still reeling from the treatment he had received and badly needing a drink.

The good smith, in fact, noticed Hans' distress and slipped him a pot of water from his smithy as he was measuring the chain for his feet. Griffo also made him tie the other prisoners' hands and then rope them together. "I am sorry, my friend," he said to each one, "I don't know what you have done, but I've no quarrel with ye and I would rather have no part in this."

All Bertram's people assured him they did not hold him responsible and spoke so kindly to him that he was near to tears as he worked upon them, especially with Bertram, whom Prince Rudolph heard talking to him about Jesus. *He never misses an opportunity,* he thought to himself, and smiled inwardly despite his situation.

They slept that night in the little village where Malka lived. Griffo turfed a family out of the nicest hut but the rest of his party slept in the open round a large fire.

Half a dozen guards were set at intervals on the edge of the village. They were not supposed to move but Ertel knew Griffo would not check on them until much later, if at all, so he wandered over for a chat with his friend, Alglis. He was the nearest guard to his position anyway, so it was convenient.

"Where do you think Stoggi went to?" he asked Alglis.

"I don't know, I've been thinking about that. You know, it's funny that he didn't come back. It's not as if there is anything in those woods to attract him. I can't see him deserting at that point. There is nowhere to go."

"You don't think he had an accident of some sort, do you? Perhaps fell over a cliff or something and broke a leg?"

"Nar, there are no cliffs near there. He might have tripped over something and hurt himself. He was always clumsy. You remember that time when he knocked the firkin of ale over. Everyone was right mad with him at the time."

Ertel nodded. He remembered it well.

"Well, I'm not going to worry about it anyway. The captain will sort it out when he comes back, and I wouldn't be in Stoggi's shoes when he does."

"Do you think the captain will remember to relieve us later?" Alglis had remembered that the captain was not always that concerned about his men and often they slept where their guard post was. And so it was this time. Griffo had other things on his mind, changing the guard in this out of the way village was not one of them.

At that moment, he was lying on his rough bed thinking over the day. He pondered Sylrac's words and thought about certain of his prisoners. He knew he had never had prisoners like these before and he was intrigued. As he fell asleep he was still thinking about them

EIGHTEEN

Morning light was just beginning to show itself, when everyone was awoken by hideous screams. Shrieks and pitiful cries for mercy echoed around the little valley where the village lay.

Griffo woke with a start, fumbled for his weapons in the dark and ran for the open.

Outside his party was in turmoil, with men-at-arms running here and there, pale-faced at the terrible screams and cries coming from the the thin woods on the valley sides. With curses and a few well-placed blows, Griffo restored order and angrily questioned his sergeant, Talmek.

"What is it, you fool? What has been happening?"

"Sir, we don't know, We just heard these terrible screams and were trying to find out where they were coming from."

Griffo glared around. The awful noises seemed to be coming from both sides of the valley. It *was* hard to pinpoint them, as the echoes were reflected from one side to the other. One thing, thought Griffo, mere screams won't frighten me. They're made by men and I can handle men, whoever they are.

"Sir! Sir!" Padeelis, one of his best soldiers was running up to him.

"What is it, Padeelis?"

"Sir, Ronka and Mastuch are both dead in their blankets,

their throats cut."

The prisoners! Griffo looked at them, but although not chained, they had all been roped together for the night. It was impossible for them to be responsible for this.

"Who was on guard duty, Talmek?"

"Pishtin and Adrakis, captain, Alglis and Ertell."

Suddenly one set of screams stopped abruptly, and then the other.

The light was better now.

Griffo made a decision.

"Padeelis, you stay here with two dozen men. Talmek, bring the rest and come with me."

His horse was brought and he rode at the head of his group up the valley side where the hideous noises had been coming from. His men were nervous and kept their weapons ready but they were mostly seasoned soldiers and were used to the screams of men.

The woods were very sparse, scattered trees really with some undergrowth. There! At the top of the hill, Griffo thought he saw some movement but looked again and there was nothing there.

The path turned. They passed thick bushes and there on the grass before a scraggy birch tree, lay a man, pegged out. He covered quite a large area, but this was because he had been pegged out in pieces: an arm here, a leg below the torso, the head separate again, and so on. He had been systematically cut into pieces.

"It's Adrakis," whispered one of Griffo's men, "I thought I

hadn't seen him this morning."

A little further on, in another clearing, they found the remains of Pishtin. Judging by what they found, it was he who had been screaming. Now they *were* frightened. Griffo knew he had to rejoin the main party and he turned and led them back down to the village.

When they got back, his men discussed their grisly find with their friends in the other group. Sylrac listened with fear gnawing at his heart.

"Sir," he said to Griffo, "this is Velda's work. We must get out of this place quickly or we will all perish."

"You pitiful coward," snarled Griffo, "how can it be? She is back in the town. This is the work of more than one person and not a woman, at that."

"Sir, I told you, she has many men and her arm is long."

The black-bearded captain snorted but he thought he had better get on the move. It would be wise, he thought. Then he thought again about his unusual prisoners. Could they have had anything to do with this?

He strode over to the little group where Manfred and Hans were, still shackled and manacled. No, it was impossible for them to have been involved and, anyway, the two men looked half dead. They would have trouble just reaching the place where the soldiers lay. They could not have climbed the hillside.

"Talmek!"

"Captain?" answered his grim faced sergeant.

"Take two men, on horses all of you, and have a quick look on the other side of the valley. See if you can see anything there, but take no risks and do not delay there. We will be on the move soon."

The sergeant went without another word, just a brief salute with his weapon, and he and his companions were off.

Griffo was puzzled and worried. Was this anything to do with his strange prisoners? He wondered again. Was it Sylrac or that fool of a mayor who had said they were under this woman, Velda's, protection? If so, why? Why would she be so concerned about these strangers to her town?

"Hmm," he mused, "a rich merchant, a servant and a boy whom they both seem unusually fond of ..." The last was particularly puzzling to him, as he himself had never seen anything in any boy to be particularly fond of. He paused and fingered his shaggy beard "... and twenty men could not take them." And he had to admit to himself, if to no-one else, that *he* had only managed it because he had had the foresight to bring those archers along.

I wish I had such men in my army ... and such concern for a skinny apprentice boy, whose eyes flash fire and shout defiance, even when he is helpless in my hands. Such a boy ... as might be high-born.

"That's it!" he spoke aloud and then recovered himself, as some of his men looked at him. *This is some nobleman's whelp and they are taking him out of the way of the Archduke's army and, unless I am mightily mistaken, his father will pay handsomely for his safe return.* He continued to muse on the matter for, although he was absolutely loyal to his master, the pay was non-existent, and every man was expected to fend for himself

161

and take such opportunities for personal enrichment as were (frequently) afforded by service to the Archduke.

Acting upon such thoughts and continuing to surmise that his captives would fetch a better price if they were returned in good condition, Griffo enquired as to whether there were a horse and cart in the village. Someone foolishly told him he had one and saw it immediately confiscated for his pains.

He turned to the sound of hooves galloping towards the village. It was his sergeant, pale and even more grim.

"It was the same that side, sir. Only this time, it was Olnat in pieces on the floor. We didn't even know he was missing."

"Pull yourself together, sergeant. Get the men on the road. See that the cart has an escort." He paused, then groaned, "What's that now?" he said for he heard the noise of men-at-arms approaching.

He groaned aloud but told his men to get ready to fight. He would not go down without a fight, yet he could not believe there *were* any soldiers near, apart from the his fellow recruiting bands from the Archduke.

He need not have feared for the newcomers turned out to be some of the Blecklinghaus town guard, not anxious to remain and face Velda's fury at the death of her henchman and the capture of her guests. With them had also come a group of six black robed priests, hurriedly deciding their duty lay elsewhere, for exactly the same reason, as Velda respected the cloth of the church not at all.

It was now quite a sizeable party, numbering perhaps a hundred, not counting the prisoners. Some were on horses but most were on foot. The priests saw the cart and, as they were unused to walking long distances, sighed with relief and started to climb on board.

Griffo's angry roar could be heard three fields away.

"Out! Out! You fat friars! Do you think I went to all this trouble just to obtain transport for non-paying guests! I have better things to do with that cart. Here, you men, put the prisoners in that cart - him, him, him and that one there, too, I think." He pointed to Hans, Manfred, Prince Rudolph and, to the priests' fury, Father Bertram, as well. Griffo still entertained exaggerated ideas as to his wealth.

The priests began expostulating loudly with Griffo, but he was having none of it. He brushed their protests roughly aside, mustered his men and commanded that they continue their journey along the highway, a strong guard being placed around the cart.

It was, indeed, just as well that Griffo had made his decision concerning the cart as neither Hans nor Manfred, nor in fact Bertram, was in any condition to walk much further. They were so weakened by their wounds that they would not have lasted long on the forced march which ensued. The other prisoners suffered too, because of the heat and lack of water. Being tied was irksome, causing irritation, but nothing that could not be born. Hans drifted in and out of consciousness but his lucid spells grew longer and, gradually, to the young prince's relief, he began to start flexing his muscles and he knew that Hans was trying to get himself ready to fight again for his prince if the opportunity arose.

Manfred, too, was feeling better physically, although his

heart was heavy as he considered the situation they had got themselves into. He wished to encourage Hans though and smiled down at him in the bottom of the cart. "It's all right, old fellow, *he* (with a quick glance at the prince) is safe, though we are prisoners."

"We have been in tighter spots than this," said Hans. "How many men have they got?"

Manfred wasn't sure they had, but he thought Hans must be referring to one of the many times they had stood side by side in battle, never knowing when the next spear might strike one of them down, or the next sword cut might be for them. At least, they were not in immediate danger of their lives as, for some reason, Griffo's hanging desires seemed to have passed off, since Sylrac's intervention.

"About a hundred, I would say," he answered Hans, "but the biggest problem is the presence of these irons. I will have to see if I can persuade our gentle captain to have them removed." Hans grunted his agreement but the Prince noticed that he began to test his strength against the irons in various places.

"There's another strange thing happening, Hans, too."

"What's that?" groaned Hans.

"Someone is picking off Griffo's men. I think it's six so far have died or disappeared. Someone is harrying Griffo's party, and I think I know who it is."

Despite his thundering headache, Hans was interested. "Who do you think is behind it?"

"Velda, but hush now!"

Griffo came sauntering arrogantly to the cart.

"Now, my fine friends, we are on our way to somewhere you will have heard of ... aye, to the castle of your King, Dehrmacht, although I don't think His Majesty is living there in quite his accustomed style."

The Prince's eyes flashed and he leaned forward as if to speak, but Manfred's hand slipped on to his arm and he sank back again, silent. Griffo regarded them silently for a few moments and then turned his horse and rode back to the front of the column.

It was a tedious journey though it should have been beautiful. Their path lay through deep woods. The sun shone, pleasantly shaded by the trees. The birds sang. The scent of wild flowers filled the air and, altogether, it was a lovely day for a walk in pleasant woods. Their hearts were heavy, though, with thoughts of failure. To be taken ignominiously back to the castle, chained and in a cart, was the last thing any of them wanted. Prince Rudolph could not stop thinking of his father. He knew it would cause him great distress to see his son dragged back after all his efforts to secure his safety. Manfred and Hans had even worse thoughts, as either would have gladly given his life to save their young master, but neither could see any escape from their predicament.

The men-at-arms too were uncommunicative and ill at ease. They looked round nervously at the sound of the wind in the trees. Strange bird calls seemed to accompany them too and, just before noon, there was a strangled squawk and the soldiers turned to see Talmek lifted bodily off his horse to hang from a branch over the path.

"Cut him down!" shouted Griffo. "Padeelis, take his horse,

and twelve men and find who has done this."

Padeelis did not look pleased as the way was thickly forested at this point and he had no desire to leave the path. He dared not disobey Griffo though and he obediently led his men searching around the tree and into the gloom of the forest.

Talmek was alive, though his throat was raw.

"What happened?" asked his captain when he could speak again, though with difficulty.

"Booby trap, captain," he said hoarsely. "I noticed a sapling bent in a strange position, pushed the branch aside, the noose fell and up went the sapling."

We won't find anyone then, thought the captain. They will be at a safe distance by now.

Strangely, that comforted the Thalesian, as he thought, his unseen enemies could not be that strong, or they would fight more openly, instead of in this secretive way.

Amongst the prisoners, the townsfolk had guessed what was happening. Crillan particularly knew that this was the way Velda's men would work until they were strong enough to attack openly. His heart lifted and he began to think they were not in as bad a state as they had feared.

NINETEEN

Prince Rudolph had not heard Manfred's conversation with
Hans and did not have this comforting knowledge. He was feeling
very low. Their high plans had come to nothing. Manfred and
Hans were seriously hurt and he feared for them both. Manfred
could hardly move in the bottom of the cart and the boy could see
that he was wracked with pain all the time. Hans too looked ill
and dopey. From time to time, he shook his great head, as if to put
it to rights, and then sank almost into a stupor again.

And how was the priest doing? Prince Rudolph could not
make him out. He was in as bad a state as any of them but there
he was looking almost cheerful and, the Prince was sure, he was
humming a little hymn to himself. What strength was that!
Bertram catching his glance, smiled at him. "Don't worry, lad.
Things will get better soon, I believe. My heavenly Father did not
send me all this way from home just to end on a tyrant's gallows.
Also, my people here... he waved his hand at his bedraggled,
bound and exhausted fellow prisoners, my people here are
wonderful pray-ers and my God answers prayer. That I *do* know."

At the end of a weary day, they stopped at a small village,
where Griffo called a halt. The prisoners were herded towards one
of the huts. As they were going, Hans forgot the chain between
his feet and attempted to take his normal stride. He stumbled and

fell heavily on Bertram who, in turn, sprawled painfully on the stony ground under Hans' great weight.

"I am sorry, Father," rumbled Hans. " I have not yet become used to this wretched chain. I hope you are not hurt?"

Winded and panting for breath, the priest smiled weakly at Hans. "I am afraid I do not make a good cushion. But do not call me Father, for our Lord said 'Call no man Father, for you have one Father that is in Heaven.'"

"But you are a priest," said Hans. "All priests are called Father."

"Not this one," said an angry voice behind them. "This one is a renegade and a heretic and is like to burn when we get to the Archduke's army."

One of the black-robed priests had come up unexpectedly and had heard their words. He kicked Bertram viciously in the shins, so that he gasped again in pain, but did not cry out. The priest continued "What do you mean by filling ignorant men with harmful doctrines, against the teaching of Mother Church!"

"I merely quoted our Lord's own words," gasped Bertram meekly.

"Don't lecture me," said the angry priest, more cross because he was tired and hungry. "I have heard your sort of false learning before. You choose carefully the words which you believe and those which you deny."

"I believe all that our Lord Jesus taught," said Bertram.

"Then why do you and your sort teach that in the holy Mass, the bread and the wine do not *actually* become His blessed body and blood, *as He himself said at the Last Supper!*"

Father Maurice, for that was the priest's name, smirked at his victory over the prisoner. Manfred, Hans and the young prince waited with interest to hear Bertram's reply. They had all grown to respect him and even to love him, but they had years of church teaching behind them and in their hearts they wondered how he dared to question things they had taken for granted for so long.

Bertram sighed, knowing that he would never convince the arrogant churchman beside them but he also knew he had to answer, for the sake of the others who were listening.

"That is a misunderstanding of our Lord's words and intentions," he said calmly. "When he said those things, it was a prophetic act. With them he was symbolizing the death he was about to suffer and its great purpose in redeeming men and women from the curse of sin and death. It was a *prophetic* act. He used the bread and wine as it was a convenient and suitable picture. He could have easily chosen meat and water but he had used bread and wine before when teaching about his ministry. To think he meant that they actually changed into flesh and blood is a nonsense and a denial of the whole of the New Testament's teaching of salvation through *faith*, not through tangible objects of this life."

Father Maurice could not contain his rage. "Heretic! Scoundrel! False to the cloth you wear and to Holy Church! False prophet! Liar! Ignorant peasant of peasant stock!" Then, to those who were listening. "Close your ears to this wicked nonsense," he screeched, purple with rage. "Father Godwin, Father Ulric!" he called to two others in black.

"This wicked scoundrel still has not learned his lesson. We

169

must be quick to save his soul."

Father Godwin was heavily built and well fed. From under his black robe he brought a short handled whip, loosing its length from a coil round his leg.

Without more ado, the priests seized Bertram, tore his outer robe from him and tied his wrists to the low branch of a tree. Prince Rudolph saw with horrified eyes that Bertram's back was already criss-crossed with scars. It was plain he was no stranger to the lash.

A small crowd of villagers had gathered out of curiosity. Strangers were always interesting and their village had prospered greatly from the many travellers on the great road from Dehrmacht to the east of the Kingdom. The men-at-arms also came to watch: careless, indifferent, most were hardened to suffering of one kind or another. Griffo was elsewhere, seeing to provisions in the village or he would probably have stopped the whole thing. Not out of humanity, but because he still thought Father Bertram might have rich relations in England who would pay for his return unharmed.

Father Godwin tried his whip out, flexing his muscles. The thong whistled and cracked in the air. Then he raised his arm, flicked his wrist and brought the lash down on Bertram's thin back. The ragged priest writhed under it but made no sound.

"Wait!" cried a boy's shrill voice, and Rudolph stepped forward. "How can you, a priest, commit this act of cruelty, and against one of your own cloth?"

Godwin turned with an oily smile. "Ah," he said smoothly, "it is entirely for his own good. It is because we love him that we do this thing. It will only hurt his body and may persuade him to turn from his foolishness and thus save his soul."

"But, look at his back! It is already marked with many lashes. It has not persuaded him to repent in the past. Oh ..." the boy pleaded, near to tears, for he had grown to respect and admire this gentle, but courageous man, "please, has he not suffered enough? Please let him go. He sincerely believes what he says and he is a good man."

"Your compassion does you credit, boy, but see how much harm he has done already for he has persuaded you and how many others that he is a good man. No," the priest said firmly, but with a cruel glint in his eye, "I am afraid we must try stern measures to save him from himself. Now stand aside, boy, and let me do my unhappy work," and he pushed the boy out of the way. He did not look unhappy though and, after thirteen years watching the intrigue of his father's court, Rudolph had learned to read men's hearts through their eyes and faces, rather than their words. He knew, as certainly as if the priest had spoken, that Father Godwin was going to enjoy whipping Bertram and that Godwin was cruel at heart. All his training and upbringing came to the fore and he seized the priest's arm.

"You *shall* not strike him again!"

Father Godwin's response was simple. He shook the boy off and struck him hard across the face.

"How dare you interfere with the work of holy Mother Church!" he hissed as the boy fell stunned beside him.

That was all he had time to say, though. Two iron-circled hands seized the big priest and flung him bodily into the side of a

171

hut nearby, where he lay still.

The soldiers did not look too disturbed, though one or two hefted their spears and watched Hans for further signs of violence. Hans, though, was helping his young master to his feet and making sure that he was not injured. Manfred was with him.

One of the other priests scurried over to Father Godwin and wailed loudly and angrily "He is dead! His neck is broken. You vile and wicked man to slay a priest of the church. I will see to it that you are brought to justice for this terrible crime." He turned to the men-at-arms. "Seize him," he commanded, but the soldier appeared uncertain whether they should obey his orders, and then Griffo appeared.

He saw the dead priest and Manfred and Hans bending over the boy. He also saw Bertram tied up with the blood red weal of the lash fresh across his back and his face darkened. "What has been happening to my prisoners?" he asked.

Father Ulric told him loudly and angrily. Griffo turned to Padeelis, who had been one of the onlookers. A large ugly fellow but loyal to Griffo and who could be relied upon to tell his master the truth. "Is this true?"

"Yes, captain."

Griffo turned to Ulric. "I told you priests to leave my prisoners alone. They are *my* prisoners, you understand, all of them." He prodded the priest's chest with his finger as he spoke each word. "You are to leave them alone," he shouted. "If you touch them again, I will hang you myself."

The priest blanched, more from anger than fear, and said "You mean you will do nothing about this foul murder."

Griffo looked at him for a moment and then seized him round the neck with muscular and non too gentle hands. "Nothing!," he hissed. "I fear not you, not holy church, nor any bishop, nor anyone but my lord the Archduke so, if you value your life, fat priest, stay far away from me for the rest of this journey!" And he flung the priest from him. Then he indicated the prisoners and commanded his men

"Bring the prisoners. I have found a hut for them, but those four, put them in my lodging first. I want a word with them."

The prisoners were led into a shabby hut while Bertram, Hans, Manfred and Prince Rudolph were taken under heavy guard to the largest house in the village, where Griffo examined them with interest.

"Now what exactly is going on with you four? Who are you? I am pretty sure that two of you, at least, are of noble birth - maybe all of you. It is hard to tell with priests sometimes, because their learning excels, but you," pointing to Manfred, "were in Velda's house, an honored guest and I see from your eye and your manner that you are used to command. You *may* be a merchant, but a very unusual one.

"And the boy," he continued, "has too bold a look, too fair a speech, for an apprentice. Also, you both leap to his defense very quickly. How many apprentice lads would be delivered from a beating? From what I have seen, most of them need every beating they can be given. Come," he said, "tell me now who you are. I could have all three of you killed, if I chose."

"Would not Balic object to that?" asked Manfred, playing for time and thinking desperately while he did so.

"The Mayor of Blecklinghaus?" he snorted scornfully. "What has he got to do with it? It was my idea to take you to the Archduke to see if *he* was interested in you. No, Balic has nothing to do with it. You are my prisoners until we reach his grace, or his highness as he likes to be called now."

Manfred's face cleared and he gave a beaming smile at Griffo, much to his surprise.

"Ah, captain, if we are going to Archduke Boris, all is well. You see," he said ingratiatingly, leaning close to Griffo and indicating Prince Rudolph, "this is His Highness's cousin, Leopold of Havanor. My friend and I were entrusted with the task of bringing his lordship safely to him, but without the knowledge of his family and, of course, without the knowledge of King Maximilian. He is heir to great wealth and the archduke suddenly remembered his kinship with the lad and decided that he would be safer under his protection than in the unruly lands of Havanor.

"That is why I warned you not to chain him. We know our royal master does not like his orders disobeyed and we were instructed to treat his lordship with every respect." Manfred lowered his voice, so that only Griffo could hear. "We have told the boy that the Archduke had learned of a plot by his relations to murder him and that we were stealing him away for his own protection. He thinks of us, therefore, as his friends and protectors, which has made our task easier in bringing him so far to meet his esteemed and powerful cousin."

"Hmm!" mused Griffo, his little eyes darting from one figure to another, "but why did his Highness not mention this to me? I could have helped perhaps."

"How could he know where you would be when we came? He had no knowledge of the route we would take, nor how long it would take us to find and speak to the young count. Also, you know our prince, he likes to keep one hand secret from the other!"

"Aye, that is true," said Griffo, but then his suspicion flared again "but if you are so close to our lord, how is it that I have never seen you in his courts or in his camp?" And his little black eyes peered suspiciously at Manfred.

"Captain Griffo" said Manfred winningly, "you know the Archduke's ways. You know he has secret agents in various places, even in Dehrmacht itself. Even so trusted a friend as yourself is not told the names of his agents or where he sends them. Is that not true?"

"Aye," muttered Griffo.

"And maybe you have heard of the name of his chief agent, which hardly anyone knows, except those highest in his Highness's councils?"

Griffo looked cautiously and nervously around. "I have heard it, but it is said to be dangerous to admit to this knowledge."

"Dangerous indeed," smiled Manfred knowingly, "but *I* know it and could whisper it to you now."

Griffo looked at him and Manfred knew that he had won. Then Griffo said heavily, "Whisper it to me but, on peril of your life, let no-one else hear it."

Manfred drew very close and whispered a name in Griffo's ear. He seemed to ponder it and then he said "Aye, you are right. That is his name." Manfred doubted if Griffo really knew the man's identity but it did not matter for *he* did, thanks to his own agents in Thalesia, and if it embarrassed his enemy to have his name blazoned abroad, so much the better.

"I should think I am right," answered Manfred brazenly, "as he is my immediate master and I am answerable to him and then his highness."

"We had a lot of trouble 'rescuing' his lordship from Havanor, without being caught," rumbled Hans, anxious to support Manfred.

"Yes," said the Prince. "It took me three days to slip away from my tutor and my guards to escape with these my friends, in order to join my noble cousin. That is why we had to pretend to be a merchant's party. As for this good priest, he befriended us along the way, when we needed food and shelter. Also," said the Prince confidently, "he is of noble birth in England and much respected and valued there. He was telling us along the way of the lands and castles his father owns and how, though not the heir, he is his father's favorite son. Methinks his family will pay well to receive him back safe and well.

"So now, my good captain, release these my friends and your lord's trusty servants from their chains, and allow us to ride in a condition suited to our rank."

"Ah well, not so fast, your *lordship*," said Griffo slowly, with not too much of a sneer. "I am only a humble soldier, you see, and I need time to think these things over. In the meantime, I am afraid I will still have to keep you confined for a short time perhaps, but I will not put you with the rest of the prisoners. There is another hut, cleaner and more comfortable, and nearer this house, where you will spend the night. I am sure my master will not mind me taking precautions with his precious cousin, and his agents."

And with that they had to be content. Griffo would not move any further yet, but he was interested and Manfred was convinced that he would, at least, see that they come to no more harm on the journey. He might even accede to the Prince's request to remove their shackles, which is more than could have been hoped for a short time ago.

There were no guards posted that night, at least outside. Griffo faced a minor revolt among his men for they were fearful of being the one found in pieces next morning. So he gave it up for a bad job but insisted on a score sleeping outside in case any attempt were made to release the prisoners.

He had to be content with that and went to bed. In the darkness of his purloined hut, Griffo remained awake for a while, considering the possible truth of Manfred's words. There was no doubt in his mind that the boy was high born. His speech and mannerisms betrayed him at every turn. The habit of command came to easily to him and it was no habit of a minor lord he had acquired. This boy could well be royal, especially from the way his eyes flashed fire when something displeased him. No boy of low birth, or even minor nobility, had that sort of pride of bearing. And his two guards or captors, he wasn't sure which, were obviously prepared to go to great lengths to secure his safety. Was this devotion to the Archduke's wishes? He had a fearsome reputation for dealing unpleasantly with any who failed or disobeyed him. *Was it fear?* It didn't look like it. But, the one who spoke so much, what was his name? He had seemed pleased when he knew they were heading for the Archduke's camp. What motive could he have for that if they were not who he said they were?

On the other hand, if this were a kinsman of the Archduke, he exhibited a curious eccentricity, considering that family, as he seemed to object to cruelty or injustice. That did not run in the family, he mused. His head was beginning to ache, with all this thinking. All considered, he would do nothing in a hurry and would proceed with caution. He would give them a few trivial comforts, would preserve them unharmed, especially the boy, but no freedom... not yet.

While Griffo and his prisoners had been talking, Bertram had been released from the tree and thrust unceremoniously into the hut which was to be their prison for the night. Alone for a moment in the darkness, he prayed "Heavenly Father, thank you for the courage of the boy and for sparing me more of the lash, in your mercy. Bless the boy, for you have promised to do good to those who do good to those who love you. May he and his friends come to know thee, the one true God, and believe in your son, Jesus, who alone give peace and happiness. And, as for me, Father, I am sorry I am so weak under persecution. Give me grace to bear whatever the priests put upon me and not to waver from the truths you have shown me. You, Lord, called me to this land far from home, and you gave me a work to do here. I seem to have done nothing so far, Lord, and here I sit, useless, weak, and in prison.

"How can I serve you here, my Lord? What good can I be in

your service here? If I am to die, as these priests say, if such is your will, then so be it, Lord, but what of the work? How will it be done?

"And what *is* the work? I don't even know what it is you want me to do? Was I mistaken? Was I wrong to come? Was it just my own wish for travel and adventure?"

Bertram sighed, but even as he sighed, he felt his heart lift and he was at peace again. He was sure he was right to come. Although nothing appeared to have changed, he felt better.

Then the door opened and the other three entered, newly released from their fetters. Manfred's words had not been entirely in vain. Food and drink were also placed in the cell and, great blessing, a large, crude tallow candle. It guttered and flickered and emitted clouds of black smoke, but it gave light too and they were grateful for it.

Bertram was pleased to see them and, somehow, they seemed to be glad to see him too.

"Let me bathe your back, Father," offered Hans.

"Thank you, my friend, but do not call me Father. Just call me Bertram."

"You are either a very stubborn or a very brave man, er… Bertram," said Manfred, looking at the evidence of today's and other beatings. He, also, found it difficult to ignore a lifetime's teachings and call the priest simply by his Christian name.

"No, neither," returned Bertram with a small smile, "just convinced about Jesus Christ and my task for Him." Then he smiled inwardly, thinking of his doubts just a short time ago. "Ouch!" he gasped as he was brought back to the present as Hans made contact with the livid welt, recently received.

"Sorry," muttered Hans, " I have no salve, only this water, but it's better than nothing."

"Just caught me unawares. Take no notice," said the priest.

Hans gently dabbed at the priest's back. They all ate hungrily the plain, but substantial meal Griffo had sent in to them. The candle continued to sputter and smoke but it gave its light and managed to give a tiny bit of comfort in their dismal surroundings.

Bertram was very interested in them, definitely not convinced that they were the merchant's entourage they feigned. He knew there was more to the boy than anyone was telling but did not yet guess the enormity of the truth. All three of the friends were on their guard, as ever, and, to turn attention away from themselves, as well as from genuine interest, Manfred asked Bertram about his life and strange beliefs.

He was a priest, as they knew, educated at Oxford in England, where he had heard the teaching of Master John Wycliffe. Perhaps they had heard of him, he politely enquired, but they said they had not. He said that he had immediately warmed to Master Wycliffe's teaching, had believed and had avidly read the Bible for himself. After a while, he had been convinced that God wanted him to travel to Europe and teach the truths he had embraced, to the people he met there. Thus, he had come to Dehrmacht but, so far, had had little opportunity to teach or preach, being much hindered by the war... and by the priests and bishops.

"Truth to tell," said Bertram, "the Church does not seem

much hindered by the war. Men say that the King, though a good man, was not much of a churchman, and that the priests would be happier if the Archduke were to rule."

The Prince tightened his lips and frowned.

Manfred spoke "Is that view widespread? Have you found that yourself among the clergy?"

"It is not widespread among the ordinary people. They have a love and respect for the King but yes, I have found it among the clergy. Of course, they have not spoken much to me but I have heard odd comments from different ones, which have made me think they have no great loyalty to King Maximilian. Also, a priest considers himself to have a higher allegiance anyway, so perhaps that is not so surprising."

"What do you mean?" asked the Prince. "What can take precedence over a man's loyalty to his king?"

"Well," said Bertram, "take me for example. I would be loyal to my king in England, but my first loyalty must be to my Lord Jesus and, even if the king ordered me to, say, stop preaching, I would have to carry on as that is what I have been commanded to do."

"Even if it cost you your life?" asked the boy.

"Even if it cost me my life, as it looks as if it might," said Bertram soberly.

"So you are saying that these priests, like Father Maurice or Godwin, would prefer the Thalesian because their higher loyalty is to Jesus?" The boy was incredulous.

"Well, I think *they* might say that, but *I* am not really saying that. They would interpret their loyalty to Jesus as being loyalty to the Pope in Rome and to the Church, so if Boris is likely to give favors and benefits to the Church they would favor him."

"But he is cruel: a murderer and a robber!" said the boy, outraged.

"Yes, but he is also, in their terms, a loyal son of the Church, whereas King Maximilian has more than once defied the Archbishop and issued decrees which it is known the Archbishop did not like."

"That is because he is king and must do his duty before God as *he* sees it."

Manfred laid a restraining hand on the boy's arm and said, looking at the boy as he said it, "These sound like matters a little high for our debatings."

Prince Rudolph looked down. "Yes, I am sorry, Master, you are right. These things are far above the likes of us."

Bertram looked keenly at them both. "I think the boy is right. How can it be wrong to debate the right of any man, king or otherwise, to choose his own path before God. You see, St Paul tells the believers in Philippi to 'work out your own salvation with fear and trembling.' This was because he, Paul, was not with them and so he is telling them to take responsibility for their own faith, although we all need help sometimes, of course.

"And," said Bertram suddenly, looking at them keenly, "what about yourselves? It is all very well to talk about the king doing what is right in God's sight, but what is your position in these things?"

"We attend Mass regularly, as good sons of the Church," said Manfred stiffly.

"Hm! A good non-answer! What I mean is, do you seek to serve the Lord Jesus Christ and to do what is right in His sight? Or is it sufficient to you to attend Mass regularly, as you say?"

Manfred got the impression that the ragged priest was very gently mocking him. It made him uncomfortable. He had not spent much time thinking about these things and, in fact, had never been encouraged to do so, even by the priests he had known. Bertram was continuing, with a gentle smile, hardly seen in the dim flickering light.

"You see, Jesus said, 'You must be born again.'"

"Wait a minute, Father, er Bertram," put in Hans. "What chance have I got? I have just killed a priest. Indeed, I have killed many men, usually in the heat of battle, where it is kill or be killed, but never a priest before, and, though I have never, admittedly, had much time for priests, I suppose it *is* much worse to kill a man dedicated to serving the Church. Mind you, I did not mean to kill him," he finished a little lamely. "I mean, I imagine the Church will excommunicate me and I shall be damned for ever. God will have nothing to do with me."

"The Church has nothing to do with it," said Bertram softly.

"What!" exclaimed Manfred and Hans together. "The bishops and priests say you can't go to Heaven unless you are a good churchman and in good standing with the Church."

"It does not depend on that. You see, Jesus died on the cross, taking the punishment there for our sins. Whoever believes in Him, whatever they have done, even killing a priest, will be forgiven. That is what Jesus said and that is what the Bible says. So, my friend, if you want a place in Heaven, whatever you have done, if you repent, that means be sorry for what you have done and turn away from doing it, and believe in the Lord Jesus Christ, your sins will be taken away and you will be forgiven."

"But I have always believed in Jesus and God."

"When I say Believe, I mean to put your trust in Him, to give Him your life because you *believe* in Him with all your heart. You see, if you really believe in Him, you must believe that He is the Lord of the Universe and King over all, so He is entitled to your absolute obedience, isn't He?"

The young prince listened intently to the man's words. They really made sense to him and he wondered that he had never thought this way before. He thought of his father, the King, and how, privately, he held the Church in contempt, for its great wealth, its emphasis on ritual and its lack of concern about a man's character. What, wondered Prince Rudolph, would he think of this man? He looked at Bertram's kind and worn face, the awful tracery on his back, and the simple logic of his words. Yes, he thought, his father would approve of *this* priest and he resolved that he would do all in his power to introduce Bertram to his father when he could.

As he thought about his father, his eyes filled up and he wondered whether he would ever see his father again. It was too much for him. He had held himself in check for so long, had seen so much cruelty and suffering, had had to be continually something he wasn't. The self control always needed at court had helped him a great deal, but this man's gentle kindness and the reminder of his father, broke through and, to his great shame, he cried like a child, forgetting that, in reality, he *was* little more than a child.

Hans and Manfred muttered something or other, but the priest seemed to understand.

"You have suffered a great deal very quietly, my boy, haven't you? Who are you? Why are you so silent? You must have many enemies to be so hidden and so well guarded."

Prince Rudolph answered nothing, but his shoulders continued to heave and evidenced the emotions he was struggling to control. Manfred came forward and put his arm round the boy's shoulders.

"It is always a strain on a youngster to be far from home and, then, to be taken prisoner by these ruffians. He will be all right and, you are right, we *will* take good care of him."

"One thing you can be sure of," said the priest, "*I* will not betray you or be your enemy. Indeed, I know nothing about you, do I, but what I *have* seen, I like, and I would like to be thought of as your friend. I will never betray your trust, for that is my calling."

"I'm sorry," gasped the Prince. "It just all came over me. I want to see my father again, and I miss Viga, my dog, and I am tired of pretending. Now that we are prisoners, I am afraid I will never see my father again."

Manfred was horrified. "It is nothing to worry about, Father Bertram. The boy is worried about his father. Under the circumstances I think I can tell you the name of his father. It is Waldo of Drachsmer and, of course, as you know, Drachsmer was one of the first of the cities to be taken by the Thalesian. Waldo was worried about Fritz and, as a personal friend, he asked me to look after him and try to get him to the north of the country, away from the enemy. The Thalesians do not have a reputation for kindness to those they have conquered. The boy has relations in the north country and his father has business interests up there, so he would be safe. I am sure that once the Archduke learns that we are merchants and nobody of any influence, he will let us go on our way. I imagine a ransom will need to be paid but I don't see any need for real anxiety. So ... cheer up, Fritz, things will get better soon."

The Prince was so amazed by Manfred's powers of imagination and his ability to lie so easily, that he was dumbfounded and not a little amused. He started to laugh and changed it quickly into a cough. "Fritz" indeed. It had been used so often recently, he was even beginning to think of himself as Fritz!

Bertram looked steadily at Manfred. "I am sorry you do not feel you can trust me yet," he said, "but I will tell you again. It may be of no moment but I would like you to think of me as your friend." Then he turned to Prince Rudolph. "Listen, my son, I have a heavenly Father who loves to answer prayer. He is real. He is alive and He grants us our heart's desires, if we trust Him. Let's ask Him now about your father. What do you think, eh?"

"Yes, I would like that," said the boy instantly.

So Bertram prayed a simple prayer, asking that the boy might be restored to his father, safe and sound. Manfred, Hans and the Prince were all astonished at the idea of praying such a simple prayer, outside church and in their own language, but the boy felt strangely comforted and easily accepted the priest's next words.

"My boy, I am persuaded that God is going to grant that prayer. When He does, you are to remember that our heavenly Father did it for you."

"I will," said the boy and cheered up considerably. And, it may be said, never again did he doubt that he would be re-united with his father and that all would turn out right in the end.

The four prisoners settled down for the night and were quiet. But Hans was troubled and, after they had been still for about fifteen minutes, he spoke "Father Bertram, are you awake?"

"Yes, but not *Father* Bertram."

"Er, no Father," said Hans meekly, while the Prince, who was listening, stifled a giggle. Hans continued "Did you mean what you said about forgiveness for *any* sin?"

"Yes," said Bertram, now wide awake.

"I have done many wrong things," said Hans, "too many even to remember. I have fought and hurt and killed, since my youth. I have been a liar and never cared for others' feelings. Can a man be forgiven everything, or does he have to do many things to make up for everything he has done wrong?"

"No," came the reply in the darkness, "our Lord Jesus Christ died once, for all, so that all who believe in Him might be forgiven. His sacrifice covers *all* sins when someone comes to Him, repents and believes in Him."

"How do I earn this forgiveness? You see it has been troubling me a lot lately, ever since I saw you taking your punishment willingly, even though to my mind, you had done nothing to deserve it. Today, when I killed the priest, I felt that I

187

had really put myself outside God's forgiveness."

"You don't have to earn His forgiveness. Jesus has already earned it for you, through His death on the cross."

"But what do I *do*?"

"Believe that the Lord Jesus Christ died for your sins," said Bertram.

"I *do* believe, though I never did before."

"Then tell Him that you are sorry for all the wrong things you have done and that you turn away from them. Tell Him you believe in the Lord Jesus Christ and ask Him to take away your sins, as He has promised."

"I am not much used to praying," rumbled Hans.

"Let me lead you in a simple prayer, Hans, if it will help you."

Hans agreed and Bertram led him phrase by phrase in a prayer, confessing his sin to God and putting his trust in Jesus as his Savior.

"Now," said Bertram, "He promises you that your sins are forgiven, because of Jesus. His Holy Spirit comes to live within your heart, if your conversion is real. Your life now belongs to him. All the years before, you lived for yourself, but now your life is not your own. It does not mean you will never do anything wrong again. You will... but when you do, tell your heavenly Father all about it and ask His forgiveness and you have His promise that you will be forgiven immediately, and all will be well."

"Thank you, Father, I feel completely different."

"Well, that is good, but your salvation does not depend on

188

feelings, but upon God, whose promises are clearly stated in the Bible."

"I can't read, Father, and if I could, the Bible is written in Latin, isn't it, so I would not be able to understand it."

"While I was in Blecklinghaus, we started translating the Bible into your language. The man doing it was not taken prisoner with the rest of us and so, I trust, is continuing the work. Of course, it will take a time, but when finished it will be such a benefit to your country as can hardly be imagined. When we are safe from all this, and the translation is completed, I will see that you have a copy. You will find someone who can teach you to read and then you must read it and share it with anyone you can. You must also try to lead others to believe as you and I do. Meet together, wherever you are, and encourage each other to be faithful, as you have seen me do. One more thing you must do, as soon as you can."

"What is that?" asked Hans eagerly.

"You must tell someone what you have just done. That will help you to live up to it."

"Right! Manfred. Are you awake?"

"What is it? What is it?" cried Manfred, awaking from a deep sleep and struggling to draw his sword, forgetting his captivity. "Is the boy safe?"

"Oh yes, yes," said Hans, waving that aside airily, "I just wanted to tell you something marvelous."

"Oh yes," said Manfred doubtfully, "and what is that then?"

"I have been forgiven. All my sins are forgiven. I have given my life to Jesus. Isn't that wonderful!"

189

Manfred muttered something inaudible but then said he was pleased for Hans, and he meant it. But another thought struck Hans.

"Can I still be a soldier, Bertram?"

Manfred groaned and pulled his hood tightly over his head but then he loosened it so that he could hear Bertram's reply.

"Yes, Hans, you can, in a just cause, and you can be as good a soldier as anyone else, better really, if you believe in what you are doing." *Though,* thought Bertram to himself, *I thought you were supposed to be a merchant's servant! Hmm.*

"Thank you, Bertram."

There was a long silence. Then, in a whisper, "Bertram."

"Yes?"

"I am not really a manservant. I am a soldier and it *is* in a just cause, but you must not tell anyone else."

"I know," said Bertram, and smiled in the darkness. "I know, and I won't."

Prince Rudolph had listened to it all in the darkness and he smiled too. It all made sense to him and he knew, that in some way, his dear friend Hans had found something very precious.

TWENTY

Another soldier died during the night.

There was not a mark on his body and he had been sleeping outside with the others. He just did not wake up. Someone had slipped up to the sleeping group and silently killed the man while he slept. Somehow it seemed to frighten his fellow soldiers more than if they could see awful wounds and they shuddered, knowing it could have been any one of them. No-one had seen or heard anything, apart from one who said he had seen a couple of gypsies at the edge of the village, but they did not come near.

Now the soldiers really *were* rattled, anxiously looking over their shoulders and talking amongst themselves of demons and evil spirits, though not in front of their captain.

Griffo was angry and took it out upon the soldiers and any prisoners who attracted his attention. The four 'specials' were now protected from his wrath and from abuse by his men but he was anxious to be about their journey. The soldiers in turn passed his anger on with blows and curses to the rest of the prisoners.

Prince Rudolph had been awake a while, because of a strange sound. It was a deep rumbling that seemed to rise and fall irregularly. He listened to it for a few minutes before he realized that it was Hans singing.

Rudolph was astonished. He had known Hans since he was

born and could not remember hearing him sing before. Hans was usually painfully quiet. Even at the royal feasts, Hans was quiet. He was always there: solid, dependable, always at hand, and silent!

Then the soldiers came into the hut and there was no more time for thinking just then.

As they went through the day, Hans continued as he had begun. Manfred did not seem to know what to think about Hans' change and said little. Prince Rudolph was intrigued. The change in his friend was astonishing. He sang and hummed all day. He laughed at the smallest thing. He pointed out the beauty of the countryside. He even delighted in the birds they saw. He was like a different man, a new person. Indeed, that is what Bertram said he was.

When the guards had taken them out to continue their journey, Hans had gently helped the priest into their cart. One of the other priests had stepped forward and roughly ordered Bertram out, but Hans had towered over him and asked politely if he might be allowed to stay. The priest backed away quickly, remembering, no doubt, the fate of Father Godwin. He loudly rebuked Hans calling him a murderer and a wretched sinner, who would perish in the flames of hell. A troubled shadow passed over Hans' rugged features and he glanced at Bertram, who smiled at him and shook his head. Hans visibly brightened and spoke out in his quiet, rumbling way.

"I am those things that you said, it is true. But I am not going to hell. I have believed in the Lord Jesus Christ and I have been forgiven."

"You have been listening to that heretic, you great fool. He has led you astray. You will perish in the fire with him, when we get to Dehrmacht."

"I *did* listen to him, you are right, but I believed and now I know the truth of his words for myself, and I *know* I am forgiven."

"Bah!" said the priest, in a great rage, and he strode away to join his fellows. But Bertram stayed in the cart.

All morning and on into the afternoon, they traveled, rumbling slowly and heavily in the cart. Hans continued cheerful and chatted away to Bertram, asking him questions all the time about his new faith and the teachings of the Bible. Manfred and the Prince listened to Bertram's replies and even Manfred had to admit that the priest's logic held together and answered a lot of the questions he had about the Church. They listened to Bertram as he said that Jesus had said "You must be born again" and that this is what had happened to Hans.

"Truly, it is obvious," thought the Prince, with wonder in his heart.

Bertram said that Hans no longer lived for himself, but for Jesus and that his life was not his own. Did this mean, asked the Prince, that Hans would have to become a priest? Not at all, Bertram had replied, but that in serving others and doing his duty, he would be serving God. Bertram spoke of forgiveness and sharing your life with God in a way none of them had ever heard before.

Manfred liked what was said and was relieved to hear that Hans would not have to give up the King's service, although he was not sure what Bertram meant when he said that Hans now served a higher king. Prince Rudolph understood more and more and, before evening came, he, quietly and humbly, asked forgiveness for his sins and trusted in Jesus Christ as his Savior. He immediately felt a release, a lightening of the load, an easing of tension and worry. He did not fully understand what he had done, but he felt a new happiness he had never known before and a lovely freedom from fear and guilt. Even his chains and captivity did not seem too bad any more.

Increasingly, the soldiers caught glimpses of small groups of men in the distance. They passed several gypsies who gazed silently upon the sad procession, but melted into the woods if any move was made towards them. Another soldier just disappeared. He was right at the back and no-one saw him go. The soldiers kept together now and were reluctant to leave the main party for any reason. Griffo's eyes were everywhere. He would have welcomed a more direct challenge instead of this Will-o-the-Wisp enemy. He even started sending individual prisoners for water and one or two of them disappeared as well, although Cryllan quietly whispered that he had seen one of them amongst a party of ragged men on a nearby ridge.

The day passed. Nothing outwardly had changed but the Prince felt everything was going to be all right. He listened avidly, with Hans, to all that Bertram said, asking such questions and showing such pleasure and interest in the replies that Manfred began to feel a little left out.

The day ended at a sizable village and Griffo came over to them when the wagon stopped.

"I have been watching you all day. You," pointing to Hans, "have been so cheerful since you learned we were going to Dehrmacht that I have decided to take a chance on what you have told me and to release you from your chains. Mind you," he said sternly, "the slightest attempt to escape will tell me that your story is false and I will have you shot down like dogs, the boy included."

Truth to tell, Griffo was frightened and uncertain what to do for the best. All day he had pondered over his problem. *If* Manfred were telling the truth, his lord would not be pleased to see his kinsman and agents arrive in shackles. Archduke Boris was a stern and cruel man and Griffo shuddered at what he might do to someone who had not treated a loving cousin with proper respect. It was known that this cruel princeling had a high regard for his own dignity and, presumably, for that of his nearest and dearest too.

On the other hand, why should he believe the word of this lean and wily-looking man, who certainly looked twisty enough to be a secret agent of the Archduke. But Griffo was a worthy servant of his lord and had dealt with prisoners often enough not to take much notice of a man's words when he was in chains and perhaps about to die. He smiled grimly to himself as he pondered over it all. Why, he would not have lasted five minutes if he had listened to the hard-luck stories and plausible lies he had heard. Well, he would err on the side of caution. He would continue to guard them well but it would not do much harm to strike off their shackles. Their traveling in the cart was perhaps an advantage as he could easily keep an eye on them and, at the first hint of escape, he was firm enough to know that they must be false and they would die.

The final deciding point had come when he had heard loud laughter coming from the cart. He had turned to see the big man laughing with one of his own guards! That had done it. The boy, too, seemed to be joining in the joke. It was unlikely that they could be doing that if they were his ruler's enemies. They *must* be on the same side and obviously thought they were traveling to safety and a hero's welcome. He had, of course, completely misread the signs, but he did not know that and, on the whole, felt he had made the right decision. He was already phrasing his words to his royal master to show how he had demonstrated proper regard and respect to his kinsman, even when he had not known who they really were.

Their chains were struck off that evening and they slept more comfortably that night. Bertram was not included in the general amnesty and but had had no chains anyway. However, he was allowed to stay with the three friends and they continued to be kept separate from the rest of the prisoners. This pleased and displeased Bertram. He was not bothered about himself. He was used to discomfort, but he was bothered about the other members of his flock and wanted to be able to talk with them and make sure they were all right. However, he also was glad to be with Hans and the boy and to continue to talk to them about their faith. He still did not know who they were, although he had guessed that the boy and Manfred were high-born. He could not know the incalculable effect his words would have on the future of the country. If he had known who his young convert was, he would have gasped with wonder at the mysterious workings of his God.

Bertram was kept under close guard because Griffo was wary of the priests, despite his brusque manner with them. They *did* wield considerable power with the Archduke, who was superstitious and fearful about such matters, perhaps knowing that his crimes were many and that he had need of re-assurance concerning the after-life. Despite the fact that the Archbishop lived in the King's palace, Griffo knew that he was, secretly, a great friend of Archduke Boris and stood high in the his favor.

Griffo had no time for the priests himself and, indeed, considered murdering them on the road so that no word of his doings would reach the Archbishop, but he decided that the risk was too great and that he would be better trying not to offend them too much on the way. Even now, they were looking blackly at Griffo and Hans, and swore that Hans, at least, would perish with Bertram when they reached Dehrmacht.

TWENTY-ONE

As usual, they started early next morning. There was much bustle as the cavalcade prepared for departure. In the midst of it, Manfred took the Prince to one side and gave him detailed instructions. Rudolph was not very pleased and tried to argue, but Manfred was insistent and, reluctantly, the boy agreed. Hans was also given instructions, which did not please him either.

It was, again, a lovely morning, sunny with fresh breezes, which usually lifts the spirits and cheers the glum. The woodland continued on either side after they had left the village and its cleared strips of cultivated land. It was not thick, overgrown woodland, but pleasantly spaced trees, with shafts of sunlight shining through and plenty of beautiful glades with lovely green carpets of grass, kept short by the innumerable rabbits that lived there. The Prince knew that this woodland stretched for miles behind them and to the north, but in the direction of their journey, the woodland thinned as the ground became hilly.

Griffo's attitude to the three companions seemed to warm and become more friendly, but he seemed to harden towards Bertram and, at the insistence of the priests, he was now expelled from the cart and made to hobble along with the rest of the prisoners. This pleased the good man and the Prince could see him chatting away to different members of his little flock and encouraging them to trust in Jesus and all would be well. They seemed to be having such a good time that the prince would fain have joined them but he could not.

As they slowly progressed they came to the beginnings of the lovely, rolling hills, still wooded, which stretched all the way now to Dehrmacht. It was countryside much beloved by the huntsmen at court, although Griffo's band had not yet reached the stretches the Prince and his companions knew from previous expeditions. They talked little among themselves and Rupert played a game from childhood where he concentrated on the sounds around him, not made by man, and tried to identify them. He listened intently. There was the gentle plod, plod of the horses' hooves on the soft floor, the soft steady footfalls of the soldiers, the buzz of insects everywhere and the different chirps and squawks of birds hidden in the trees. There was, of course, the low murmur of voices among the soldiers and among the prisoners. He wished they would be quiet for a while. Could he hear water far off among the trees? No, he thought not, just a gentle breeze in the treetops. That was all, and then, what was that! Surely he was mistaken. It had been very faint, very far off. It did not come again, as he listened, but he was sure he had caught, a long way away, the faint call of a trumpet.

He looked to see if anyone else showed signs of having heard it. No-one seemed to have done so. He looked round quickly. Everyone was plodding on unconcernedly. Anyway, it might have been a patrol of the Archduke's men out looking for more hapless recruits to join his usurping army.

Then his heart began to quicken. Among the trees on his

right, he had seen a large boulder on its side. He saw another, and another. They were scattered on either side of the path, huge rounded boulders, some piled on top of each other, others lying alone.

Manfred had said to look out for these boulders and, when they were plentiful, a line of thick, dark trees in the distance. And now he saw them. They looked impenetrable. He looked at Manfred who returned his gaze steadily. Half an hour later, they were almost up to the trees and Manfred gave a slight tug on his arm. It was a good moment. The men-at-arms were dozing on their feet, relaxed, and concentrating on putting one foot after the other. Prince Rudolph leaped over the side of the cart and ran for his life towards the dark trees ahead of him.

Behind him, he heard an angry shout and the sudden quickening of hooves as Griffo spurred his horse to chase him. To catch the boy, he had to pass close to the cart, as Manfred had hoped and, as he passed, Manfred hurled himself at him and pulled him from his horse.

The nearest crossbowmen hastily fitted quarrels to their bows but their aim was too hasty and the boy was twisting and dodging among the boulders as he ran. The archers did not have much time either for with a fearsome roar, Hans launched himself from the cart amongst them. It was forlorn, of course. Hans and Manfred were easily overpowered as soon as the soldiers had recovered themselves and they were born down by sheer weight of numbers.

Griffo was beside himself with rage. He beat Manfred with his bare hands. Then he remembered Father Godwin's whip and

lashed him until he was unconscious. He screamed at his soldiers
to catch the boy, but it was too late, he had vanished into the thick
cover of the dark oak woods in front of them. They did follow
him in, but there was no sign of him. Griffo's men searched for
hours until, at last, he angrily ordered the march to be continued,
leaving behind a small party to leave no stone unturned.

Before they left, Hans, too, had been beaten senseless.
Griffo berated his men and gave orders that Manfred and Hans
were to be tied up tightly, until they reached the next village with
a blacksmith, where they would be chained again or hanged. His
orders were carried out with great zeal. The men feared him and
knew that their lives were as much in danger as the prisoners'.
Their treatment of the men was not gentle, therefore. Trussed like
chickens, bruised and unconscious, they were unceremoniously
thrown in the back of the cart.

Unmoved by the events of the last hour or so, nature
continued exuberant. The sun shone, the birds sang and the
insects hummed contentedly in the lovely greenery of the hilly
glades. Few among the soldiery had any thoughts for nature's
joys. They were angry and resentful. Griffo's temper had vented
itself in blows on everyone that came within reach, his own men
included. No-one dared approach him now. Even the priests, who
considered themselves a law unto themselves, kept away from
him. He sat on his horse, his massive bulk hunched on the high
saddle, his scowling, bearded face resolutely set against all men.
He conversed with no-one, of course, but those just behind him
heard him muttering angrily from time to time. Some even found
time to pity the two battered and bleeding men who lay in the

cart, who would surely pay dearly for their treachery.

Hans regained consciousness more quickly than Manfred. He found he ached from head to toe. He tried to gently ease his muscles, but the thongs cut into his arms, his ankles, his wrists. He could not move. Furthermore, they had fastened a leather thong from his knees to his neck so that he could not straighten his back. It hurt like fire, but he could not move.

Deep in his heart, he remembered his God, so recently discovered. Despite his desperate pains, he was conscious of a joy deep down, which circumstances did nothing to explain. He remembered that Jesus had suffered before He had died and, somehow, in a strange way, Hans felt better for sharing a little of the experiences of his Lord. In his heart, Hans thanked God that He had chosen to suffer and die, so that men might be forgiven. His heart thrilled with the wonder of it all and he forgot *his* pains for a while, as a deep peace filled him. He prayed for his young master, and for Manfred, still unconscious beside him.

He sensed, rather than saw, Manfred's return to consciousness. He could not see him but heard his pain-filled groans as his senses returned to him. Manfred rose through red mists of pain to the knowledge of the jolting cart beneath him, and the remembrance of what had passed. Had the Prince got away? He must have done. He had last seen him heading for the dark trees he had told him about. They had been planted long ago by his grandfather to hide an escape route for his robber bands. It had been a favorite place from which to attack peaceful travelers on the road to Dehrmacht. It was the very crimes perpetrated from those woods which had finally led to the King's determination to eliminate the troublesome hornets' nest that was Tata, and now that very escape route had, he hoped, saved that King's only son and heir.

Later in the day, Bertram spoke as Griffo passed him. "My lord Griffo, if you do not loosen these men's bonds, I doubt your prisoners will reach Dehrmacht alive."

Griffo cursed loudly, swung round and struck Bertram full across the face with the his heavily gauntleted hand. "Renegade priest! What do I care if they are alive or dead when we reach the king's castle? They will die there if I have my way, and slowly. And you, you have been their friend throughout this journey. I will hang you from that oak tree yonder if you speak to me again."

Blood trickled steadily from his mouth and nose, but Bertram was undaunted. "Take care, Captain. The man, Manfred, may not have told you the truth, but it is easy to see these are not common folk. I think Archduke Boris would rather receive them alive to question them himself than have two worthless corpses delivered to him." He went on relentlessly. You have lost the boy. If these men were to die as well, I don't think you would enjoy facing your master. I'm told he is not patient with those who do not please him."

A dull red flush of anger mounted Griffo's bull neck and into his face. He looked as if he was going to burst with rage. His sword shot out of its sheath and flashed in the air as he raised it over Bertram's head.

"Wait, Captain Griffo!" shouted one of the priests. This time it was Father Bruno, a smooth-spoken, high-born priest, whose father owned much land on the border of Thalesia, and who was widely tipped to be a bishop before long. He was the youngest of the priests and, hitherto, had said little to Griffo having arrived somewhat later than the others. "That man is a priest. His life is forfeit to the Church and, I imagine, his fate at the hands of the Church will be worse than a quick blow from your sword."

Griffo knew Bruno and he knew his father was a powerful lord. His reaction was not, therefore, as violent as it would have been if one of the other priests had intervened. Indeed, if it had been Maurice, he would probably have killed him. He also recognized the truth of his words. Bertram might well fare worse if he were handed over to the Church. Even so, it was terrible to see the battle for self control which raged across his features until he finally had himself in order again.

The whole party slept that night under the trees but Griffo did give instructions for Hans and Manfred's bonds to be loosened, including the cruel halter around the neck and hands of Hans. The pain they both experienced after they were untied was indescribable. They were quite unable to move for some while as the blood started to circulate through their veins again, bringing agony with it until, at last, they began to have some sort of normal movement. Even then, they were very sore and bruised with their beatings. Neither was able to sleep much and Manfred, especially, suffered agonies from his lacerated back all night.

Only forty miles separated them now from Dehrmacht, but their progress was slow. The chains and the poor condition of the prisoners made Griffo think that it might take them as much as four days to reach the castle. Still, he thought, they would probably meet one of the Archduke's patrols or foraging parties long before then and he could probably be relieved and allowed to make his own way to the Archduke's court, leaving the prisoners to be brought in by others.

Dawn came slowly through the stately trees but Griffo had his men up and ready before the path could be clearly seen. He urged them and none dared argue. Manfred and Hans were tied again, though not so tightly, and were thrown back into the cart. This was not from kindly motives but they were so hurt and bruised that Griffo thought they would slow the party down and he did not want that. Also, if walking, they would have had to have more freedom from their bonds, in order to walk, and he did not want that.

The wearisome bumping of the cart was agony to the two men. It seemed, at one stage, to be penetrating Manfred's brain. One wheel must not have been quite true and, occasionally, the cart lurched sickeningly as the wheel twisted. Unfortunately, it was irregular, so that when Manfred tried to anticipate it, it did not come, and then when he relaxed, the cart would heave over dreadfully again and his bruises and nerves screamed for peace. To take his mind off it, he screwed his neck to try to see their surroundings.

The path here was broad but the wood on either side was dense here. He knew it now. It was the last thick belt of woodland before the trees started to thin and the rolling downs before Dehrmacht began. Whatever awaited them in Dehrmacht, if they fell into the Archduke's hands, Manfred knew it would not be pleasant, but at least the boy was free. If Manfred and Hans were to perish, at least he would have the compensation of knowing that he had protected the boy.

He found he could twist round and through the open tailgate of the cart, he had a reasonable, if uncomfortable view of the country. What a good place for an ambush, he thought idly. The trees here were interspersed with leafy bushes. An army could hide here without us knowing, he mused. No wonder my ancestors were robbers. This forest invites it. No one really knows all its hiding places, he thought, though I know a few. His mind floated back over the places he had been shown and the tricks he had been taught by his father, long ago. And what would his father think now, if he could see him. He could almost hear his derisive laugh. He would not have been sympathetic and would probably have said it was his own fault.

Ouch! There was that dreadful lurch again but this time the cart stopped. He could not see what was happening ahead but men nearby seemed unusually tense.

Griffo had been leading the column, as usual. His heart and mind were full of black and murderous thoughts. He knew he could reach the castle in a day if he could leave the little convoy of prisoners. It was a tempting idea. Revenge upon those who had tricked him was foremost in his mind, and he could hardly wait to receive permission to vent his spite on Manfred and Hans. He would also enjoy seeing that wretched, foreign priest burn at the stake. He almost, but not quite, felt sorry for anyone who fell into the hands of Holy Mother Church. He had seen strong men reduced to trembling hulks. All done in the name of love, he marvelled dimly to himself.

At this point, the wood was very dark. The path had been broad, was still broad, but the trees were thick and the gaps filled with leafy bushes. Sunlight filtered through but only on the path. He was so deep in thought that he hardly lifted his head as his horse found its own way along the path, but something glinted ahead and he looked up.

TWENTY-TWO

Thirty yards ahead and across the path lay a tree, blocking the path. In front of the tree, facing them, waiting for them, was a knight. Even on his horse, it could be seen that the stranger was unusually tall. His horse was white, and magnificent. A beautiful and snowy mane lay along the graceful neck. A noble head tossed impatiently, while a silken tail swished the early morning flies from its body.

The rider had chosen his position so that he sat in a shaft of sunlight. He was in full armor except that, in the modern fashion, he did not wear a full helm with visor. Instead, a steel, or was it silver, cap sat upon his noble head, topped by a tall plume of white feathers, which stood tight-packed and regal in the early morning sun. His armor was painted white and, even at this distance, Griffo could see that it was richly chased and ornamented. Such armor would have cost a king's ransom. A long shield hung by his horse's side. It, too, was white, with a scarlet device painted on it, a snake thought Griffo, with a spear pinning it to the ground. His heart stood still. He knew who owned that badge. Over the man's armor lay a loose surcoat with, across its chest, the same device of the pinioned serpent. In his hand, resting on the stoop was a long, long lance; tipped for war.

Griffo's startled gaze discerned, a little distance behind the

208

knight, two young men, similarly caparisoned, but without the armor. His squires, he thought. He was in a state of deep shock for he recognized the device upon the shield. Half the world knew it, he thought bitterly. Only one man wore that device and he was spoken of as the finest warrior in Europe. What was he doing here, Griffo wondered. He should have been miles away. Indeed, Archduke Boris had timed his invasion with this man's absence at the fore-front of his mind. For the device was that of Prince Henry of Felden, Archduke of Eltzenberg, Count of Nimendorf, whose armies had won for his lands complete freedom from all overlordship. He was also King Maximilian's younger brother.

Strikingly handsome, fearless in battle, courteous and practiced in all courtly procedures, it was rumored that the maidens in his domain swooned whenever his name was mentioned. His sword was for hire but only for a prince or king whom he considered had a just cause for war. He had gained a reputation for putting down tyrants, hence his heraldic device, and he had grown rich in using his army wisely.

Not all this passed through Griffo's troubled mind just at this moment. He hesitated before the stern blue eyes, fixed upon him now.

"Hold!" cried the knight. "Who are you and what is your business this day, as you go armed upon the King's highway?"

Griffo's legs started to tremble on his horse, but he was not really a coward. He answered boldly, feigning not to recognize the man before him. Then his heart lifted a little. After all, however great a warrior this man, he, Griffo, had nearly four score armed men at his back. It had been a hundred but it was rather less because of the enemy along the way.

"Griffo of Tastag, escorting malefactors to justice. Out of my way, Sir Knight, and I will proceed on my lawful business."

"How praiseworthy, captain, to be escorting malefactors to justice," sneered the knight, "and what crimes have they committed in order to deserve your righteous attention?"

"Enough of this, Sir Knight. I have no quarrel with you and wish you no harm but I have no need to state my business to every traveler upon the road."

"Oh, so true," replied the knight, "but you *will* answer me, or I will find the answer anyway. Who are these prisoners and what are their crimes and what right has Griffo of Tastag to travel with armed men in the Kingdom of Dehrmacht. Tastag, as I recall, is not very far from a certain arrogant archduke's domain, Thalesia. Now, answer me, knave."

Griffo sneered. He looked behind and signaled to his men. They began to move forward, weapons in hand.

The knight laughed and raised his arm. Griffo heard a rustling among the trees and from the bushes stepped forth, short, swarthy black haired bowmen. They were not tall but everyone was powerfully built, with massive arm muscles, and they carried the longest wooden bows that Griffo had ever seen. The knight raised his other arm and, from the bushes and trees on the other side of the path, a motley crew of beggars, gypsies and various ragamuffins dropped into sight. They were variously and curiously armed. They carried knives, some carried fearsome clubs, some home-made pikes and several had longbows made from the trees around them. They were grinning at the discomforted soldiers.

One of them was a singularly twisted man, not tall, with his head at a curious angle on his neck. Wrynack had reason to be pleased. He had obeyed his mistress. His ragged band had seen Prince Rudolph's escape. They knew of Felden's army and had taken the boy straight to his uncle. There Rudolph had told Prince Henry all that had taken place, not forgetting to give praise to the tattered men from Velda, without whom he might have wandered for weeks. It had all happened better than Wrynak could have dreamed.

"Tell your men to lay down their arms, if they want to live," commanded the knight quietly. "They tell me that the bows of these archers can put an arrow through a suit of armor at two hundred paces, and I would say, captain, that you are about ten paces from the nearest. Oh … and they hardly ever miss."

Griffo cursed angrily, but commanded his men to lay down their arms. He knew he was beaten but, he thought, he might still be allowed to go on his way. This royal knight would hardly know of his doings in Dehrmacht, may not even know his loyalty to the Archduke. No need to despair yet.

He turned and looked around. The ruffians were amongst his soldiers, collecting weapons (and purses) while the Welshmen waited, bows still at the ready. There may still be a chance of escape, he thought. One lone horseman, however many archers, and Griffo might be able to ride away at the right moment. The first chance that offers, he thought, I will be off.

No sooner had he made this decision when his attention was caught by the jingle of horsemen approaching. Ahead of him, behind the knight, a party of horsemen, all in armor, with pennants flying, appeared.

"Look behind as well, my Captain Griffo, and forget all thoughts of escape," said the stern young man before him.

He looked behind. He was in truth cut off. Another party of mounted men filled the path behind his men.

Prince Henry rode slowly towards him, closely followed by his squires who, he saw, carried a sword and a dagger each.

"You have two friends of mine with you, I think, although I cannot see them." He turned and Griffo wilted before the anger in those clear, blue eyes. "If you have killed them, you will die as painfully as I can devise," said Prince Henry.

He continued to move along the line of prisoners and stopped at Manfred and Hans, both chained, bowed and shuffling because of their injuries. Manfred lifted his eyes and tried to smile. "So, he managed it, Your Highness. I knew he would. He is a fine lad and a worthy member of your noble house."

"My lord Manfred, my dear friend. Yes, he managed it. I was never so proud of my nephew as when he arrived, brought in by some of Breclan's foresters, in fact. But what have they done to you, my friend, and is this Hans?" he asked wonderingly, for indeed, Hans was bent and racked with pain, hardly able to lift his head. "Hans? Hans, have they reduced you thus?"

"Not in my heart, Your Highness," gasped Hans, barely able to stand, "and my body will recover."

"How cruelly they have bound you, faithful friend!"

He made a quick gesture and men rode quickly to cut their bonds.

Prince Henry raised his voice again. "Ranulf, Espen, put these, my friends in the cart and see that their wounds are attended to," and his pages stepped forward to do his bidding. "Be gentle with them. They are high in my brother's kingdom. Did we bring balm?"

"Aye, Your Highness, as you ordered, and Emlass, your physician."

"See to it then."

They bowed low and a short, fussy, little man came awkwardly forward on a horse. He almost fell off it and then came bustling forward to look at the prisoners, muttering and tutting all the time. His name was Emlass and he was a skilled physician, however comical his manner.

Prince Henry's eyes narrowed to slits. His mouth set, his features hardened and he drew his sword, riding towards Griffo, who shrank from the fury in his eyes.

"A treacherous merchant, Sir Knight, and his servant: not people of any account," he stammered, backing his horse away, "w-w-worthless scoundrels, I swear."

"Worthless scoundrels!" hissed the knight. "You unspeakable wretch! These men were as much your superior as the stag is to the worm. One, at least, is as high born as any in the land, and the other is as noble in his character as I have found in any of my travels. *And you chained them!*

"You low varlet! Knave! Ruffian! Worthless scum!" And Prince Henry accompanied each word with a blow from the flat of his sword, so that Griffo writhed and twisted to escape the blows. "You are not fit to occupy space upon the earth. Now I will tell

213

you what I will do to you," ceasing to belabor him.

"You will be bound hand and foot, as they were, for as long as they were. Then you will be untied and, as you return to consciousness, you will be flogged, and then you will be hanged from the highest tree I can find. I dare say none will mourn your departure from this earth. Now," he turned to some of his men, "bind him tightly, hands and feet, with a halter from his neck to his ankles tied up behind him.

"One of your prisoners, a mere apprentice boy, you deemed him, told me to look for a priest. Ah, here I see four priests. Three of them are fat, well-fed, prosperous, well dressed, obviously learned and respected fathers of the Church."

His cool and searching gaze rested in turn on each of the priests, while his men bound Griffo with savage delight and threw him roughly into the cart, still occupied by Hans and Manfred rubbing their wrists and thighs. Dr Emlass was fussing over Manfred's back, red raw from the whipping he had received.

"Tsk, tsk," he muttered, "very nasty, very nasty. Still, I have the very ointment to soothe this, my lord," and he liberally laid a sweet-smelling yellow ointment over the skin.

"Feels better already," smiled Manfred. Both the men were recovering. In fact, for both of them, the knowledge that their beloved prince was safe with his father's friends had made them feel a hundred per cent better immediately.

Prince Henry rode over to them now. Anger flitted across his face again as he saw Manfred's lacerated back. "He will pay for it, Manfred. I promise it," he murmured.

"He must die, Your Highness," said Manfred grimly. "He

has been responsible for many deaths amongst our King's subjects."

"It is already decided," Prince Henry replied, "and now, which of these fine priests do you think a prince of the realm would have me honor."

"I knew he would be safe," said Hans joyfully, who had hardly been conscious when Prince Henry had come upon the scene earlier, "and he asked for one of the priests, did he?"

"He *is* safe, Hans. He obeyed Manfred's instructions to the letter and this gallant band of ruffians brought him safely to our camp. He is even now with my lord of Berenal, but he was anxious about this priest," a little smile appeared on the prince's face, "not to mention his anxiety for two other friends of his. I think he realized you would suffer for helping him to go. I have always known that you are both unshakably loyal and true to my royal brother, but I will never forget this and, if it were possible, you will have double honor at my court when you visit. Let us get on though."

"God be praised!" said Hans in a loud voice, and he grinned a huge grin.

Prince Henry looked surprised and gave Hans a keen glance.

"I prayed he would be safe, you see," the giant soldier said sheepishly.

Manfred sighed and Prince Henry looked at him strangely. "Has the King's Guardian now become a priest? Certes, strange things have been happening in this realm of late," he mused gently.

His gaze then turned to the prisoners again. "Ah, I see

215

another priest, this one in rags and, what, have you not had your bonds cut yet, Father? You, men, what are you thinking of! Strike off the good father's ropes immediately. I see you have done most of the others."

One soldier stepped forward. "I offered to do him first, your honor. He would not hear of it."

"Well do it now, good Faston, although I trow it is not often I see a priest in bonds. Who would dare to chain a priest? Unless ... his crime was against the Church itself. He bears all the marks of experiencing the tender mercies of the Church against one who offends them," he shuddered a little.

"He has indeed sinned against our Holy Mother the Church, noble knight," said Father Hugo, not recognizing the august prince, "so do not have his ropes cut off. He is a vile and guilty sinner and must be taken to the Archbishop at Dehrmacht, where he will be justly tried and helped to see the folly into which he has fallen and," shaking his head "sadly, led many others astray, including some of these ignorant folk here."

"Ah, so the holy Sigismund is still at Dehrmacht? A prisoner, no doubt, with the King, in the dungeons?"

"Well, no," said Father Hugo, "the Archduke has recognised his Grace's great qualities and spiritual wisdom and our lord, Sigismund, is continuing to exercise his papal office in the Archduke's court."

"Yes, I have heard something of his 'wisdom' in accommodating the usurper of Dehrmacht. Rest assured, master priest, he will not continue to exercise his office, when *I* arrive in Dehrmacht, papal or otherwise. Release the ragged priest!" he commanded Faston, who was only too pleased to oblige.

"Father," Prince Henry said to Bertram, looking with interest and curiosity at the gaunt figure in a faded brown robe before him. "I know little of theological niceties but I do know that you received a whipping ... perhaps one of many, from your appearance. I know ..." he continued, "that you received a whipping on behalf of a young kinsman of mine. For that you will be greatly honored when his father learns of it. But, greater than that, to my mind, I know not how, you have given a priceless gift to a noble boy: that of happiness in adversity, a great gift indeed to give to a prince."

Prince Henry was a fierce and proud man, a warrior from his youth and much feared by his enemies, but he smiled at the man in rags before him. "The boy that you helped without knowing who he was, is Rudolph, Prince of Dehrmacht, only son of the King and lawful heir to the throne. He asked me to give you any assistance you require, and commands that you come to our camp, where you will be a most honored and welcome guest."

Bertram smiled at him and bowed. "I am honored by such friendship. I thank God that my young friend is safe. God grant success to your plans. The only assistance I would ask is that these my friends," indicating his fellow prisoners, "be returned to their homes and families, from whom they were so rudely torn away, and I look forward to meeting His Royal Highness in safety. I told him things would work out for him and his friends."

He smiled to himself and thought *I didn't know who he was, but I did know he was not a mere apprentice. The very idea!*

TWENTY-THREE

Manfred and Hans passed through the rest of that remarkable day as in a dream.

Prince Henry chatted gaily to them as they rode by his side. He was in high spirits. Kings and princes are used to treachery, double dealing and flattery. Unselfish faithfulness, as he had seen in Manfred and Hans, was rare and greatly to be prized. He told them about his delight when the little prince had arrived at his camp, accompanied by the most tatterdemalion bunch of ragamuffins he had ever seen. But, they had looked after the boy, and he would honor them for that for the rest of his life.

Which camp? The friends asked.

Prince Henry laughed cheerfully, What other sort of camp would there be, but an armed camp. You will see, he had explained. Berenal was there, he said, and Breclan with a large party of men. Rudolph had told him of his flight from Griffo, how Hans and Manfred had risked their own lives to save him, for the boy was sure the archduke's fierce captain would take some revenge for being outwitted in this way. Prince Henry had lost no time in selecting a strong party and setting out to find the boy's faithful friends. He had had great difficulty in persuading Prince Rudolph to stay behind but he saw that he was exhausted and insisted that he rest before having any further adventures.

Manfred and Hans looked at each other and each was satisfied. Their beloved prince was safe. They were also relieved. Their mission was accomplished. They had both known it would be a difficult and dangerous one and now it was over. They knew Prince Henry's reputation. They also knew there were many old friends in the army which had been gathered, and now all that remained was to release Dehrmacht from the grasp of the archduke. It would not be an easy task but they were confident they would be successful. Their only fear was that the Archduke might have ill-treated or even murdered the King, as the castle must have fallen several days since.

Hans even started to sing softly to himself and Manfred watched as his huge friend rode, painfully, a large smile creasing his grim features. He wondered if he would ever get used to this ever cheerful Hans.

Manfred scowled in mock anger at his friend. "And what does the Captain of the King's Guard have to look so happy about?" he asked. "I suppose you will tell me you knew all along that his highness would be all right, will you. I guess you might even say you *prayed* about it, eh?"

Hans smiled again and nodded.

Manfred looked fondly on his friend. He was pleased for him although he did not know that he could go along completely with all that the good Bertram had said.

He looked back at him now, chatting with the soldiers, seemingly unheeding of the fact that he had been beaten and whipped unmercifully. *What a man!* thought Manfred. Whatever happens, I will personally see to it that he never lacks for anything again in this beloved kingdom of ours.

Prince Henry was also looking quizzically at Hans. Like Manfred, he had known him since he had come to Dehrmacht, orphaned, homeless and, at first, friendless. What power could turn this grim warrior into this happy, smiling giant? Religion couldn't, he was sure. From the priests he had known, most had revolted him with their love of good living, their ignorance of goodness and their arrogance. No, this was something deeper and, thought the prince, impressive.

At last, the path lay over the brow of a small hill and there, spread before them, lay the camp of the King's friends. Crude tents and rough bivouacs, made of branches and trees, were everywhere. Unusually, there were no fires, at least none that could be seen.

Hans and Manfred realized this was a *large* army. The trees were thinning now and they saw one or two larger pavilions. Then, at last, a large white pavilion with Dehrmacht's blue and gold flying above it and, although where they had got it from, Manfred could not think, there was also the standard of the royal house of Dehrmacht. This must be the tent assigned to Prince Rudolph. A group of stalwart men-at-arms were encamped nearby and two of the blond warriors of Selden stood at the door. Next to the royal pavilion, was another, slightly larger and, above this flew the silver and red of Selden, Prince Henry's residence, and his badge of the pierced serpent flying from the roof.

And there, coming out of the tented porch, was a small erect figure, beautifully dressed in colorful silks. He was flanked by the short, wide Breclan and the large jovial Baron Christov de

Berenal. Behind them, a large party of knights and noblemen followed, many of them armed.

Word of Prince Rudolph's presence had obviously got around, for someone raised a cheer and then men everywhere, as they caught sight of the boy, were whipping off their hats and hoods and cheering lustily. It would have lasted much longer, but their leaders commanded silence. Their presence was a secret, which they wished to maintain until the last possible moment. Prince Henry could see no sense in letting Archduke Boris know they were there one minute before they had to.

Prince Rudolph seemed taken aback at the show of enthusiasm, but he smiled and waved his cap at the men. Then he spotted his friends and ran to welcome them.

"Manfred! Hans! I am *so* glad you are safe." He waited while they dismounted and then they knelt before the boy.

"Your Royal Highness," said Manfred, "I am so glad *you* are safe and that I can at last address you properly once more."

"Ah Manfred, you never for an instant failed in your loyalty towards me, however you addressed me," and he beamed at his father's adviser. Then he paused, a twinkle in his eye, "even when you rebuked me vilely in Velda's vestibule!"

"My prince, do you still hold that against me? I trusted you had forgiven me for that."

"No, I jest, Manfred. What have I to forgive? You and Hans," and he held out his hand to the burly warrior, "I know well that I owe you my very life, and it will never be forgotten, by me at least.

"But where is Father Bertram? Did he not come with you?"

222

"Yes, nephew," said Prince Henry, "he is somewhere, talking to the soldiery, some of whom are badly in need of a good priest, I fear. Though I doubt they will listen much."

Hans' eyes brightened. "By your leave, Your Highness, I will go and find him. He might need some help in persuading men to listen."

Prince Rudolph grinned. "Leave granted, but mind you tell him he is to attend me in my pavilion this night and provision is to be made for all his accommodation and, my royal uncle, has kindly provided servants to wait upon him … whether he will or no."

"It will be so, Your Highness, I will see to it," rumbled Hans happily.

That night the royal party feasted and made merry. Prince Henry wanted to hear all their adventures and was much impressed by Father Bertram, who sat at the High Table as an honored guest. He, of course, was delighted to be able to tell again the simple message of salvation and to show how ordinary people had gladly embraced the truth of the Scriptures, leading to changed lives. Prince Henry listened intently but said little. He had seen so much of the pomp and glory of organized religion that he found it hard to believe even this sincere man. However, a man that would willingly suffer a savage whipping to save an unknown boy, at least deserved the right to be listened to and he decided he would give further thought to it when he had less pressing matters on his mind.

Prince Henry was also deeply interested in Velda. The idea of a sort of underworld queen, ruling benevolently over thousands, intrigued... and disturbed him a little.

They sat up late that night but were awake in good time the next day, as the Prince Henry had called a Council of War. Both princes were there, gorgeously appareled. Christov of Berenal clapped Manfred and Hans, and almost everyone else on the back, but when he saw how they both winced he apologized and, for a while, was almost subdued. He was there by right as the King's cousin and a member of the King's Council of State. A few, a very few, were there as leaders of companies of men from Dehrmacht, more were leaders of groups from Selden, and some were powerful nobles who supported Dehrmacht's king or hated Thalesia for their own reasons. One of these was a venerable and very deaf old man, whom hardly anyone knew but of whom all had heard. He was the old archduke Prince Simon of Igritsenberg: kindly, benevolent, immensely rich and a warrior of some note in his young days. Despite the advice, much of it tearful, from his family and councillors, he had insisted on coming to the aid of his old friend Maximilian the Good and, besides, Archduke Boris had recently stolen some of his possessions in Makenstadt, a province too near to Thalesia to escape its depredations. More to the point, he had brought with him, five thousand pikemen and fifty knights, a doughty contribution to any army.

Another was a lean, dark-faced individual, speaking a strange language. He wore battered half armor, even here in Prince Henry's council. His face was crossed and lined, his nose hooked, his mouth grim and predatory, half hidden by a straggling black mustache. Apparently, he was Lucis di Cazo and had brought with him the wildest looking horsemen Manfred had ever seen. He had observed them the night before. They had oriental faces, wore a breastplate of leather armor, studded with iron, carried round shields and were capped by a round helmet with a down-turned brim. Each carried a short spear and a gleaming, curved sword, which they seemed to spend every spare moment sharpening and polishing.

Prince Henry called the meeting to order. Manfred was introduced and asked to outline the plan he had already formed for the assault on the castle. For the castle had been taken, not long after the young prince had escaped.

As was usual in Dehrmacht, Manfred was given no title, other than the King's Friend or Counselor, which raised eyebrows among the noblemen who were not familiar with the court in this country. Some were frankly skeptical, amongst whom was di Cazo

"Who ees thees man? A common peasant, a nobody, a nothing. I weel tek no orders from heem."

Prince Henry flushed and looked sharply at him, but said nothing.

Manfred heard him but ignored his jibe and went on to describe the current situation at the castle, information supplied by spies and clandestine patrols. Dehrmacht had been taken by the enemy, as most of those present knew. The causeway across the river was still intact but there was a strongly fortified gate at the castle end. Within the bailey was a massive keep, damaged when the castle was taken by the Archduke, but now repaired and said to be stronger than ever.

Somewhere in the keep, they believed the King was alive

and well. To rescue him and get him out alive was of paramount importance. Therefore, a normal siege and assault on the castle was not to be contemplated at this stage as the Archduke would not hesitate to use the King as a bargaining tool. Manfred also thought the archduke would execute the King if things went badly and he was forced to leave the castle.

Furthermore, the Thalesian army was still encamped around the castle. Most of it was on the plain this side of the river, which meant that an attack on the castle would first have to defeat the army outside, leaving the defenders free to do whatever they wished with their prisoners.

However, the army this side of the river was vulnerable to surprise, as the plain was rimmed with low hills, behind which an enemy could mass. Spies had reported that the Thalesians had a system of lookouts posted on each hill leading to the highway down to the castle. This was the reason no fires were lit in Prince Henry's camp. The smoke from the fires of a large army would have been easily visible to the lookouts and a long battle and siege would be inevitable.

Manfred continued his plan. It involved Griffo.

He was an important member of the archduke's entourage and he was expected back at the castle any day now. In fact, if he had not been intercepted, he would have arrived by now. So, no questions would be asked when he did arrive and his fifty men should be admitted to the castle. Griffo *was* going to arrive, but it would not be *his* fifty men with him when he did. These would be hand-picked warriors from the royal army, who must take and hold the castle until reinforcements arrived. The lookouts on the hills would be taken care of before the little cavalcade passed down towards the causeway.

As soon as Griffo's force entered the castle, the main Thalesian army would be attacked on the south and east. A raiding party should be dispatched at once to cross the river far up north and attack the camp across the river soon after the main attack had begun.

It was vital to the plan's success that as the main camp was attacked in the south and east, a strong party of knights and cavalry should smash its way through to the causeway and reinforce the advance guard which should, by now, be in the castle.

Manfred finished and looked at the group. He wished he knew more of the people present. There were too many unfamiliar faces, too many whose strengths and weaknesses he did not know.

For a few moments, there was silence while all present thought about the plan which had been outlined. Some were openly hostile. Di Cazo spoke first: "Ees a crazy plan! By a crazy man!" But numerous voices were raised in favour. The main problem seemed to be that everyone wanted the spectacular parts and nobody to be in reserve or be sent on the more prosaic task but vital of the raiding party across the river. Even Archduke Simon wished to be in the first party to enter the castle.

With difficulty, Prince Henry restored order. "Your Royal Highness, Your Grace, my lords and gentlemen," he said sternly, "this is not a plan for debate. It is already adopted and approved by me. Four thousand men under Count Fidelski are preparing to leave at this moment, to cross the river north of here.

"Manfred will choose the party to enter the castle with Griffo."

"I have already done so, Your Highness."

"And I ..."

"And I will go with them," cut in a young, clear voice.

Manfred turned pale. "Your Highness, it cannot be. I cannot agree to this."

A great shout came from the back of the tent.

"Who eez zis, to question the wishes of the royal son? 'Ow dare 'ee speak thus! In my country, 'ee would be flogged for such behaviour."

Di Cazo had again voiced his dissenting opinion.

Prince Rudolph turned red with anger, but spoke quietly but clearly.

"My Lord di Cazo, I know that you are a great nobleman in your own country, and our royal family appreciates your assistance against our enemies, but, there is something which you must know.

"This man, as you call him, is nobly born, as high as almost any man here. Because of deeds of infamy, not his own but his father's and forefathers', he renounced all titles and all claim to his estates, which were considerable. Now, he is my father's friend, and mine. None stands higher in our royal father's councils than he. Times without number he has proved his devotion to our royal house and, if any further proof were needed, these last months has risked his life, suffered imprisonment and flogging like a common felon, in order to keep me safe. I declare before you all, he is our Friend and loyal counselor. I will hear no word against him. If any man is his enemy, he is ours also. It is true, no man can defy our royal will without our displeasure, but if Manfred says I cannot go with his party, although I would dearly love to, then I willingly bow to his wishes. I were an ungrateful churl to do otherwise." He smiled at Manfred and then, "My trusted friend, I will serve wherever you want me."

Manfred breathed a deep sigh of relief. "I thank you, my prince, for your love and friendship to one so unworthy of all the kindnesses of your gracious house. I am conscious of the honor you do me in heeding my word. I shall enter the battle at ease in my mind, if you would stay with your royal uncle while he directs the battle, and with his staff if he leaves to fight with his knights."

Then that nasal, sneering voice spoke again. "What about my men! We weel lead the dash for the causeway, yes?," said Di Cazo. "We are much better zan ze slow, lumbering knights. We will be in, Pow! And we weel smack them like se hand smacking ze wasp. Kapow! Eet will be over quickly."

Manfred looked at him carefully. He could be right. If only he, Manfred, knew his man better. Under that sneering, sardonic mask, there could be really great fighting qualities.

Then he thought the man is right. Berenal, as brave as a lion, would do wonders and his loyalty was without doubt, but fully armoured knights *were* slow. If they smashed a way through, di Cazo's swift horsemen could be in the castle while de Berenal was paving the way. He decided to trust him.

"My lord di Cazo," Manfred turned to him. "I thank you for being so willing to hazard your men in a daring and dangerous escapade. We need such a man as you to do this great and glorious deed I have in mind."

Di Cazo preened himself under these words.

"My lord," he said, "I thank you and weel do whatever zis great thing is you have thought of. You may be not so mad, after all," and he smiled with pleasure.

Manfred then explained di Cazo's part to the rest of the meeting.

A small party under Manfred and Hans were to capture and hold the gatehouse to the castle. If possible, they would force and entrance into the great keep itself, but they would need help very quickly. De Berenal, with his party of magnificent knights would smash its way through the soldiers gathered before the castle. This was no small task and would probably fully occupy them. Speed was essential though, so di Cazo's group of light horsemen would follow and give immediate support to the initial band in the castle courtyard. They would then be further backed up by a division of men-at-arms following more slowly. Di Cazo was delighted. It was just the sort of thing his men would do well. They would sweep like lightning to provide the first much needed bracer to the tiny party going into the castle.

Now all that was needed was to persuade Black Griffo to take his part in the plan.

The meeting broke up soon afterwards. Prince Henry made his depositions, giving orders to different officers as to where they were to use the troops under their command. A large contingent was ordered to prepare immediately to travel to their position south of the Thalesian army. Another officer was in charge of the essential lookouts, other nobles and knights were told to be part of the main assault force, others to be held in reserve, others to advance only when they were signaled to do so from his command group, and so on.

Manfred muttered something about "preparing for tomorrow" and disappeared into his tent. His lamp was seen burning late into the night, but only Hans and Breclan knew what he was doing. Strangely, no man was allowed past the threshold. All visitors were turned away.

TWENTY-FOUR

Griffo *would* cooperate. He had little choice. Prince Henry would certainly carry out his threat to hang him. Griffo's face when he had seen Prince Rudolph and recognized his boy prisoner had been, as they say, a picture.

Blue was the sky, perfect the day. Birds were everywhere, hunting food for babies in nests. The air was sweet scented from wild honeysuckle and countless wild flowers and the buzz of early morning insects was all around them. A lovely day, a beautiful, heart-lifting day, a day to live and not to die on, but some would die, as this was the day to fight.

A thousand different thoughts passed through the minds of the columns of determined men now plodding along the main highway to Dehrmacht. Fear certainly, resolution, the nervous thrill and excitement of impending action, mixed thoughts and emotions surged in many a keyed up mind.

Out of sight of the main army, way ahead, Griffo's cart rumbled along the dirt road, accompanied by about fifty men-at-arms, all in the uniforms of the Thalesian soldiers captured by Prince Henry. Griffo rode at the front of the column, just as he did in the days of his freedom. The difference lay in two stalwart men riding immediately behind him, both armed with crossbows, hidden beneath their tunics, but loaded and aimed at his back.

Hans was in the cart. As far as he could be, consistent with his role as a prisoner, he was exuberant, more cheerful and buoyant than Manfred had ever seen him. Breclan was in the cart too, dressed in priest's clothes, and Manfred was near him. Usually ebullient and cheerful, Breclan was struggling to stay quiet and subdued, as befitted a captive on his way to his enemy's stronghold.

Manfred, in his place, was dressed unusually. A plain, brown cloak wrapped him closely round, yet somehow it was loose at the chest, so that his arms could move freely. The hood was very deep: so deep that nothing at all of his face could be seen. Indeed, some said it wasn't Manfred at all until his voice reassured them. On his hands he wore enormous gauntlets, despite the promise of a hot day. When questioned, he just laughed, saying he was hiding his face in order to frighten the enemy later. The rest of the men were hand-picked soldiers, several of them archers, skilled and brave. It was unlikely many of them would survive their role in the day's events.

They plodded on. Two hours before dawn they had started in the cart. Behind them, all over the forest, men were on the move. By now, Fidelski's force would be over the river and marching down. Archduke Simon's men, backed up by Pirenath and his hillmen, should be in position behind the southern ridge. Berenal's knights were near but hidden by the hills. Di Cazo's wild horsemen were, with difficulty, being restrained from undertaking a lone headlong assault of the castle. Behind *them* the main body of the army was ready to sweep over the hill down towards the castle when the signal was given.

Everything hinged on the parts of the plan coming together at the right time. If any part of the army arrived too soon, the alarm would be raised and the castle's formidable defenses would ensure a long and difficult siege. Prince Henry knew they must avoid this if at all possible. Although he was sure a siege would be successful eventually, it would put the King's life at risk and the struggle would be long and costly.

It promised to be a beautiful sunny day. Already its heat was chasing the night's chill away. The cart rattled and swayed on the uneven road, while the band of picked warriors in it prepared mentally for the fierce fight they knew lay ahead for them.

Onwards the wagon rumbled. All the wheels squeaked but Breclan noticed that one at the back, nearest to him, seemed to have a particularly loud and annoying squeal at any change in the road's surface. They could see the river, shining and glistening in the morning sun. A blackbird caroled its joy at the new morning and bees were already stirring in the sunlight

Here were the first lookouts. It would not have been human to be relaxed. This was the first challenge.

A swarthy individual in the Archduke's colors of red and black held up his hand and the driver heaved on the reins of his horses. It was the first watch of the day and the man had no doubt been woken early for it, but his eyes were bright enough for all that. He glared at the cavalcade, looked at the drivers on the cart and swept his eyes over the 'prisoners' in it. Manfred, peering out from the depths of his cowl, saw a small group of soldiers sitting by a fire and, he noticed, one with a trumpet slung from his neck. *If that one blows his trumpet, we are lost,* he thought to himself.

"State your name and business!"

Then Griffo's voice rang out. "What, Carl Jantinck! Do you not remember your old master-at-arms?"

The man fell back a little and peered at him. "Your pardon, Captain Griffo. I didn't expect to see you so early in the morning."

Manfred thought grimly that Griffo had done his part marvelously well. He had been promised great things to do so and a very quick death if he didn't, but still his performance was much better than expected.

"All right, Captain, I will give the signal and you can be on your way." He waved a small flag towards the castle gatehouse and signaled Griffo to proceed.

Manfred released his pent up breath.

As the column moved past the little group of soldiers, a few of the men marching at the rear hailed them. "Hey mates! Care to wager on the fate of these prisoners?" They turned aside from the rest of the men and approached the guards.

Interested, the Archduke's men advanced to meet them, joking roughly as they did. They were young: bronzed and healthy, from living out of doors. They were not well fed though, for the Archduke had had great difficulties feeding his army in the face of a partially ruined and mostly hostile population.

It was very quick and very quiet. The men who had stopped were 'Breclan's Browns'. Short, strong, hard as the wood with which they worked, they attacked the small band of unsuspecting guards with swift and sudden ferocity. The lad with the trumpet died quickly for his importance had been noticed straight away.

Down the path and up the next little hill, they were challenged again, but not so rigorously. This time a grizzled old veteran, with a mean eye, recognized Griffo and waved them on, first giving the signal to the next lookout.

He was just in the act of muttering insults and imprecations against the men in the cart, when he and his band were suddenly and violently overwhelmed by Breclan's formidable woodsmen. None escaped.

So they passed through the third and final checkpoint and down into the plain, the wagon's wheels squealing and complaining down the hillside as the brake checked them on the descent.

Breclan thought Dehrmacht looked beautiful in the morning sun. He had always loved this view of the castle, from the last hill. The sun was on it now, as it sat on its little spit of an island and its low causeway gently washed with a thin layer of the river flowing over it. From this height it looked close enough to fly into it. The flags fluttered bravely on the ramparts, the archduke's own standard depicting a black wolf on a red background flying impudently from the keep. Five hundred men, Manfred had said were in the castle and their party in the cart and cavalcade were seventy. *Hmm, well, we'll see ...*

Below them, too, as they plodded gently down the path, the Archduke's army was vastly spread on both sides of the river. Fires, tents, pavilions, horses and men were everywhere, busy about innumerable tasks, mostly to do with making breakfast probably.

A column of horsemen and mules was snaking off to the

south, on the interminable search for food for an army in the field. *Their* day was likely to turn out differently from their expectations anyway.

Two or three other troops, smaller and on foot, were going in different directions and other patrols seemed to be setting out on the other side of the river, too. Hopefully, anyone interested in the little column of horsemen, soldiers and wagons would think it just another of the routine patrols, returning from their task. Today, however, would not be routine for any of them.

Most of the camp lay slightly to the left, or south, of the causeway, to allow passage through, but also because there was more room for the army to spread. On the north side, the hills came down closer to the castle.

Truly, it was a beautiful day and a beautiful and interesting scene. Soon, though, this lovely landscape would be filled with the clash of arms, the shouts and screams of men, acts of bravery and, perhaps, of cowardice. The scene afterwards would be anything but beautiful, with the wounded and dead lying scattered over the soft green grass. Breclan thought briefly of home: his wife and his little ones. What would they be doing now, he wondered. He sighed and then thrust such thoughts firmly out of his mind. Thinking of them would soften him, unman him and spoil his effectiveness, when every ounce of his strength and ability would be needed this day for his King.

They were very near now: near enough for Griffo to shout an alarm, or bolt for the sentries on duty. He was well covered, but Breclan thought it worth hissing to him "My bow is a yard from your back. At this range, the bolt would go right through you and come out the other side. No tricks, Griffo!"

A smartly dressed guard held up his hand and stood in their path.

" Welcome back, Griffo. Have you been successful in your searchings? You have more willing soldiers for His Highness, I trust?"

"Ah, Gildak, you seem to be well installed already. Yes, I have some fine specimens to join his army, and some prisoners."

"We had heard that you were coming but we expected you some time since. You must have been detained somewhere on the way. We also heard something about some priests."

"We are here, my son," intoned a foreign voice, its owner robed in black, a little behind Griffo. This was actually an Italian mercenary, Pitrinaldo, tall and thin, normally with a gleaming smile, but keeping it well under control for the present. He had begged to be allowed to be a priest, for one day at least. He held them in great respect and had paraded in priestly robes among his fellow mercenaries for at least an hour yesterday evening. Breclan gave him a stern look, but it was entirely lost on those dark twinkling eyes.

Gildak, captain of one division of the Archduke's own guards, seemed happy.

He sauntered over to the cart and looked curiously, and perhaps a little sadly, at Hans and Manfred sitting apparently bound there.

"Well, you look fine fellows," he said. "I'm afraid my master does not treat his prisoners well, but perhaps you will find some favor with him.

238

He looked at the cart.

"Curiously high these carts are, you would get far more in them if you lowered the floors."

A slight pause from Griffo, which was then accompanied by a slight prod from the soldier on his left. Then "I don't bother myself with the construction. I just use them as they come."

"Yes, I suppose so," and Captain Gildak waved them on, idly watching the second cart, apparently laden with barrels, pass him.

On, through the northern edge of the camp, they passed. Although there were men everywhere, few took much notice of the procession passing through. One or two cracked jokes, made comments, as men do, especially if they noticed any irregularity in uniform or appearance. In truth, thought Breclan, the Thalesians were reasonably smart and the camp in good order.

The carts jolted on. These carts are not built for comfort, thought Manfred, as he eased his position. Better than last time, though, and he wondered how the archers were faring beneath him and in the barrels on the next cart.

Breclan frowned as they drew nearer to the river. A company of pikemen was exercising. He hoped fervently that they would move away before Berenal's knights came down. Such a company, well disciplined, could seriously hinder them.

Nearer and nearer they approached. The great, grey walls loomed over them. Breclan tried to count men on the walls but couldn't see many. The gatehouse faced upriver, so that, too, was largely hidden. He could hear men inside. Somewhere near that window a man was shouting at an underling. *Sounded like a cook,* thought Breclan. The chink, chink, chink of a hammer on metal floated clearly across the water from inside the castle. The armorer, too, was awake early.

Another challenge. This time, it was guards before the causeway. The ground here was muddy and the river high, overflowing its banks and the causeway itself. It wasn't turbulent but there must have been heavy rain in the mountains, where the river rose.

Griffo was again cleared to proceed and the horses" hooves splashed in the water awash the causeway. Those pulling the wagons strained and heaved as they hauled them up. For a second it looked doubtful, but the team of eight managed it and the wagon lurched onto the stone.

"Those wagons are heavy," said one of the sentries, "must have good food for his highness, I think."

And the others grumbled their agreement. Manfred gathered that the Archduke was not overfeeding his men.

They were well on the causeway now, turning the bend and there were the massive gates: wide open, though they could be shut quickly, as they well knew.

Breclan was as still as stone, as he sat, but his eyes ranged over the gatehouse. He knew where the ropes were for pulling up the drawbridge. He knew the guardroom and the stairway to it. These would be his responsibility.

His bow was steady under his robe. If Griffo intended treachery now, they would all be lost, but he would die first.

Every man in the procession was as taut as a bowstring, from Griffo and Breclan at the front to the brave and stalwart swordsmen at the rear who, if the plan sprung too soon, would perish miserably on the causeway or in the river. The 'Browns' who had been at the back had dropped off to replace the last lookouts they had overcome.

The final challenge came from a sleepy sergeant-at-arms who was waiting for his relief. "What's your business? … Oh, it's you, Captain, many things have happened since you left. His Highness will be glad to see you."

"Yes, sergeant. Let us through will you, we have been on the road too long already."

"Yes sir, pass on."

TWENTY-FIVE

The horses' hooves clattered on the stone floor of the courtyard. The rest of the procession followed; one cart, the one with Manfred and Hans in it, rumbled up to the very door of the keep, the other coming to rest in the center near the gatehouse.

The sergeant saw them pass without interest but suddenly came to life when he saw where the first cart was stopped. He came bustling forward, full of his own importance. "Captain Griffo, you can't stop that cart there, in front of the main door. You know better than that, all carts and produce have to go round to the kitchens and storehouses, and His Highness can't stand anything in front of the entrance. He says it is too easy for his enemies to get close. Sir, you will have to move it."

"Sergeant," Griffo spoke sternly to him. "When have you ever questioned my orders before? Do you not know that I receive my orders directly from the Archduke himself?"

The man looked discomforted and unhappy. He gathered his courage to reply for he knew Griffo had a fearsome reputation, but so did his master the Archduke. He was spared the decision though for, in the distance, a bugle blared, and then another, and then another.

He froze, then turned to shout to the bugler on top of the

gate. He died before he could open his mouth, shot through the heart by Breclan. The unfortunate bugler followed quickly after, this time shot down by one of the archers at the rear of the procession

Manfred and Hans sprang for the entrance to the keep, accompanied by a dozen men. Two men by the first cart began heaving up the false bottom and archers scrambled to leap out and head for the keep as well. Breclan flung aside his bow and seized his weapon of choice: a large battle-ax, which had been hidden on the floor of the cart ready for this moment.

The few Thalesians which had been on duty were all disposed of quickly, but there was still the man or men on duty in the room above the portcullis. That must not come down. Breclan sprang for the door of the gatehouse, while the other party made for the keep. He charged up the short staircase, followed by a small group of his own men.

Three men were in the room, one of them in the very act of raising his sword to sever the rope that held the portcullis up. Breclan never hesitated. He flung his ax and split the man's head, as if it were a turnip. Now Breclan was in danger for the other two guards flung themselves at him.

They were too late. Breclan's men were there and parried the sword thrusts of the guards before killing them.

Others of his men had already gone on to the room above, where the huge wheels were which heaved the drawbridge up, and soon the gatehouse was secure under their control. The first objective of the royalist army was achieved.

These things happened quickly but bugles were sounding on

the walls and outside in the camp. There were sounds that the castle was coming awake in a hurry.

Manfred, Hans and their men were already involved in fierce fighting. Comparatively few soldiers were actually in the keep itself, most of the garrison being housed in barracks around the bailey or yard inside the castle walls. Manfred's men had three objectives: to take and keep the gatehouse, to secure and render impotent the men of the guard inside the keep, and to find and rescue the King. The gatehouse was done and Manfred knew that it could be in no better hands than Breclan's. He was to hold it until Berenal's knights could force their way across the field and enter the castle. Hans and most of the men would stay in the keep, take the guardroom and, if possible, shut and keep closed the great doors of the keep, again until Berenal's force should arrive. He, Manfred, would take a small group and find and rescue the King.

Most of the men of the guard had been slain at the entrance to the castle but there still men on duty inside the keep. There were also, of course, more men on the upper floors of the keep, but some would be needed to man the walls and, hopefully, not be spared to attend to the disturbances downstairs. Those that did come down would probably descend the spiral staircase to the right of the main doors and Hans knew that there was a barracks room up there for the use of the men on duty in the castle. He also knew he would be better not to wait until the men came down and gathered in the entrance hall. He would be better to seek out those he could now, so he leaped for the staircase.

Unnoticed by anyone, Griffo slipped away by himself.

The phenomenal strength possessed by Hans carried him up against the flow of men coming down. His massive shield protected him while he thrust vigorously at each body as it came. Another man would have been quite unable to cope with the weight of bodies coming down. As it was, he was unable to swing his sword much, as the spiral of the steps was against him but his thrust was enough. Men were falling past him and he found himself clambering over the bodies of the slain.

At last he reached the barrack-room he had been aiming for. There were few men there now and Hans and his followers cleared them after a few minutes of bitter hand-to-hand fighting. Then, they scrambled down over the bodies on the stairs to re-join their comrades and defend the hall and doors.

Their arrival was timely. The entrance hall was not large but the main hall lay beyond it. A huge oak screen shielded the doorway to the hall and Hans could hear men gathering behind it. The screen was actually a help to him, for it prevented the archduke's men rushing his little party at the entrance. His archers were cutting down any individuals trying to slide round the edge of the screen. Hans knew there was not great danger there as it was unlikely there were great numbers of troops inside the main hall.

A sudden cry and a thud made him turn in time to see one of his men fall with a crossbow bolt in his back. It had come through the doorway, probably shot by one of the men on the walls of the castle. His main danger came from outside, that is from the large body of troops barracked in the bailey. Breclan would hold the gatehouse and were keeping heads down outside by well-aimed arrows, but there was a limit to how much could be done that way. If he shut the door of the keep and he and his men perished, the royal army would find it difficult to enter and the danger to the King would be increased. If he could jam the doors open, then all he and his men had to do was survive until help arrived.

He looked at the massive doors standing open. He looked at the huge iron hinges and the great iron bars which were used to bolt the doors, and he prayed for guidance.

His eye fell on one of the bars. It was huge, and when the doors were shut, it stretched right across from doorpost to doorpost. With an effort, for it was heavy, he picked it up. He hefted the huge bar in his hands, grunted, and lifted it above his head. With his arms stretched upwards, he strode forward into the doorway.

A bolt hissed viciously past his ear and another narrowly missed his middle, but he did not hesitate. Hans marched forward and rammed the bar, with immense force, into the middle of the two doors standing wide open. Thus, the doors were jammed, with a great iron bar, well above the height of most men. It would take skill and a lot of effort from several strong men to move that bar now.

As he turned to rejoin his comrades by the staircase doors, a bolt struck him full between the shoulder blades. He staggered a little, made to continue, but his knees buckled and mighty Hans fell full-length in the entrance of Dehrmacht Castle keep.

TWENTY-SIX

As the wagon made its way down the hill towards the castle, Berenal sat and waited at the head of his knights. The smell of horses, of leather, of grease on armor joints filled the air and the noble Christov, Count of Berenal, sniffed deeply and appreciatively. He loved it. He loved horses. He loved excitement and he loved action. He pulled at his long, droopy, ginger mustache and shifted his seat impatiently.

"Much longer, Your Highness?" he asked anxiously.

Not much longer, my active friend," smiled Prince Henry, who was beside him. "Manfred's party is well inside the camp and nearing the causeway, according to the lookout."

"Safe so far," put in Prince Rudolph who, clad in exquisite silver armor, sat a white stallion on Henry's other side.

"Boris," he called to a lad given to him as a servant, "go and see what is happening and especially look out for the noble lord, Manfred, and Hans, the King's captain."

Boris rushed up the little hill for the twentieth time and returned.

"The King's Counselor and the captain are sitting still in the back of the cart and they are about to mount the causeway, Your Highness."

One of the lookouts, a Brown from the first party, then

shouted "Your Highness, the cart seems to be stuck. They are having difficulty getting it onto the causeway. They seem to be struggling."

"Oh no!" wailed Prince Rudolph, "they must get through. They MUST!" and he bowed his head in prayer.

"They seem to have done it," shouted the man. "It seems to be all right and is on its way on the causeway."

They sighed and released their pent up breath. Behind Berenal two hundred knights waited with much the same thoughts, hopes and fears that the brave little advance party had felt. They were quiet mostly, except for the odd one nervously jesting with his companions. They came from the noblest families in Dehrmacht, Selden and a few other kingdoms as well. They were mostly young, superbly fit, at ease in the saddle and skilled from their youth in the arts of war.

"Sire," said one, Igor of Madritch, in Prince Henry's country. He spoke with a lazy drawl. "Sire, can't we go soon, my horse is becoming impatient."

Before the Prince could reply, a lookout ran up to him. "Sire, they have passed the outer gate."

"Give the signal quickly," said the Prince. The man ran back to the hill-top and flashed the "Friends" signal they had picked up from the original Thalesian lookouts. He did it with a piece of bright, shiny metal, reflecting the rays of the sun to the sergeant of the guard at the camp. Twice he flashed. Then he paused and flashed twice more.

"Go, my lord of Berenal, and may God grant you success!"

With these words, Prince Henry turned with his staff to

direct the rest of the troops, and Prince Rudolph went with them.

Berenal led his magnificent force down the path, quickly, but not too quickly as the path needed care. They rode three abreast over the hill, the sun glancing and reflecting off their lances, their shields and their armor. They carried no pennants, in order to keep the element of surprise for as long as possible.

Pedric, eldest son of the lord of Garavor, a powerful noble from the far north, saw the river and remarked breathlessly to his brother "I knew it, Gidrach, the river is high. I said it would be."

"Yes, it will stop any Thalesians crossing the river to aid the castle I think, but what is that strange noise?" asked his brother. There were noises all around them. The horses were trotting and their hooves rang on the flints in the road. Armour clanked and weapons clinked. There was noise everywhere but Pedric knew what he meant. He laughed with boyish enthusiasm and pleasure.

"It's my lord Berenal. He is singing!"

And so it was. Berenal was singing lustily. He was in his element. Without a nerve in his body, the danger was that he would be too rash. He loved every part of knightly warfare. The fact that he might, within the hour, be lying fearfully wounded or lifeless on the field, never occurred to him. If it did, he did not harbor such a thought for very long. This was his life and he would sooner die here than on an invalid's bed in his castle or even linger on for years in old age. No, this was the way for a man to live, or die.

He checked his sword was loose in its scabbard. He hefted his lance. He listened to the noise of movement all around him, and the rhythmic clatter of hooves and jingle of armor thrilled him to his core. He surveyed the camp below him and saw the uplifted faces as men watched the shining column approach. His heart lifted within him and he sang for pure joy.

The sergeant at arms was in a quandary. He had seen the signal saying that friends were approaching, but these friends were a large column of heavily armed knights, equipped and dressed for war, and not coming slowly either, like that other slow-moving procession before.

Pass the buck, he thought, and then, aloud "Call the captain. Quickly now, lad," and the man beside him ran to the captain's tent.

Every man in the vicinity had stopped to look at the approaching knights and then, it happened.

One of the hill-top guards had gone for water and, returning, found his companions gone and a body of strange knights riding into his camp. He immediately was suspicious and, thinking he would err on the side of caution, sounded the alarm on his bugle.

The sergeant and all the men in the camp looked towards the sound of that trumpet and the moment of surprise was lost.

Men threw aside their food, their cards, their business in hand, whatever it was at that moment, in a frantic dive for their weapons. Pots were overturned, cups and platters thrown away, fires kicked aside, tents even pulled down in the sudden frenzied panic everywhere. Trumpeters seized their instruments and alarms sounded in every part.

The timing was bad for Berenal and his knights. He had no alternative but to increase his speed and his knights followed him. The going was easier as they had negotiated the slope of the hill and he knew that every second counted for the men already in the castle.

"Sound the charge, my boy!" he shouted to the lad galloping beside him, and the shrill clear notes swept out to the column of men behind.

Berenal shouted with delight and leveled his fearsome lance as he pounded at the head of his beloved cavalry.

Only the company of drilling pikemen showed no panic. Their officer heard the shrilling trumpets, saw the knights, knew a charge when he saw one and gave his orders.

Slowly, the company of men swung round, slowly advanced towards the enemy, slowly took up position across the path, swiftly and efficiently embedded the ends of their pikes into the ground and grimly awaited the coming shock of the hurtling horsemen.

The knights fanned out a little: four, five, six a-breast, galloping hard.

The men in the camp fled before them with the captain of the guard dying immediately as he bravely tried to rally his men. The sergeant perished too, lifting his sword as the lance swept through his body. The crash into the pikemen was terrific. The fearful smash of galloping horses and heavily armed men against the long and heavy pikes was heard across the camp.

Berenal and those in the front rank fell at the first clash. He never even saw the pike that skewered his horse from shoulders to withers. He flew through the air, crashed heavily to the ground, and lay still.

TWENTY-SEVEN

Even as de Berenal's magnificent knights met the pikemen, di Cazo's men were sweeping down the hill. Small and wiry horses, their riders superbly in control, moved swiftly over the ground. The pikemen were still fighting a bitter battle with the knights from de Berenal's troop, when the little dark-skinned horsemen with their vicious curving swords were upon them, amongst them and... past them.

Following orders, they stopped not for the pikemen, saving only when one was unfortunate enough to be in the way, when he was unceremoniously cut down by a sweeping blade and passed by.

At their command position, on a hill-top, Prince Henry, Prince Rudolph and the rest of their staff, had watched the knights pass down the path with mixed feelings. Some had wished they could have been with them. Others were worried about the timing of the different attacks, upon which so much depended. Now they watched with wonder as the swarm of dark horsemen swept on to the causeway.

The command party fretted with the inactivity. Theirs was not a class which was used to waiting. Behind and around them, still and quiet, fifteen thousand foot-soldiers, pikemen, halberdiers, and archers, also waited.

"I can't bear this waiting," cried Prince Rudolph, "and, especially, not being able to see anything."

"Not much longer now, my nephew," replied Prince Henry. "Archduke Simon's attack should begin any minute now. Wait for it."

The air was full of tension. The very trees and bushes seemed hushed and still.

Then, at last, it came.

First they heard the shout of their own lookout. "I see the banners of Igritsenberg, Your Highness!"

Then, faintly, the first frantic trilling of a distant bugle, followed by others, and the distant, urgent rattle of drums.

"Up!" cried Prince Henry. "Forward Dehrmacht! Attack Selden!"

On his command the massed soldiers from Dehrmacht and Felden, along with the mercenaries from various countries advanced on a broad front so that they crossed the brows of the rolling hills ranged round the eastern plain of Dehrmacht Castle. There were none at the northern hill, as little of the Thalesian army was encamped at that end of the plain.

The crucial point in the battle was the castle itself and Henry knew that if Manfred's plan was successful, they would win the day. If not... who could know what would result?

As the soldiers poured over the hills to the plain below, the two princes rode to the hilltop beside the path with a group of knights, all eager to see the progress of the battle.

Prince Rudolph alternated between, on the one hand, acute anxiety for his father and Manfred and Hans and, on the other, excitement at the magnificent spectacle being played out below.

They had arrived at the hilltop in time to see Berenal's magnificent charge. The boy's heart had thrilled to the stirring sound of the bugle call to charge, which came to them clearly. He watched with bursting pride as the knights allowed hidden pennants to fly clear. He watched their powerful steeds thunder from trot to gallop down the path. He shouted with delight as the Thalesians fled in all directions before them and they cut a wide swathe towards the causeway. He caught his breath when he saw the company of pikemen waiting so ominously and he felt his uncle stiffen beside him.

The smash as that beautiful phalanx of pounding horses and armored men met those vicious rows of sturdy pikes floated clearly up to them. The boy saw men fall and some rise. He saw Thalesian soldiers quickly run in to sink knives and swords into those still on the ground, but he also saw that the following knights thundered on to wreak havoc amongst the pikemen.

Prince Henry smiled, and said "de Berenal did his part but look now at di Cazo's men. You know, I think he was just what we needed at this moment. See, they are almost at the causeway already and the pikemen don't seem to be able to cope with those tiny horses and the astonishing way in which they twist and turn!"

It was true. Di Cazo's little wild horsemen were cutting the pike company to pieces. They were in, around and behind them before they could turn their heavy unwieldy pikes and by then it was too late. Not that they stayed, the fierce little men were already on the causeway and sweeping aside any resistance.

Prince Henry sighed with relief. One crisis was over,

although it had been a serious one while it lasted. It was time to dispatch the group of infantry which would support and finish the work in the castle itself. To send them now would be right, as it would take a while for them to get down the hill, probably fighting their way through some of the Thalesians en route.

He turned to another, older man seated on a beautiful, black horse, and smiled at him.

"Now it is your turn, my lord of Altrecht. Take your division and finish taking that castle for me. Assist in its taking, at all costs."

"Your Highness commands and I obey," he replied gravely and wheeled his horse around to fulfill his commission.

TWENTY-EIGHT

When Manfred left Hans defending his entrance hall position, he took with him six of Breclan's Browns and four of those superb, sturdy Welsh archers. He himself wore light chest armor under the blue and gold of Dehrmacht, topped by a small iron helmet. Although entitled to it, he wore none of the elaborate trappings of knighthood of those days: no plumed crest in huge ornate helmet, no surtout emblazoned with his coat of arms, no gaudy shield proclaiming his high birth and nobility. It was not his way but, in any case, he had another purpose this day and was covered in a drab hooded cloak, which clung about him and completely covered his face. This day he wished to be even more inconspicuous and retiring than usual. Only his trusted friends, Hans and Breclan, knew what he was about.

Followed very closely by his chosen band, also hooded and shrouded, he ran to a small side door, not much used, which he knew led into a passage directly alongside the great hall. None knew Dehrmacht Castle like Manfred and, at this moment, he knew exactly where he was going.

They had a good view of the hall as they flitted along. Men at arms were muttering in groups. Some were clustered at the great arch leading into the hall and beyond which was the screen, and Hans. There was a somewhat bewildered air and, so far, the archduke was not to be seen. As usual in the great hall of most castles, the light was not good. The blazing fire at one end gave illumination and there were some rush-lights, but windows were high and small and gave little sense of the day outside which, of course, suited Manfred and his hurrying group.

Near the end of the hall, Manfred led the way from the passage into the hall itself. From that point, about two thirds of the way down the hall, he slipped along beside the wall until he came to another door. This time it was shut, recessed and heavy.

It opened easily enough, though heavy. He waited for his group, shut and bolted the door, and passed on.

All safely through, Manfred fairly flew down the passage. He knew he had very little time. If the Archduke thought his rule under serious threat, he would either seize the King and transport him swiftly away, or kill him so that he could not be a rallying point for the loyalists attacking the castle.

Manfred's men had to work hard to keep up with him. Left and right he turned, descending deeper into the bowels of the castle.

Several times men appeared and tried to stop his headlong rush. They died without mercy on his flashing blade.

Down yet another passage they ran, round a corner and Manfred stopped. Steps were before them and, at the bottom, a door.

"Guardroom!" he hissed. "Ready?"

"Aye!" They growled a response.

Down the steps he sped and flung open the door.

Six startled men looked up and reached desperately for their weapons. They had no chance. The invaders swept through like a tornado, leaving them dead or dying. Manfred paused long enough to seize two large bunches of keys from the wall and they were on their way again, through dark passages, lit by flickering torches and, at last, Manfred slowed.

He knew the castle intimately. They were in the dungeons. Where was the King? He stopped at a locked door and slid back a shutter.

"Anyone in there?" he called.

"Yes, Master," a quavery voice answered. "Only old Negritch in here. Is it time for dinner, Master?"

"No, Negritch. Where is the King?"

"The King? Why, the King is in his castle, Master, where he ought to be. Can I have my dinner now?"

"Later, Negritch, later," and Manfred ran to another door. Then he heard a noise and remembered there were bigger dungeons further on.

"Come on," he said, pointing to a stout door at the end of the passage.

There was no shutter on this door, so it would have to be opened. He tried the keys frantically until, at last, one fitted and turned. The door opened and they stared into blackness.

Voices rose and shouted questions.

"What's happening? Who are you? We heard noises. What *is* happening?"

"The castle is attacked and we are searching for the King. If any of you are here because of your loyalty to King Maximilian, you are released. Where is the King?"

A few of the men had crept nervously nearer to the door.

"The King?" they said. "He was put on the level below. Had it almost to himself, just two servants with him."

Manfred had to ask, though he trembled at the reply he might receive. "Is … is the King in good health?"

"We don't know, Master," one said, "we have seen and heard nothing since we came into this dismal place.

"Who are you, anyway, that wants to know?"

"I am Manfred, the King's servant."

A shambling wreck of a poor fellow came forward and peered at him with weak and watery eyes.

"Oh, Sir!" He said, bursting into tears. "I knew you would come back, but I can't see your face. Is it really you, my lord? Him they call *The King's Friend?*"

"Yes, I am he, but who are you?"

"Havel, my lord. I served you often at the King's table."

"You can't be," said Manfred. "Havel was a young man …" and then, "I'm sorry, Havel, it really is you. Is this what they've done to you, then?

"But where is the King? I have no time to lose."

"Below, Sir, on the floor below. Go quickly, my lord. Forget us. We can get ourselves out now."

"Here are the keys to this block, then. Release all who are loyal to the King, but watch out for the Archduke's soldiers. They will not treat you kindly."

Manfred turned to his little troop and nodded back towards the guardroom.

"Back that way, lads. Keep your eyes open. There are bound to be men coming soon."

Towards the guardroom they ran but just before they got there, Manfred turned at a passage on the left and descended more steps.

At the bottom a passage ran right and left. Manfred turned left.

It was grim. It was damp. Two or three flickering torches illuminated a dismal chamber at the end of the passage. It contained a rough hewn table, half a dozen chairs, a few odds and ends of leather and metal, even keys, huge and heavy, but no people. An open door led out of it at the other side.

Manfred stopped.

"This is strange," he mused. He turned to his faithful band of followers "Go carefully, now. This has all the appearance of a trap."

They went carefully. They passed through the door into a smaller chamber with two rough beds.

"Ah!" though Manfred.

Beyond this was another larger chamber, into which they rushed and … stopped.

A line of men, clothed in steel breastplates, helmeted, wearing the Thalesian black and red, armed with sword and shield, ready for war, stood waiting.

Towering above them, smiling a little satisfied smile was Griffo. He almost laughed out loud at Manfred's face, but another was there to whom Griffo gave way.

Boris, Archduke of Thalesia, universally disliked, widely

feared, sometimes despised, often hated, was sitting in a stately chair. A man of around forty years, he was slim, tall and well-built. Cold blue eyes gazed from under hooded lids, in a mobile and intelligent face. His nose was thin and in proportion, his mouth was wide, thin lipped and cruel. Richly dressed, but with steel beneath his robes, he carried himself nobly and his cold eyes regarded Manfred steadily for a few moments.

"Ah!" he said, "I was expecting … someone else. You have come for your King, I imagine. He is here. Behold!" And he motioned with his hand.

Some of the soldiers drew aside to reveal three figures: two soldiers, with drawn swords, and the King. Manfred's heart jumped when he saw him. Maximilian the Good was alive: gaunt, thinner and paler, but erect, proud and unafraid.

"Manfred?" he said. "Is it really you, my friend? I can't quite see your face."

"Your Majesty," said Manfred, "I am so glad…"

"Yes, yes," interrupted the Archduke, "of course, Manfred, the so-called King's Friend. Well, I have heard of you and I offer you a post with me. I have heard you are skilled in all the arts of war. I pay well, and my service is, let us say, more secure than that of your present master."

"Your Highness," began Manfred.

"Your Majesty, you should say, Manfred, as I am now King here and only keeping your former King alive in the hope it will attract someone else," said the Archduke.

"Your Highness," repeated Manfred, "Maximilian is my King and will be till he dies, or I die."

261

"Either or both of which may happen soon," said the Archduke easily.

"Now then," he went on, and the smile vanished. "Call off your attack, both inside and outside the castle, and I will allow you and your king to live. Refuse and I could have him slain now."

"Archers," said Manfred quietly, and his four bowmen lifted their weapons.

"Enough of this, Your Highness!" burst out Griffo, who could keep quiet no longer. "Kill the King and let me finish off this upstart."

"Well? What is your answer, Manfred the Wise?" sneered the Archduke. "Griffo's way or mine?"

"May I talk with the King for a moment?"

"Why not? By yourself you can hardly save him. One of my men will go with you. You might see reason more easily if you talk of the hopelessness of your situation."

So Manfred was allowed through the group of men, but a Thalesian went with him.

He fell on his knee before the King and kissed his hand. The King raised him up and immediately asked, "Is he safe?"

"Yes, Sire. He is with Prince Henry at this moment."

The King sighed with relief and seemed to relax.

"Then it doesn't matter what happens to me. Now, Manfred," said the King earnestly, "don't surrender whatever you do. Preserve the kingdom at all costs, for him. Will you do this, my friend?

"And, Manfred, why do you not uncover your head? You

262

hide your face. Why?"

"You will see, sire..."

"Enough," came the Archduke's voice. "Give me your answer!"

Manfred returned to the room they had left. He approached the Archduke and then turned suddenly to the men at arms, flinging back his hood.

They shrank from him in horror, for his face was bandaged to hide the awful wounds and erosions of leprosy!

"Yes," he said. "You are not afraid to die, I suppose, but such a death as this... and if I so much as touch you... if I smear my fingers across your face..."

They backed away from his outstretched hand, from which he had removed his gauntlet to reveal more bandages and what appeared to be mere stumps of fingers.

"If I touch *you*," he whispered, leaning close to a young guard, who shook visibly, "or your archduke?" He moved towards Archduke Boris, who turned pale and opened his mouth to speak, but no words came.

"It is a slow and lingering death, shunned by all men, living apart, dying alone..." continued Manfred, emphasizing each word.

"Kill him, Griffo!" gasped the Archduke. "Kill them all!"

With that, he shot from under Manfred's hand, slipped through a side door and was gone.

TWENTY-NINE

It was both utterly thrilling and fearfully frustrating to be on top of that hill, watching the fascinating spectacle spread below them.

Rudolph could not be still, even to the point of jumping off his horse to squeeze between two boulders to get a better view, which wasn't in fact better. He was very excited and yet fearful. The odds for him were enormous.

Upon the outcome of this battle depended not only his own future but the lives of everyone he loved. Somewhere in that beautiful sunlit castle was his father; alive or dead, he knew not. Manfred and Hans, friends and companions since childhood, were in that same castle, probably fighting for their lives, against appalling odds. The past few months, too, had made their friendship so deep that the thought of their being killed, or even badly wounded, was unbearably painful.

A huge variety of sounds floated clearly up to them through the morning air. The constant roll of drums from all over the field formed a patterned and martial background to the harrowing sound of screams and cries, the neighing and, sometimes, shrieking of horses, the clash of arms, the blare of trumpets and hoarse commands.

Prince Henry was unhappy, too.

"See there," he said. "The Thalesians are fighting well under pressure. They are holding Igritsenberg's men on the bottom edge. Also," he continued gravely, "the army on the western bank are crossing in small numbers, but steadily, to help their fellow Thalesians. Where is Fidelski? He must come soon!"

It was true. Thalesians were crossing the river in long, low boats and helping the embattled troops on the near side. Worse, some were rowing towards the causeway to reinforce the soldiers in the castle.

The remnant of Berenal's knights had made it to the castle and fierce fighting seemed to be taking place there.

The Thalesians had well overcome their first panic and had formed well-disciplined companies, which were defending the ground well.

Henry's practiced eye swept the field. A group of Berenal's knights had become isolated and could be seen fighting desperately close to where the first valiant charge had come to grief. They were hopelessly outnumbered and in imminent danger of being overrun and wiped out. The main body of the royal army was meeting fierce and well-organized resistance. Something needed to be done immediately.

"Kesternich!" said the prince sharply.

"Yes, Your Highness?" Count Leopold of Kesternich, a colorful individual from the eastern part of Dehrmacht, rode forward. He sported a bright orange plume above a rather old-fashioned suit of armor which, he claimed, had belonged to his father.

"Kesternich, take that overgrown, orange feather of yours, your troopers, the rest of the archers and Spilnick's men-at-arms, and place that feather of yours over Berenal's body."

For so it was, Prince Henry's sharp eye had seen that the little group of knights was around its fallen leader and would stay until they fell too.

"At once, Your Highness!" shouted Kesternich joyfully, and turned to his men.

"Where is Fidelski!" muttered the prince to himself again, for he realized the situation was in danger of teetering into defeat. "And, also," he said angrily, "where is di Cazo? Where did he disappear to?" He had watched with approval the little horsemen's headlong charge and whirlwind passage to the castle, but now nothing appeared to be gained.

"I think it is all or nothing now, my dear nephew," said Prince Henry to Rudolph, with a smile.

"Geldstein!"

"Highness?"

"Take all the rest of the troops. Reinforce the center in the field. Cut the northern half off from the south and secure the northern end around the causeway."

"Yes, my prince," and he was gone too.

"Your Highness! Look on the right." One of the knights with Prince Henry shouted.

He looked and it was a sight to behold.

Out of the gateway of the castle burst a mob of fleeing Thalesian soldiers, closely pursued by a body of small, dark horsemen.

"Di Cazo!" breathed the Prince.

They watched breathlessly as the dark mass of hustling animals and terrified men spilled out along the causeway. Di Cazo could be clearly seen at the head of his men, while bodies jumped or fell into the river. Others were slain by the flashing swords of the fierce tribesmen until, at last, a few of the terrified castle defenders reached the end of the causeway and joined their brethren on the field.

Di Cazo turned his horsemen round and started to return to defend the castle against further attack.

"Good man," breathed the Prince, but then held his breath.

While the horsemen were clearing the causeway, a huge barge laden with men was approaching the end of the causeway near the castle gate. Di Cazo saw the danger at once and, again, his fierce little men charged to meet the new threat. The men clambering awkwardly from the boat were in no condition to meet battle crazed cavalry, thirsting for blood, and they fell in their dozens, staining the river for yards in an ever-widening circle.

Then faintly, from across the river, there came the sound of bugles sounding.

"Fidelski!" cried the prince. "Fidelski, at last."

More bugles sounded on the opposite bank and the little lines of ant-like figures, which had been waiting to cross, turned to face the new threat from their rear.

"Just in time! Well done, Fidelski," grinned Prince Henry at Rudolph. "There, look to the right, round the edge of the hill, and you will see them."

"Yes, Uncle, I can see them," replied Prince Rudolph,

whose sharp, young eyes had picked out the marching men before his uncle. He felt like cheering again, but it was undignified for the heir to the throne to show too much emotion. In his heart, though, he was relieved, for he knew his uncle had been anxious.

THIRTY

In the gatehouse, Breclan saw Hans fall.

He had watched with bated breath, as the mighty man had picked up the massive bar and walked fearlessly to close the massive doors to the castle proper.

"Give him cover, you archers!" he had growled fiercely.

"We can't, lord," one of them replied. "They are out of our range of vision."

Then it was too late. The vicious bolt had thudded solidly into Hans, piercing his great breastplate and felling him at one blow.

Breclan groaned deeply.

"Come with me: you, and you, and you, and you!" he said, pointing to different men.

"Now, archers, cover us, and no nonsense about not being able to see. Come into the yard if need be, but find targets and make them keep their heads down. Remember you can shoot three or four arrows to every one of a crossbowman." He knew they knew that but it would make them faster if they thought their reputation was at stake.

The gatehouse was secure and Breclan knew that while they still had arrows left, there was little chance of it being re-taken for a while, so he was free to make an excursion.

Huw, Breclan's right hand, stepped forward.

"Indeed, my lord, some of us will come outside and see if we can stop all the crossbowmen."

"Good, friend Huw, but don't take too many, mind. The gatehouse must remain safe, even if we have to be left outside. Understand?"

Huw nodded gravely and stumped off to collect a small band of his superb archers.

Out of the gatehouse door, they streamed: a dozen determined men. Huw and his men let them go and stepped smartly after them. The door slammed shut and they heard the bolts go home.

An arrow whizzed from above and a man in Breclan's party flung up his arms and collapsed without a sound.

Huw looked up and behind him.

"There," he said, "in the angle between the gatehouse and the wall," and, almost as quick as the eye could follow, an arrow was dispatched followed by two others in quick succession.

They were not wasted. There was a short scream and a clatter as a crossbow fell from lifeless hands and hit the roof of the building tucked into the foot of the wall.

Breclan ran to the open doorway, followed by his men. He bent over the still form of his friend, while his men looked to pick up the bar dropped by Hans.

"He's alive," shouted Breclan joyfully and straightened up.

That was the moment chosen by the men, chosen by the men in the great hall to launch their attack. Round the huge screen they came and fell upon Breclan and the others in the entrance.

Breclan roared with rage. A pike caught him a blow on the head, but he was unaware of it: a dull, red mist hovered before his eyes. Both his powerful hands seized his two headed axe. He jabbed its end viciously into a fellow not two feet away, swung it backwards in an awful arc, which ended in splintering bone, and a scream of agony. He jumped round on his feet and let the axe follow, slicing another poor fellow's neck, as it did so, and cleaving a third man's skull.

Breclan roared again, fighting mad. Friend and foe alike fell back from the powerful figure with the glittering ax.

For a second he stood there, panting: a short, squat, angry bear of a man, round skull-cap helmet on his head, shining breastplate under Dehrmacht's blue and gold, now splattered with blood.

Slowly, he advanced on the Thalesians. Then, with a great, angry bellow, he hurled himself at the Thalesians. With his ax at the full stretch of his short, tree-like arms, he whirled round and round in the midst of his enemies.

While it lasted, it was fearful!

Men fell to left and right, screams and cries filled the air. None could attack him successfully, so quick were his movements and so powerful his swings. His men backed him up, but at a respectful distance, for Breclan knew no man in this state, and would quite possible have cut down his best friend without mercy.

Suddenly, there was no-one left between the great screen and the doors. The Thalesians broke and ran for cover, leaving their dead and dying, lying in heaps along the passageway.

With a final twirl, Breclan buried his ax in the screen. He tugged at it wildly for a moment and then stopped. The madness cleared from his eyes and he gazed stupidly around him.

The ax stayed but Breclan left. Recovering his senses, he marched to Hans, turning to the remnant of his friend's men.

"Keep them off as long as you can, while I get him out," he said. "The rest of you come with me."

They nodded grimly, though it could well have been a sentence of death for them. The Thalesians were cowed for a while but who knew when they would return for another attack. They desperately needed reinforcements.

With the help of two of his men, Breclan hoisted Hans into an upright position, let him fall across his back and staggered with him to the courtyard. His men surrounded him while he tottered unsteadily across the yard to where Huw and his men were still keeping watchful eyes upon the battlements.

Abruptly a bugle sounded, a single clear note, and more Thalesians poured out of doors opening onto the walkways and down the ladders and steps from the walls.

Huw and his men shot arrows at lightning speed, one after another, as fast as the eye could follow, but there were nowhere near enough of them to quell the flow of the enemy. The first of the men from the walls were down and running at Breclan's party. Some fell from Huw's arrows, but more came on.

Huw fell, mortally wounded, the long evil point of a pike skewering him to the door, even as he drew another arrow. The men with him all fell and the way to the gatehouse was barred to Breclan.

He stood irresolute under the great weight of his friend. His men closed ranks around him and, one and all, prepared to die.

They fought with animal ferocity. Breclan had chosen his men well. Every one of them was a seasoned and skilful warrior and each one seemed to fight with the strength of ten.

Breclan lowered his precious burden gently to the ground and, just once, lovingly stroked the lank, black hair and the pale face.

Quickly, he straightened, drew his sword and threw himself into the fray alongside his steadily decreasing little band of men.

At that moment, with a roar that could just be heard on the princes' little hilltop half a mile away, Lord Altrecht's party of knights clattered across the drawbridge and hacked, cut and speared their way into the seething mass of men fighting in the outer bailey.

There was pandemonium. The noise was deafening: clash and shriek, bang and roar, crash and cry, as men fought and died. Some of Altrecht's knights fell on the paved yard in full armor and were dispatched swiftly by the Thalesians. Others were missed in the confusion and, thus, lived. The soldiers thrust and parried, hammered on shield and helmet, cut and were cut, bled and perished. Horses neighed and whinnied, reared and plunged and, a few, died.

The courtyard was a boiling mass of men and horses: colorful confusion. Many of the knights wore their own colors and their coats of arms covered their richly caparisoned horses. Squires were there, too, fighting by the side of their masters and wearing their master's arms emblazoned on their tabards.

It was magnificent and exciting. It was brave and valiant. It was heroic, but it was a losing battle. There were simply too many soldiers coming into the courtyard and too few knights left. Despite superhuman efforts and extreme courage, the knights were being overcome. His head ringing with the din and aching from a blow which had almost split his helmet, Breclan stood in the cauldron of death. Blood streamed from his sword, and from a dozen wounds on his body. Dead men were all around him but, with a sense of wonder, he realized he was not, at that moment, being attacked. The fighting continued everywhere else but not around him.

He stooped again to his friend, sat him up and, with a stupendous effort, hoisted him on to his shoulders and continued his journey to the gatehouse.

Five of his men were left. Faithfully they gathered round him as he staggered the last ten yards to the door.

The battle raged around them. His men fought off any Thalesian who came near but the Thalesians were currently occupied almost entirely with the knights. One of Breclan's men, Tarus, a brawny, good-humoured fellow from Breclan's own village, fought a small, stocky Thalesian with a long sword. His foot slipped on the gory ground and his enemy was upon him. Breclan saw Tarus fall and groaned, but he did not stop his walk to the door. Two more died fighting a desperate rearguard action just as Breclan reached the steps up the door. At last, he was there. Willing hands reached out to pull him and his two last faithful friends inside and the door slammed shut behind them.

THIRTY-ONE

Below the dungeons, in the dismal chamber, where the King had been imprisoned, Manfred still held the moral advantage, for a while at least. Despite the Archduke's departing order, Griffo and his men shrank from the prospect of a fearful, living death.

It was Griffo who moved first, though. He too had shrunk from those horrid bandages, stained and dirty, but then he rallied and spoke loudly and decisively.

"It's a trick!" he burst out. "He can't have leprosy. His skin was clean seven days hence, when he was my prisoner. Get him!"

Manfred moved like lightning. He seized the sword out of the hand of the nearest guard and brought it crashing down on the man's head. He then plunged at Griffo, with the sword in a thrust that was easy to parry. Griffo grinned contemptuously: such an opponent was not worthy of him. He gripped his sword firmly and prepared to deal Manfred such a blow as would separate his head from his shoulders in one strike.

However, in the very act of lunging, Manfred unfastened the clasp of his cloak, with his other hand. With a flick of his wrist, he swept it off his shoulders and swung it into Griffo's face. It seemed to gather speed as it moved and it struck the burly, black-visaged soldier with tremendous force. Manfred made no attempt to pull it back, but followed it and, with a deft twist, wound it round the unhappy man's head and pulled.

Off-balance as he was, Griffo teetered and crashed to the floor. Manfred was instantly astride him, long dagger to the man's throat, as he faced the room.

"Get back!" he ordered. "Drop your weapons, or Captain Griffo dies."

The Thalesians stared. Griffo's strength and fortitude were legendary in the Archduke's army, and here he was, overthrown in less than half a minute. They hesitated, but Manfred's men didn't. They moved quickly to disarm the guards before they were tempted to allow Griffo to perish. He was not a popular leader.

"Bar the door," said Manfred to his men. He did not want an inward rush of extra guards.

He unwound the cloak from his victim's head. Not too soon either, for his captive's face was purple and his eyes bulging ominously. The Archduke's feared captain had not been breathing easily.

Manfred's eyes glittered as he gazed intently at the man in his power. He was sure that this man had committed many crimes against his royal master's people. He was tempted to administer justice there and then but a quiet voice spoke.

"Manfred."

He stiffened and answered. "Yes, sire?"

How good it was to give that familiar answer of obedience! It had been so long since he had uttered it.

"We cannot stay long here," said the King. "We must find the Archduke."

"Yes, sire." Then, to his men, "Tie them all up tightly."

They left them there, trussed like so many bundles of wood. The King, Manfred and his men went through the same side door which, the King and Manfred knew, led to the private apartments of the castle.

THIRTY-TWO

Christov of Berenal, fourth baron of that title, and absolute lord of several thousand families, awoke from a confused and chaotic dream.

Musicians had come to his castle. They had banged and clashed their instruments together, so that he had an awful headache. Margaretha, his wife didn't like them either, and she had taste! He kept trying to rise from his seat at the High Table to tell them to go, but every time he did so the big flashy fellow knocked him down with his drumstick.

"Ouch!" There he went again. He would just lie there a few seconds until his head cleared and maybe they would take this soup bowl off his head. How dare they, anyway! Putting a soup bowl on his head. He was far too easy-going. He'd have a word with Glinistein, his steward. He shouldn't let such cheeky fellows in.

Slowly, his head cleared. He had difficulty seeing as well.

Suddenly, like a blinding flash, he remembered.

The noise of battle was all around him. He couldn't see clearly, because that ridiculous old helmet of his grandfather's had slipped slightly and, with the visor down, his vision was obscured.

With a great effort, he struggled to sit up. Not an easy thing in full armor, but he managed it.

Crash! Down he went again. Ooh, how his head hurt, and his side, and his chest!

Someone with silver legs had bumped into him. There was a cry of surprise and delight, and strong arms were helping him to his feet.

"My lord! I'm so glad you're all right. The Lady Margaretha would not have forgiven me if I had returned without you."

It was Simon of Dreisel, his own squire who, truth to tell, had not left his side since he fell and whose armor was now sadly dented and battered. His sword ran red with blood and he seemed near to exhaustion.

Berenal looked around, his head clearing rapidly.

"Where are the rest?" he asked, and ducked as a Thalesian aimed a vicious swipe at him with a pike. It was a reflex action for him to grasp the pike as the man lurched forward. He wrested it from his enemy's hands and brought it crashing down upon its former owner.

"Ah, I am beginning to feel better," he remarked to his faithful squire.

No more than a dozen of his knights were with him, fighting vigorously side by side in a little group near him.

Now the Baron of Berenal was lion-hearted. Generous, warm to his friends and popular, he was fearless in battle, and a great leader. Despite his aching head, he quickly assessed the situation and knew they would all perish unless help came soon. His men were fighting bravely, and were the pick of the royal knights, but they were hugely outnumbered by their many foes.

He picked up his sword, still where it had fallen and squeezed in to fight beside his men. He rallied them and encouraged them.

Briefly, his eye caught a bright orange feather, bobbing ridiculously a hundred yards, or so, away. Parrying a sword thrust from a Thalesian soldier, who certainly did not seem to have gone short of food, he thrust his own sword along the inside of the man's arm, piercing his opponent where his breastplate ended.

There was that silly feather again, bobbing and weaving about, and there, with it, the blue and gold of Dehrmacht.

"Look, my friends! It's Leopold of Kesternich, over there with that beautiful feather," and he knew that his fears of being overrun were unlikely to be fulfilled. Steadily, he urged his men to join Kesternich and his gallant band.

THIRTY-THREE

Far above them, Prince Henry watched the battle rage. "Look, Rudolph!" he cried, "de Berenal is up and fighting."

"Hooray!" shouted the boy, for he loved the bluff and genial baron.

"And there, Your Highness, is my lord of Kesternich," said another knight nearby, "you can just see his feather."

"You have good eyes, Sir Ranif. You are right. He has almost reached them."

Henry's eyes swept the plain.

There was fierce fighting everywhere he looked. He knew they were at that stage where the battle could go either way. It would be decided within the next hour, whatever happened. His reinforcements were making their presence felt, but the Thalesians were fighting bravely.

"Another thousand men would do it," he mused to himself. "Nay, five hundred. Oh for another five hundred men!"

Prince Rudolph looked at him. He knew his uncle was troubled. Though he did not have his experience of battles, he sensed they were nearing a crisis.

He did not know where they could possible come from, but he remembered Bertram the priest saying that God loved to answer specific prayers, so he prayed. "Heavenly Father, all the men in all the world belong to you and you govern nations according to your great will. Please would you let us have just another five hundred men at this critical point in the battle. In Jesus' name. Amen."

Igritsenberg's force was beating the enemy back in the south and Fidelski seemed to be triumphing on the eastern bank. Altrecht's knights were in the castle courtyard. A force of infantry were doggedly fighting their way through to join them.

No, it was the centre where the Thalesians seemed to be gaining strength. The bulk of their forces had been there and had had no difficulty resisting the initial attack. They had regrouped well and were advancing on two fronts, one to meet Geldstein's reinforcements, trying to drive a wedge between them and the causeway. The other was pushing back the first group that had come over the hills in the center.

The sun had been climbing steadily and the day was becoming hot. Then, it happened.

Out of nowhere it seemed, over the central ridge of hills, there appeared, running, the oddest collection of rag, tag and bobtail peasantry ever seen on a field of battle. They wore every color of garment, but many sported a blue sash or ribbon over their smocks and shirts. They carried cudgels, farm implements, kitchen knives tied to sticks, home-made bows, and even some swords. Fearsome yells floated up to the command group as they hurled themselves enthusiastically into the battle. More and more of them poured over the top of the hill. There were at least two thousand of them.

"Who are these? They remind me strangely of those ruffians

who found you and brought you to me," murmured a bemused Prince Henry. "Whoever they are, they appear to be on our side and they are just what we needed. Now, victory is ours!"

Prince Rudolph watched with awe as the strange mob poured down into the battle. "Thank you, Lord Jesus," he breathed, and then, "but where have they come from? How did this happen?" And then he knew the answer.

"It's the Lady Velda!" he cried. He could see her clearly, near the front, in a little cart, being pulled by two lovely black horses. He shouted again in delight for he saw that even she was brandishing a sword, which seemed too large for her dried up body to carry. Beside her, massive and calm, lion head of hair waving in the breeze, her faithful servant, Igor stood and deftly slashed and struck any unfortunate enough to come near his lady.

"That's done it," said Henry gleefully. "That will win the battle for us. It is just what we needed, although who she is or why she should come, I know not. She seems like a sort of bandit queen and her men the most fearsome collection of rogues I have ever come across. Nonetheless, she is more than welcome and Dehrmacht owes her a great debt."

"I've heard vague rumors of a sort of queen of the underworld," said Perrit, an old knight of Dehrmacht, "but I never knew if she really existed."

Prince Rudolph grinned broadly. "My royal uncle, I think you will find that Manfred knows all about this lady and... she showed me great kindness when we needed a friend."

"Then we are doubly in her debt," said Prince Henry. "I shall be delighted to meet this wonderful lady."

They watched with fascination as she directed the mob, her dry, clear voice carrying to her lieutenants over the din of the conflict.

It was a mob, a tatterdemalion horde of simple peasants, gathered from the town and country, as Velda passed through.

Then something else began to happen. Rudolph noticed it first. His sharp, young eyes saw something strange in one or two of the companies on the plain below.

"Look, Uncle!" he cried. "The Thalesians are fighting each other."

Prince Henry and the other knights looked keenly at the battle. It was true. Some of the Thalesian soldiery had turned on their officers and were fighting for Dehrmacht.

"The mob did it," murmured Prince Henry. "Some of the men in the Archduke's army were ours, forced into his service. The sight of the common folk fighting reminded them of their loyalties and gave them heart to rebel.

"Now we have definitely won," he said, and leaned back, smiling, in his saddle.

THIRTY-FOUR

When Breclan reached the gatehouse door and staggered inside, the bitter fighting in the courtyard was nearing its climax. The gallant company of knights had fought itself almost to a standstill. They had fought fiercely against overwhelming odds. The floor was littered with dead and dying men and horses. Many Thalesians had died bravely for their Archduke, but however many fell more seemed to appear. In fact, their numbers hampered them, for they filled the courtyard and got in each other's way. Inevitably, knight followed brave knight in a crashing heap, until it could be only a matter of minutes before the dozen or so left would also perish.

Suddenly there was a rush and clatter of hooves and di Cazo's wild horsemen burst again upon the crowded yard.

They carried only swords but their swords were everywhere. Thin, curved blades flashed and gleamed in the morning sun, with fearful speed and deadly effect. The tough little horses seemed oblivious of men or battle. Their riders were fearless of spear, bow or pike, and were rarely unhorsed.

The effect of their arrival was dramatic.

The Thalesian defenders had fought bravely but this latest invasion was too much. They broke and ran, in any direction they could. Many even fled back up on the walls to escape those awful riders.

Di Cazo's men did not follow the fleeing defenders up the steps onto the walls, but they did follow their leader, on horseback, into the crowded doorway of the keep. There the last survivors of Hans' valiant little band were fighting a losing battle against the soldiers who had poured out of the hall and were fighting their way back into the stairways that led to the guardroom above.

Others were vainly trying to dislodge the huge bar, which Hans had jammed with such force into the great wide-open doors.

Into this melee, laying about him to left and right, charged di Cazo, followed by his fierce little men.

How they kept their seats in that surging crowd, up the steps, under the bar, just at head height for a rider, and still managed to fight, was amazing. They cleared men before them like a brush clears water from a yard, but di Cazo did not stop.

Like a river in flood, he and his men flowed round both sides of the oak screen into the great hall. The people in the hall fled: through doors, under the tables, out of the hall, into the kitchen, down passageways, anywhere to escape those terrible blades.

Count di Cazo was undisputed master of Dehrmacht Castle's great hall, but still he did not stop.

Spitting out commands in the strange tongue of his men, he leaped from his horse, vaulted over the High Table and disappeared into the royal apartments behind.

His men followed, leaving their horses in the hands of a few grim-visaged warriors, who indeed looked disappointed that there appeared to be no more foes to fight.

Fourteen knights were left in the castle yard. None was mounted, though horses milled about.

For a while, there was a lull, and they leaned, panting, on their weapons. Their eyes were red-rimmed, their cheeks hollow, they hawked and spat like old men, though they were mostly in the prime of their manhood. As they stood, the horror of the scene impressed itself upon them. Appalled, they gazed at the carnage around them.

The yard was heaped with men. Some writhed and cried out in their agony. Some moaned. Some wept quietly. Some neither moaned nor wept, nor ever would again.

Pedric of Garavor, the laughing young man, one of a tiny handful of Lord Berenal's men who had ridden with Lord Altrecht into the courtyard, felt as if he had aged sixty years.

He ached. How he ached!

Five minutes ago, fighting, he had felt nothing. He had fought, in a blind frenzy, anyone and anything in black and red.

Now that he had stopped, his head ached. His shoe seemed full of something warm and sticky. There was a deep, deep ache in his thigh, and he didn't seem to be able to move his left arm at all.

A sharp fear stabbed at his heart: his brother, Gidrach! Was he alive? Was he among the dead?

Panic swept over him. What would he say to his mother? She had begged and pleaded with them not to go. Their gruff old warrior father had seemed more understanding, but Pedric had seen the tears standing even in his father's eyes, when he had turned abruptly away.

Gidrach! Where was he? Pedric tried to shout, but only a hoarse whisper escaped. His throat was so dry.

The castle started to spin before his eyes and a strong arm steadied him. He looked into the clear, gray eyes of his brother… and he burst into tears.

"I thought…" he whispered.

"I, too!" smiled his brother.

"You're covered in blood, Gidrach."

"You should see yourself," said Gidrach and started to laugh, a little hysterically.

The noise seemed to awaken the little band of weary men and one of them made his way to the castle well and drew water. He brought it to his comrades first, allowing them only sips.

Then, Ziprevski, a leading knight of Altrecht's part of the country, took the leather bucket and gave to wounded men, wherever they lay, whatever the color of their uniforms.

It could not last thus. They were a handful of exhausted men. Di Cazo's wild invaders had all vanished into the keep and such had been their speed and skill, not one was found among the dead or wounded in the yard.

Ziprevski, in the act of allowing a poor, broken Thalesian to drink from his bucket, heard the rattle of a drum, and his heart sank within him.

Pedric heard it too, and the sound of marching men. He clutched his brother's arm.

"Oh, no!" he murmured. Then "Where is my sword?"

288

Gidrach paled but spoke firmly.

"You are holding it, my brother."

Pedric smiled sadly at Gidrach.

"We can at least show them that Garavor dies bravely."

Ziprevski was back among them.

"Brace up, my friends!" he called. "Close order. Defend each other's back."

And through the open doors, under the arch of the gatehouse, still held by Breclan's tiny band of men, marched row upon row of soldiers in Selden's silver and red.

Baron Altrecht supporting infantry had arrived and the Kingdom of Dehrmacht was once again in the hands of forces loyal to its King.

THIRTY-FIVE

Deep in the castle itself, Manfred, Bertram and the King knew nothing of events outside. Hurrying through passages which, of course, they knew well, followed by the faithful band of soldiers, their main thought was to find the Archduke. For, he had to be found. He had to be overcome. He had to be destroyed or there would be no peace for Dehrmacht in the future. Manfred knew that such a man would find a way to raise a new army and return if he were not utterly destroyed.

They met no opposition and wondered at it but, in fact, all the fighting men were engaged in the courtyard or the hall. A few servants scuttled out of their way.

The King turned to Manfred. "I've been wondering about that cloak."

"Just an ordinary cloak, Sire… with a few modifications."

"That's what I meant, Manfred" said the King dryly.

"It's an old trick of my father's men, Your Majesty. They used it in case of capture. They sewed weights or, sometimes, sharpened metal into the edges of the cloak. Then, if their weapons were taken from them, they still had something to fight with."

"Sometimes, my old friend," said the King looking fondly upon Manfred, " I wonder how we ever managed to defeat your father."

Manfred did not enjoy talking about his family but there was little time for conversation anyway.

The rich tapestries and gracious width of the passage showed they were in the royal apartments. Not at all damaged in the first siege of the castle, they seemed just as they had been when their rightful owner had been in residence. Now, he put his royal hand on the door of the room which had, long ago, been his wife's favorite, the south-facing solar, and her memory touched his heart for an instant.

Manfred was at his side as he opened the door.

It was a lovely room. The walls were brightly painted with garden scenes and the window in the south wall was large. Stone pillars, arched at the top, supported small frames filled with expensive glass, so that the sun on this lovely summer morning, streamed into the room. A number of bench seats were there, covered with richly embroidered hangings.

Manfred noticed that a magnificent tapestry, brought halfway across Europe, and specially made for the King, had gone. The King noticed it too, for his grip on Manfred's arm tightened and he drew in his breath sharply. It had shown the young Maximilian and his wife, Edrina, entering Dehrmacht after their wedding fifteen years ago.

A small group of women rose from the window seat as the men entered.

One, a tall, slim woman, of middle age, advanced. She wore a loose fitting outer dress of deep blue, which covered her feet and trailed on the carpet. Beneath this cotte, or dress, she wore a shimmering bodice of green silk. Her yellow hair was beautifully braided and coiled, with a thick circlet of gold around her head.

Twin spots of angry red burned in pale cheeks as she bore down upon them, followed by her group of gentle ladies.

"What group of wandering vagabonds is this that dares invade a lady's chamber?"

She had a high, clear voice, used to command: a voice that brooked no argument.

She looks magnificent, thought Manfred, terrible as a warship sailing down upon the enemy. She was beautiful too, with a well-shaped face and blue eyes, but her eyes were hard and a downward curve of her lips hinted a latent cruelty.

Armed men had burst into her room, but there was no fear in her voice, or hesitation in her carriage. And indeed, though drawn swords were in their hands and they would have backed away for no other foe, Manfred's men retreated and hung their heads. Over-awed by her beauty and her bearing, they retreated before an enemy they could not fight.

The King and Manfred stood their ground. Maximilian leaned heavily, as before, on Manfred's arm, but he spoke firmly.

"No vagabonds, Your Highness, but the rightful lord of this castle, stolen by a true vagabond of cruel and greedy heart, of noble birth, but far from noble deeds."

Her eyes flamed for she was Vitrena, Archduchess of Thalesia, and the daughter, herself, of a king.

"You!" She spat at the King and with dreadful contempt, hissed at him "You, who can hardly stand without a servant's help! You, who screamed as the hot iron seared your flesh. You

292

dare to speak of my husband as ignoble. You will never compare with his magnificence."

The King wilted under the cruel hatred of her words.

"Have a care, Madam," he said sternly.

"Have a care!" she sneered. She totally dominated the situation, and now she stepped up to the King.

"This is how much I care," she cried and, stepping forward, she struck the King hard across the face!

Now Manfred loved the King more than any other man or woman upon earth. In the horrified silence which followed the blow, he advanced upon the woman. His face was deadly pale. His mouth was a grim line in a seamed and weary face. His eyes were mere smoldering pinpricks. Indeed the menace of his approach was so great that even the Archduchess quailed and retreated before him.

"I swear to you, Madam," he said, between clenched teeth, "I swear to you that you deserve to die. Lift your hand to my master again and I will cut you down, like a bitch from its kennel."

Trembling now with anger, she drew herself up to her full height, which was slightly taller than Manfred.

"You varlet! You peasant! You low-born animal! I will have you torn apart. I will put you on the rack until you scream for mercy. I will have you cut into little pieces and burn your body parts before your eyes."

Suddenly Manfred realized something. This woman was formidable. Her husband knew that few would be able to stand before her and the laws of chivalry would prevent most men harming her. The Archduke was using her to buy time.

"Enough!" he snapped and beckoned to two of his men.

"Guard these women! Keep them here. If they look like being dangerous, cut them down. Don't be misled by charm or beauty, they are deadly enemies of your King. And don't be intimidated by the Archduchess, she is no less dangerous because she is a woman. Treat her as you would any enemy."

He turned to the King.

"Sire, the usurper has used this woman to delay us. We must away and seek her husband."

The woman screamed abuse and insults at them as they passed through the solar and out of the door in the east wall. They took no notice. Now that they knew her craftiness and the trickery of her husband, they saw through her grand manner and high hand.

Through the little chamber next door and the maid's room next to that, they passed into the large audience chamber beyond.

There an astonishing sight met their eyes, and they stopped in amazement.

The vaulted room was full of people. Soldiers of the Archduke stood, disconsolate and disarmed, in a group on the left. Fierce little men with curved swords stood guard over them.

The Archduke himself, black-visaged, scowling, swarthy, stood sword in hand, facing another swarthy, scowling warrior.

Di Cazo's long leathery face, with its queer, droopy mustache, had a look of inexpressible triumph upon it, even while he scowled.

He spoke in perfect Thalesian.

"At last! I have waited fourteen years for this moment, my brother!"

Manfred looked at the King and then at di Cazo, and then at the Archduke. The likeness was unmistakeable, when you saw them face to face like this.

"Now, even now, in front of all these witnesses, we will settle who is the rightful heir to our father's throne. Here it will be settled, for ever, in the castle of Dehrmacht; another kingdom you tried to steal."

Di Cazo's lip curled in contempt.

"Was it not enough to take my inheritance? Was it not enough to steal the estates of my mother, even to send your ruffians into Irgonia, your own sister's land? No, you wanted Dehrmacht as well. It will be enough, today. Judgment is come upon you.

"Defend yourself, brother Boris!"

Di Cazo threw aside his cloak and attacked his brother. The Archduke was no weakling. Taller than di Cazo, he was broader and heavier, and he exchanged sword blows vigorously.

All in the room were quiet as the two men fought, steel upon steel, back and forth all around the great chamber. The walls echoed the clash of arms but no-one spoke. Even the two combatants said nothing, but with set face and grim concentration, each did his utmost to destroy the other.

Di Cazo was lightly clad, as befitted his style of lightning warfare. The Archduke wore breastplate, steel apron and grieves on his legs and so moved more slowly and clumsily. Again and again, the light curved sword of di Cazo, slashed across the plated metal of his brother's mail. The Archduke's heavy sword in turn hissed and whistled as he strove to cleave di Cazo: one good blow would be enough.

Although the Archduke was a soldier, he had not lived the hardy outdoor life of his brother. Slowly, the watchers in the hall saw him begin to slow and labor for breath.

Then di Cazo slipped and fell.

The Archduke raised his massive sword and brought it crashing down. If di Cazo had been in full armor he would have died then. As it was, with his brother's sword descending upon him, he twisted and rolled away. As he did so, he struck out with his feet, hitting the Archduke's legs just as he was off-balance with his sword stroke.

He wavered, and fell, with a tremendous crash. Di Cazo was astride him immediately, dagger in hand.

With a shout of triumph, he slid the dagger between his brother's chin and chain-mail and plunged it home.

"So the usurper dies," exclaimed di Cazo breathlessly, "and I, Lucis Alonzo Pietro Nestra di Thalesia di Cazo claim my inheritance!"

THIRTY-SIX

On the hilltop above the plain, Prince Rudolph suddenly jigged up and down in his saddle, making his horse snort and stamp.

"Look! Look, my uncle, blue and gold flies above the castle."

Prince Henry smiled. It had been touch and go for a while, but now it was all over. The battle was won. There were a few minor skirmishes still on the field but Velda's peasants had tipped the balance and the Thalesians were surrendering everywhere.

"Rudolph," said Prince Henry quietly, "another flag is climbing the mast on the eastern tower."

"My father's eagle!" shouted the boy joyfully. "He is alive!"

And Prince Rudolph, heir to the throne, of the blood royal, whooped and cheered.

"Can we go down now?" he pleaded.

"Yes, we can go down now, but stay with me. Not everyone has surrendered."

So the royal party and its escort left the hilltop and cantered down the long path, upon which so much had taken place that day.

Prince Henry looked at the sun. It was just at its height. All this, he thought: a battle fought, a castle taken, a kingdom won, all before noon!

Banners and pennants flying gaily in the midday sun, armour shining, spurs and harness jingling, the two princes, their knights and squires, crossed the battlefield.

Soldiers in Dehrmacht's blue and gold, or Felden's silver and red, were everywhere herding the Thalesian prisoners into groups, where they sat disconsolately. Their own late leader had dealt mercilessly with those who opposed him and, judging by their faces, many feared similar treatment from their victors.

Men cheered as the gay little cavalcade passed by and the two princes smiled and waved.

Many had died, on both sides, and the young prince was appalled to see so many fine young men sprawling lifeless, in grotesque and horrid positions on the grass, as the royal party cantered through.

Then a shout made them look and Prince Henry held up his hand for a halt.

A burly figure limped towards them, a great bear just visible on his bloodstained and muddied tabard.

"Berenal!" exclaimed Prince Henry. "Is it really you? I feared you had perished."

Then,

"But what has happened to your helmet? Or your head!"

Berenal was still wearing his old-fashioned helmet, with its full visor still firmly clamped down, but somehow it gave the impression that its wearer's head was not quite attached correctly.

"When my poor horse fell," said the muffled voice, "my

helmet suffered a mighty blow. But what a fight, noble prince! I thought I had perished too, until I saw yon orange cockerel Leopold approaching."

"Kesternich!" called Prince Henry, grinning.

"Sire?" said that worthy, sauntering nonchalantly towards them, orange feather still flamboyant above his helmet,… but shorter and not quite so straight.

"Kesternich, your feather has suffered a little."

"The knight removed his helmet and gazed mournfully at his feather.

"Your Highnesses," he said, "I crave pardon for appearing in your royal presence with only half a feather. A Thalesian warrior took a violent dislike to my poor head. Thankfully, he missed all but my feather."

Rudolph was smiling at the men, but his eyes were drawn to the dead men beyond Berenal and Kesternich. He suddenly went very white and tears sprang to his eyes.

"Oh, Baron Christof," he said, with trembling voice, "are all these the men who rode with you this morning?"

De Berenal sighed and nodded.

"Aye, Your Highness, many of them, and not a few of the enemy as well. They were grand lads and they fought like tigers."

The Prince was silent. His eyes blinked through his tears as he looked at the gay tabards, the fine armor, the broken bodies of men he had saluted and smiled at, had encouraged this very morning: men who had ridden so gaily and so bravely down this path.

"Let us go on, Uncle," he said quietly, and then he thought

of something. "Count Leopold," he called. "Thank you for going to help them."

Kesternich bowed and Henry ordered the cavalcade to continue.

If Prince Rudolph was shocked by the dead and wounded on the battlefield, he was totally unprepared for the awful carnage in the courtyard of the castle.

Here the dead were two and three deep in places. Dead and dying were everywhere. The groans and cries of the wounded were piteous, and the warm air was sweet with the sickly smell of blood and death. The horses' hooves slipped and slithered on the bloody cobbles and stumbled over men's bodies.

The boy was appalled. He hid his face so that he might not see the awful scene. He groaned as he saw more men he knew among the dead, more brave knights from Berenal's group, brown clad figures lying still and sombre, from Breclan's men, and then…

"Huw!", he cried, for he had spotted the Welshman's body spreadeagled on the gatehouse steps, his sightless eyes staring upwards.

As he gazed in horror, the gatehouse door opened, and a bloodstained, weary figure, leaned on the doorpost.

"Your Highness!" he called, "my Prince!"

"Breclan!" shouted Prince Rudolph.

"Help me down," he cried to a squire nearby, for even the indomitable Breclan was weak from his wounds.

Breclan was hardly recognizable. A deep gash across his forehead had just stopped bleeding, one arm hung limp and useless, his iron breastplate and helmet were hammered and dented.

"Breclan!" said the Prince again, as he approached.

"It's Hans," said Breclan weakly. "He is badly wounded."

A chill finger of horror stabbed at the boy's heart.

"Not Hans," he whispered. "Oh, please God, don't let Hans die."

The little prince followed Breclan into the gloomy gatehouse, up the steps and into the darkened chamber, where Hans lay.

The big man lay on a rough bed. They had taken his armor off and wound cloth round his chest. Dark red blood oozed ominously through the bandages.

With difficulty, Rudolph knelt beside his friend.

The great head was so still, so peaceful, and so pale. The Prince put his face close to his friend. He could just feel a faint breath as the wounded man breathed.

"Oh Lord," prayed the boy, "please don't let Hans die. So many have died already. Please let Hans live." His tears fell on the rugged soldier's cheeks.

He looked up from his knees. "He is to have the very best attention. He must not die. He must not!"

He turned to Breclan. "Will you see to it, Breclan?" he asked and then noticed Breclan swaying on his feet.

"Quickly, somebody!" he shouted. "Breclan is wounded too."

"Come away now, my boy," said a kindly voice. "We must find your father."

It was Prince Henry, who had come quietly in behind the young prince. He gave orders concerning Hans and Breclan, and indeed the rest of the wounded, and led Rudolph back down into the courtyard.

Together, they walked through the main doors, marveling at the massive bar, still jamming them open. They wondered at the many bodies in the entrance, by the doors and up the stairs; awful testimony to the fierce fighting that had taken place there.

Men told them of the great heroism shown by Hans and others, not least among them, Breclan's mighty rescue of the wounded giant.

"What of Manfred?" whispered Rudolph, hardly daring to hear the answer.

But the weary soldiers knew nothing of Manfred. Rumor was that he was alive and with the King, but no-one around seemed to know anything certain.

Into the castle they went and, with a trembling heart, the little prince made for the royal apartments.

There, at last, the boy saw his royal father, much weakened by his imprisonment, but nevertheless alive and well.

Great was their joy: both father and son. In a very un-royal way, the young prince hurried to his father, hampered still by that irksome armor, and flung himself into his father's arms.

Manfred, standing quietly nearby, smiled. He was well satisfied with the outcome of his task.

THIRTY-SEVEN

Splendor filled the audience chamber at Dehrmacht. The same hall, which had witnessed the violent death of the tyrant, was now filled with color and gaiety.

Men-at-arms lined the walls. Each man was dressed in the blue tabard of Dehrmacht. Golden sleeves clothed strong arms, grasping pikes with shining blades. The very shafts of the pikes were covered with woven blue and gold, with tassels at the head.

The room was full of people and a feeling of joyful expectation was everywhere. The greatest in the land were gathered; the noble, the rich and the powerful. Beauty and color rioted in the great hall.

Weeks had passed since the great battle. The soldiers of Selden and Dehrmacht had been everywhere in the kingdom re-establishing law and order. Justice also had to be done. The Lady Velda claimed Black Griffo as he had murdered her trusted servant, Aspin, and she handed him over to her tattered army with instructions that he was to be taken back to Blecklinghaus for execution. Velda's men were fiercely loyal to her, but they knew nothing of kindness and gentleness. Aspin had been the friend of Gilflower and Wrynak, and they made sure Griffo paid his debt in full. Velda's orders were carried out and his death was not an easy one. His remains were displayed in four separate parts of the city and his head placed on a pike outside the Golden Tower which had been the mayor's residence.

Many days were spent burying the dead, tending the wounded and mourning the lost. Parts of the castle had to be re-decorated and re-furbished; the courtyard and entrance hall had to be cleared and cleansed. Maximilian the Good was, at last, in firm control of his realm once again.

Three weeks were not, of course, enough to set everything to rights. The King wanted to strengthen the power of his law in more remote areas of the country. He thought it was a good opportunity to introduce some new laws and his counselors, mainly Manfred and Prince Rudolph, were urging him to curb the power of the priests. He also wanted to use some of his vast treasure to help the poorest of the people and he was sending commissioners into the countryside to see what the needs were and how they should be met. All this would take weeks and months.

Clearing up and setting to rights, finished or not, the King wanted to meet his loyal subjects and reward those who had served him well in the recent invasion. Hence the meeting now in the great hall of the castle.

Heralds sounded their trumpets and a hush fell on the great crowd. The King and Prince Henry had been swift and decisive in re-establishing royal authority, but this was the King's first public appearance since the war.

Doors opened. More soldiers came in, followed by gorgeously dressed ladies and gentlemen, many of the men in the new fashion with one sleeve huge, floppy, colorful and useless.

Manfred entered: quiet, watchful, alert, as always. Simply, almost humbly, dressed as a man at arms in the standard blue and gold tabard, but with a gold chain and the royal seal about his neck, proclaiming him as the King's Chancellor. He also carried the great staff of Dehrmacht, as he was exercising the office of Lord Chamberlain to the King.

Then the King himself came in, still limping, still thin and drawn, but erect and smiling, and with a light in his eye.

As he entered, every hat came off. The men bowed and the ladies curtsied. Close behind him came Prince Rudolph, hardly able to maintain a royal dignity, because of his happiness and, with him, young, vigorous and handsome, Prince Henry. Behind them, followed an old man, gorgeously dressed in a long crimson and gold robe, sleeves slashed with silk: Archduke Simeon of Igritsenburg, whose son had served so nobly on the field of battle.

The King took his seat on the throne. The princes, Rudolph and Henry, sat at either side.

Manfred stood before them, then turned his to face the congregated nobles and banged the great staff on the floor. The King's Grand Audience had begun. Every noble in the land had been summoned and was required to re-affirm his allegiance to his sovereign.

Rudolph was first. Those close by saw tears in the King's eyes as his son knelt before him, put his hands in his and pledged his loyalty.

"My son," said the King, "you have proved yourself loyal, brave and true. Already you have passed through many hardships

305

and quitted yourself as a man. We are grateful for such a son and you have made us proud. In the eyes of some here, you have proved yourself worthy of knighthood already, but I think you are too young and in need of more formal training in the gentle, as well as the martial, arts of knighthood.

"We have decided, therefore, to send you as squire to your uncle, my brother, the noble and royal Prince Henry of Felden. There he has agreed to see to it that you will be trained in all the proper and ancient ways of chivalry, courtly manners and the arts of war. Upon completion of that training, we intend to bestow the honor of knighthood upon you, always assuming," with a twinkle in his eye, "a satisfactory report from our royal brother.

"From what we have heard, though, you already have a higher law than that of chivalry in your heart and you will be true to the ways of God, whom you have come to know."

Prince Henry did not need to pledge his allegiance, as he was an independent sovereign in his own right, but the King called him over and, embracing him, publicly acknowledged his indebtedness to his brother. He also formally committed his son to his brother's charge.

To everyone's surprise, Manfred was called next to kneel before the King. This appeared to be a break from protocol, as his subjects should have come in order of nobility and next, as everyone thought they knew, should have been the old Archduke of Igritsenburg.

The King, though, did not appear to have been aware of making a mistake and Manfred himself did not object. The King continued:

"Long ago, our loved and faithful friend, you renounced all claim to lands, title and inheritance and came here to Dehrmacht as an unknown orphan, a boy not much older than our own son is now. You also pledged allegiance to our royal crown. That pledge has been more than faithfully kept and you are our well-beloved and loyal servant and friend. Although we would not have required it of you, you faithfully kept to your resolve to keep your true title and position hidden and everywhere have been known simply as Manfred, the King's Friend.

"As King over all this realm of Dehrmacht and rightful ruler of this land, conqueror of your father and all his dominions, it is our good pleasure to restore to you all your titles and the full inheritance of your estates and realm."

The King reached out his arm. A retainer standing by handed him the sword of state and King Maximilian lightly tapped the kneeling Manfred on his shoulders.

"Arise, Manfred, Duke of Tata, Lord of Bisroth and Neslader, Baron of Selskopf!

"Furthermore, we release you from your oaths of fealty, granting you sovereign rights in your own domain, and the promise of our undying love and friendship."

Here there were gasps of astonishment throughout the chamber. Very few knew Manfred's true identity, but everyone knew of the infamous dukes of Tata. Their reign of terror and wickedness had been known and feared far and wide: their depredations felt in many lands.

But Manfred spoke.

"Sire, I thank you for the honor you do me but, in turn, I

renounce the sovereignty you graciously offer. By your royal leave, I will retain the title Duke, but never again will Tata be independent of Dehrmacht. I renounce that sovereignty and place myself and all the realm of Tata under your rule and that of your descendants."

"So be it, Your Grace," replied the King, who had been expecting such an answer. He nodded to a nearby page, who stepped forward bearing a ducal crown upon a red velvet cushion.

It was a beautiful piece of decorated gold, with a single lustrous pearl upon each golden stanchion. Diamonds alternated with rubies on the headband, which was lined with ermine and enclosed a blue velvet cap. Another page brought forward a green velvet cloak slashed with red silk and topped with an ermine collar. A third brought a small banner, green and red stripes, with the badge of the house of Tata, the head of a wolf, upon it.

Manfred started up.

"Nay, Sire. This cannot be. That badge struck terror into the hearts of good men everywhere. I will not wear it."

"What shall it be then, Manfred?" asked the King. "It is yours by right."

Manfred frowned and thought.

"I will wear the green of Tata, if it is slashed with blue and gold, and my badge shall be a wolf submissive under the eagle of Dehrmacht, if it please your Majesty."

"Your Grace is our dear friend," replied the King. "We owe you our life, under God. All that you do pleases us. Even so, let it be as you say."

So the ceremony continued with one nobleman after another

pledging his loyalty to the Crown.

Many were publicly thanked and rewarded.

Christov de Berenal, grinning broadly at everyone, stepped forward to pledge his allegiance. He, too, was made a duke and commanded to strengthen his castle to be the main defense of the northern part of the kingdom.

His wife, Margaretha, as open-faced and pretty a woman, as her husband was open-hearted, clapped her hands with pleasure, as the King expressed his gratitude to his friend. They received their ducal coronets together from the hands of the King.

Breclan, still swathed in bandages, leaning upon his son, Garth, and moving with difficulty because of his many wounds, knelt before his king. He was confirmed in his baronry and given further sundry lands in the kingdom. The King knew he owed this man much and marveled to himself that he had such loyal friends and servants. Because of this, he was at a loss to know how to reward him adequately. He knew Breclan desired nothing more than to be allowed to return to his beloved woods and yet, he had loyally served his King and should he now be dismissed out of hand because of his own unselfishness. Then the King had had an idea, which he had discussed with his son and with Prince Henry. Manfred also had been consulted and had approved.

Prince Rudolph was standing nearby when Baron Breclan knelt and the King spoke publicly of the Crown's debt to the wild boar of Klein. He beamed at Breclan and clapped heartily with the rest when the noble woodsman was about to retire.

Breclan, a short figure in his baron's robe and crown, still almost as broad as he was tall, raised a bruised and battered face to the little prince, and winked.

Like many strong men, Breclan loved the fresh vigour of young people and had asked to be allowed to bring his brood of children to see the castle and the King. As he had almost given his life and had lain abed since the battle, his request could hardly be refused.

So those same little urchins Prince Rudolph had watched playing in the dirt of the compound in Klein now arrived at the castle. In Breclan's house little distinction was made between one man and another so, in the King's castle, Breclan's children played with the servants' children and with anyone else they could find. They were only persuaded with great difficulty not to swim in the river, which was dangerous.

As Breclan made to withdraw he was recalled.

"My lord of Klein," said his Majesty, "we were minded to have your son, Garth, here at the castle, as a companion for our son. My son, however, will be at Felden in training for knighthood. Would it please you, my lord, if your son were to join him as a fellow squire and candidate? They are about the same age and Prince Rudolph has said he regards him as a friend already. In truth he needs true friends, as we have ourselves so recently have discovered.

"Also, your second son, Ilya, we notice is of courtly manners and grace. We command, if it please you, my lord, that he be brought up here in our court, to learn ways of justice and government, possibly with a view to a position of lordly authority in the future."

Breclan's stern, warrior face relaxed into a smile. He looked at his wife quickly and she nodded and beamed her approval.

"Sire," said Breclan, "you honor us greatly, and the Lady Elena and I thank you sincerely for this mark of your royal favor."

"There is just one thing more, my lord," said the King sternly. "It has come to our ears that a certain brood of children have all but turned the castle household upside down by their wild exuberance."

Breclan looked at the King, but said nothing. His lady, Edwina, looked anxious. She had heard this sort of thing before.

The King looked fiercely at the couple before him but then his eyes twinkled and he could not restrain a smile flitting across his face.

"It seems to us, therefore, that we have benefited greatly from this breath of fresh air in our royal household. We now grant to your children the right to come and go in this house of ours as long as their childhood lasts. We further grant them the right of access to our royal presence for the rest of their lives."

"Sire, this is too great an honor for my family."

"No honor is too great for a family which has shown such loyalty as yours, my lord and, indeed, we are at a loss to know how we can honor your loyalty enough."

"My liege, I can only say how profoundly we thank you and appreciate your Majesty's gracious favor," and the noble woodsman withdrew, well pleased.

Then Hans was called for.

Hans had been very ill. For days his life had hung in the balance. Bertram appointed himself physician and had watched over him, plying him with gentle brews and strange concoctions. He would not allow him to be bled, which caused great concern, but when the King was appealed to, he supported Bertram and the matter was left in his hands.

The strange foreign priest had other patients too, whom he nursed with equal care. Breclan was in his charge, as were Pedric and Gidrach of Garavor.

When Hans was called he was carried forward, still very weak, on a litter supported by six stalwart soldiers.

The King rose from his throne and walked to meet Hans. Of course, when he arose so did anyone else who was seated. Then, somebody cheered and, within seconds, the room rang with shouts of acclaim and cheer.

Prince Rudolph and Manfred had spent hours at the sick man's side, but as Rudolph looked at that massive body, helpless and weak still, tears welled up in his eyes and he grasped the great hand that lay on the litter.

The cheers rang in the rafters as the King stooped over the bed and spoke to Hans, who was smiling at his lord and master.

King Maximilian held up his hand for silence.

"It is our wish and pleasure," he said, "that this, our faithful friend and servant, should be known from this day, as Count Hans of Peslok. It is further our wish, that he be Constable of Dehrmacht. Thus, he that saved Dehrmacht, almost at the cost of his own life, will have the governance of our arms, and the defence of our realm, as soon as he has recovered from these his honourable wounds."

So the ceremony continued. Many were mentioned and

praised for their efforts and valor in the battle. The two brothers from Garavor, Pedric and Gidrach, were honoured with the Star of the Golden Eagle, and were entitled to have an eagle emblazoned on their arms from that day forth. All the knights who had survived that glorious charge were also honored. Sadly there were only thirty left of the two hundred young men, in the flower of their youth, who had ridden that day to rescue a kingdom.

Igor of Madritch, who had complained that his horse was bored, survived the charge but died in the courtyard of the castle, from a bolt shot when the battle was almost over.

The new Archduke of Thalesia, di Cazo as was, had stayed only a few days. What was left of the Thalesian army had readily recognized his claim to the title. With his little band of fierce horsemen and his army at his back, the eighth Archduke of Thalesia had ridden off to claim his inheritance.

Before he went, he leaned confidentially over Manfred and, smiling hugely, said "Eet was a great plan. I thought eet wass crrazy but eet wass not. It only needed me!"

He then beamed at Manfred, turned his horse and rode off at the head of his men.

The ex-Archduchess, much chastened, fled the castle, with her ladies, and was rumored to have entered a convent. Manfred was much impressed by the lady and seemed almost sorry to see her go.

The only woman to be called forward in her own right was, of course, Velda of Blecklinghaus.

Her thin body, straight and erect, her mouth just a slit in that

313

dry old face, her gray eyes watchful, she approached the throne, curtsied and knelt before the King.

The King watched her with some interest.

She pledged her allegiance and rose but the King continued to hold her eyes with his.

"You killed my brother, your Majesty," she said at last.

"Yes, I did," said Maximilian. "He deserved it."

She sighed sadly but agreed. "Yes, he did, but I was sorry. I remembered him as a boy, you see."

"I understand," said Maximilian. Then, "*I'm* sorry it had to be that way, too."

"Can't be helped," came the firm reply. "The family had to be stopped. Couldn't carry on like that. Had to be done."

"My lady Velda," said the King, "We never met. I knew about you. You never pledged allegiance to me before and I was not sure whether you were alive or not.

"Now," he went on, "I find you looked after my son, when he was alone and friendless, and I owe you a great debt. Furthermore, when all was undecided in the battle, Prince Henry tells me that your appearance turned the battle in our favor. Why have you done us such kindness, when we have done nothing to earn your devotion?"

The old woman looked at him.

"Your Majesty, you are a good man. I knew that, but I loved my family and could not pledge my allegiance to you, so soon after you had destroyed my kin. My nephew, the boy, Manfred, saw more clearly than I. He made the right decision."

"Madam, we are deeply grateful for your good opinion and

314

for your outstanding services to our royal throne.

"We are pleased to appoint you as our Royal Governor in Blecklinghaus, with absolute power of judgment and justice. We further grant a Royal Charter to the city, with all that that means in terms of trade and reduced taxes. Not," the King added, with a twinkle in his eye, "that the city paid much in the way of taxes anyway."

Loud cheers and some laughter came at this point from a small group of citizens of Blecklinghaus who, up till now, had been over-awed by the company around them.

"I further command every man you name that helped in the fight against the usurper, be given ten gold pieces from the Royal Treasury."

"That is more money than most of them have ever seen in their lives. It might even turn them into honest men! Think what you are doing, Your Majesty."

The courtiers laughed.

Lady Velda bowed, saying that she would see that the money was wisely distributed, but she was pleased. Her grim face did not smile but there was a glimmer of a twinkle in her eye.

Then the King beckoned to the English priest, Bertram. He came and bowed before Maximilian.

"Master Bertram, for we know you do not like to be called Father," and he smiled. "Bertram, many here have occasion to be thankful to you. What will *your* reward be?

"Would you have riches? They shall be yours. High office in our realm, or in the church? An honored place at our court? Would you wish that? What shall be done for the man who nursed the King?" for Bertram had also ministered to the hurts the King had received at the hands of the Thalesian. The King continued "and, furthermore, gave King and Prince the best reason for living a man can have? Even as Hans found peace and forgiveness, so I confess did I through your faithful teaching."

Bertram faced the King and, for a moment, neither spoke. Then he answered.

"I desire no reward, your Majesty. God himself commands that all men everywhere should believe in the Lord Jesus Christ. By your leave, I will continue to proclaim this wherever I go."

The King thought for a few moments and then said.

"It is also our royal desire that you should take this message and teaching throughout our realm. It is our command that the royal treasury shall be open to you and that you be allowed up to a thousand marks a year to train like minded men who will teach our people the ways of the Lord Jesus Christ. It is our further wish and pleasure that if any man oppose you, he will incur our displeasure and we will visit that displeasure upon his person with vigor. The King's officers are hereby commanded accordingly."

Bertram smiled and bowed low before the King.

"I could not wish for more, Sire, and I thank you with all my heart. God will surely prosper any kingdom whose ruler has such a heart to honor Him."

A great service of thanksgiving was held next day, which thousands attended and many more waited outside. Afterwards, a great feast was given, which lasted many days, and many gifts were given to the poor, and to those who had lost much because of the war. Ballads and songs were composed, and stories told, so that many a minstrel grew rich and fat on the stirring events and deeds of valor seen at Dehrmacht Castle.

As she left the service, a gaunt, but iron-willed, rather lonely old lady, with a large and disreputable band of followers, prepared to return to Blecklinghaus. She caught sight of Bertram in the castle courtyard.

"Young man! I think it is time for you to return to Blecklinghaus to nurture the flock you established there And perhaps you might care to visit a certain old lady, who is old enough to want to know something of the life she may be going to next."

"My lady," said Bertram, bowing and kissing her hand, "I should be delighted."

"Good," she said, "I think you should arrange to accompany me now. My faithful rabble could do with your spiritual solace along the road. Look at them! Don't you agree?"

He looked. He agreed. He went.

Historical Note

Dehrmacht is an imaginary country and none of the characters in the book actually existed, except for John Wycliffe, of whom Bertram was a follower. Wycliffe was a brilliant theologian, living through most of the fourteenth century. He translated the Bible into English and he taught that priests should be poor and should teach the gospel according to the Bible. They were called 'ragged' or 'poor priests. By the time he died, Wycliffe had a large following of ordinary people and some lords and ladies. They were called 'Lollards'. Despite fierce persecution by the established church, they remained true to the Bible's teachings and many of them suffered death and imprisonment at the hands of the authorities.

Printed in Great Britain
by Amazon.co.uk, Ltd.,
Marston Gate.